FILTHY

Lies

BLACKSTONE DYNASTY II

D1522231

RAINE MILLER

THIS BOOK IS A work of fiction. Names, characters, places and incidents are the product of the author's imagination or are used fictitiously. Any resemblance to actual persons, living or dead, business establishments, events or locales is entirely coincidental.

NO PART OF THIS BOOK may be reproduced, scanned, or distributed in any printed or electronic form without permission. Please do not participate in or encourage piracy of copyrighted materials in violation of author's rights. Purchase only authorized editions.

DEDICATION

Italian Greyhounds, "BILLY" and "MINNIE."

for the two Z's

"I'm much more me when I'm with you."

— (Unknown)

ACKNOWLEDGMENTS

What a journey. Some days I don't know how I got here. True story. To the people who have supported me throughout the process of creating this book probably have only a fraction of the understanding of just how important their input was to me at the time they gave it, I can never thank you enough. The only thing keeping me tapping away on a keyboard has been my readers.

The email love-bombs, the private messages on Facebook, the late-night sprints organized by Kristy Bromberg, the fun promo events created by Vi Keeland, the awesome Tweets and Insta posts, the support from the amazing ladies of *Raine Miller Romance Readers* who offer nothing but love and joy in the words, the confessionals from people who shared with me something positive my books have brought to them in some fashion—all were part of the process for *Filthy Lies*.

These were all pretty much "render-me-speechless" moments along the journey, but most of all, the special magic that made *Filthy Lies* even possible at all. I can hardly express what your support has meant to me throughout the long creative process.

To Wendy, Martha, and Miria, your holding down the fort at RMRR is more precious to me than I can ever say.

To Simba, your random doses of humor and ridiculousness make me laugh with much-needed pure joy.

To Jena, your patience in putting up with me as I made ten million revisions to this stunning cover for James and Winter is noted and much appreciated.

To Marion, for always making my words read so much better after your thoughtful input.

To Luna and Franzi, I hope you realize the importance you play in getting books out of me. I couldn't have done it without either of you.

To Jana Aston and Katie Ashley, I NEED you in my life in order to do this writing gig. Seriously, I am not kidding even a little—I'll need to keep you guys around indefinitely.

To my better half, thank you evermore for taking this journey with me.

I am so very blessed.

xoxo R

PROLOGUE

Winter

On the day I turned fifteen, I knew I loved James Blakney. There was a look in his eye that told me he'd finally noticed I existed in a realm beyond best-friend's-much-younger-off-limits-don't-even-think-about-it-little sister. Call it womanly intuition, despite the fact I was barely qualified for being an actual woman at fifteen—and only in the biological sense—but still, I knew my own feelings.

I shared those feelings with no one.

James came to my birthday that year. To the gathering at Blackwater on the island where my family summered and vacationed as often as my father could convince my mother to spend time at the old estate perched on its coast. We were in the pool playing chicken fights when it happened. Wyatt was carrying me on his shoulders while Lucas carried Janice Thorndike, and the two of us squared off. Janice was one of those people we were forced to tolerate because our parents were close. She was a manipulative attention whore most of the time, and it being my birthday didn't change that one iota. Why she would go out of her way to humiliate someone who was much younger than her, and during their birthday celebration no less, was beyond me.

But she did.

Janice yanked on the tie at my neck that held up my bikini top and announced to all within shouting distance to have a look at my tits when it fell down. I was mortified to the depths of my soul as I frantically tried to cover back up after jumping from Wyatt's shoulders into the water. Awkwardly struggling with my chest submerged, I turned away from everyone and pulled myself together as best I could through hot tears. I think my brothers were either too freaked out or oblivious to what had happened, because neither said anything to me as I made for the edge of the pool to leave. Maybe they figured I didn't want any more attention drawn to myself—which I most certainly didn't—but a little compassion would have been nice too. Brothers can be stupidly dense.

It was James who met me at the steps with a towel and told me Janice was a jealous bitch who wished she looked as good as I did without her bikini top.

"You saw?" I asked him on a sob.

His striking greeny-brown eyes burned right into me before he answered. "You have nothing to be ashamed of, Winter, and you didn't do anything wrong. You can't help that you're beautiful and sweet." The way he looked at me told me we'd moved beyond our big brother/little sister relationship in that moment. It wasn't him being pervy with me either. It was simply James being my champion when I desperately needed one.

"Thank you," I mumbled, still mortified that he'd seen my boobs, but strangely aware the incident had given me the gift of James Blakney's attention at the same time.

"Don't let this ruin your special day, Win. You are perfectly lovely in *every* way," he said before grinning at me in a way that could only be described as a tiny bit wicked. My skin pebbled along with my nipples, as I stood there like a mute.

James winked as he took a swig of his Sam Adams before going back to his group of friends on the grass as if nothing had ever happened.

And just like that I fell in love with him.

Not even my twin sister, Willow, was privy to the innermost secrets of my heart concerning James Blakney. Within the safety of my dreams he was mine alone, and I didn't have to share him with anyone else. Or be humiliated because I'd set my sights far too high on a man who could never possibly be interested in a young girl like me. And that right there was the division between us. James was a *man* at twenty-three, and I was merely a *girl* at fifteen. Those eight years spanning between us was gargantuan—far too great of a distance to cross over.

Then.

But I'd always known him. James had been around and in my life for as long as I could remember. He met my oldest brother, Caleb, at St. Damien's when they were ten years old, and they'd been friends ever since. I was two. Willow and I went to St. Damien's eight years later when it was our turn to be shipped off to boarding school—our twin brothers, Wyatt and Lucas, five years before us. In the Blackstone family, children were schooled away from home because it built character and toughened them up for the real world. Even though the "real world" was so far removed from our lifestyle it was laughable. Things like: twenty-year-old mothers who worked the streets so her children could have food and a place to sleep; or homeless vets struggling with wartime PTSD manifested in drug abuse and suicide were the *real* world.

Those things just weren't the "real world" examples my parents referred to.

Boarding school was only one of the many requirements that came with the territory of growing up rich. James understood completely because he'd been raised in much the same way. The Blakneys owned a beach retreat on Blackstone Island not far from my family's ancestral estate, Blackwater, and so our time had been spent at the same gatherings and social functions for as long as we both could remember.

As the years went along, I loved James from afar, watching him grow more serious…and more cynical. I think his fiancée dumping him at the altar five years ago to run away with a senior partner in his father's law firm had a lot to do with the change in his personality. Leah Rawlings turned out to be a money-hungry bitch who'd left a trail of destruction in her wake. She broke my James' heart. And she did it publicly in a way that was cruel and unnecessary, and on the day they were to be married. With the guests already arriving at the church. I'll never forget the look on James's face when Caleb led him out of there.

Crushed.

I didn't know *all* the reasons for his devastation at the time. It was more than just Leah leaving him hanging at the altar. Worse than that, I would discover in time.

I couldn't have known all of the machinations that went on behind the scenes in our world when I was barely nineteen years old, but I'd learned enough to know a lot of it wasn't nice.

Despicable was a much better adjective.

James had been twenty-seven when he found out there were many secret deals and plenty of depravity in plain sight if you knew where to look.

I think the discovery of just how depraved was part of my interest in choosing social work at Boston University. I wanted to live my life differently than the people in my "social" circle. I didn't desire to be impoverished, but I didn't desire to waste my money on frivolous excess either. I wanted to use it to help make a difference for people who desperately needed someone to care, and had no one.

No one at all.

After his wedding-that-didn't-happen, I heard that James stayed drunk for about a month before pulling himself back together. With fierce resolve to overcome the betrayal of those who'd done him wrong, a mask descended over his handsome face. James lost his carefree manner and the easy smile he'd always had for others, and most importantly, in my mind, for me. He became more closed off, and far less engaging after Leah worked him over.

I missed the old James terribly at first, but I didn't have many encounters with him during the years I was an undergrad at BU. I was busy being a student, and James was busy separating himself from his father's firm. There was drama over that decision at the time. I remember my parents discussing it, but in the end, James made his own stamp in the legal community, establishing himself as the go-to guy for contract law in New England. James R. Blakney & Associates, P.C. was retained by my dad for Blackstone Global Enterprises as soon as James had set up on his own. Nothing had changed with Caleb heading up BGE since Dad's death. In fact, James probated his will—a complicated undertaking for anyone faced with settling the billion-dollar personal fortune our father left to us—and he handled it without a blip. On top of being a close family friend, James knew the conditions of my trust fund. He knew what was required for me to gain access to it before my thirtieth birthday, too. He was the one who'd explained it to my sister and me at the reading of the will. Lucas and Wyatt had nothing to worry about given they were twenty-nine when Dad passed away.

It's fair to say I hated Leah. Not so much for being with James in the first place, but for wounding him and leaving him a changed man. For that reason, she was on my unforgivable sinners' list. Because I was not confident he was as capable of forgiveness and goodwill toward people who grieved him as he might have been in the past. Which was what worried me the most, because now *I've* done something to hurt James. Something that could make him hate me, even though it would kill me inside if he did.

I stole from him.

I took advantage of James in a weak moment. I knew it was wrong, and yet I didn't care as I crossed over a dangerous line with him. I indulged nearly a decade's worth of craving to experience the magic of being loved by James Blakney. Loved? Probably more like fucked. It was done lovingly, so I didn't care. Carelessness indeed. I knew the risks and took my chances anyway.

Still, it was so very wrong of me to let it happen, because the circumstances were too close to how Leah betrayed him. My betrayal was even worse, because the ripple effects would be felt by many.

And now?

I'd have to face up to the consequences of what I did.

To James.

To us.

To our unborn child.

CHAPTER ONE

James

Three months earlier.
Boston

There was one reason and one reason only why I was at my father's law office today. The woman who birthed me. My mother asked me to see him, so I agreed, even though I'd rather take a swim in the Charles River. That I would prefer immersing myself into a polluted-as-fuck body of water to meeting with my dad, spoke volumes.

The truth? I loved my mother, but I couldn't say the same about my father. Harsh as it was to acknowledge, pragmatism told me I wasn't the first son to feel this way about a parent. History was filled with examples.

I dreaded this meeting because I knew whatever message he wanted to deliver to me personally wasn't anything I'd want to hear. Nothing he ever imparted was good news, but this felt like walking into an ambush. To say we had a *stiff* relationship was a polite way of describing it. I kept myself guarded because I had to. If your father sat on the First Circuit Court of Appeals that would probably do it for most people. The fact I practiced law in the same city as him required the appearance of family solidarity even if there was none. I had a fuck-ton of valid reasons for feeling the way I did.

Even though I'd been in his presence at family dinners and holiday occasions, I hadn't been in his office since the day I left it five years ago. The feelings of anger and disgust simmered below the surface where I'd forced them to stay. After this, I'd need a release to bring me back down to level. I knew where I'd be heading tonight. Annnnnd wasn't the irony just fucking beautiful considering where I was right now?

"He's ready for you, James." Patricia's smile held a touch of sympathy. She probably knew the reason for my summons. My father, the judge, only hired the best, and every lawyer with half a brain understood a smooth running office existed in direct correlation to the skills of his or her legal secretary.

"Thanks. Oh, before I forget, tell Chase to get in touch with Marguerite at my offices if he's interested in an internship." Patricia's oldest son was a first year law student at Suffolk and probably a smart kid if he was anything like his mom.

"Oh, that's so kind. I know Chase will jump at the opportunity, James." She smiled with genuine thanks before leading me into my father's inner sanctum.

He tracked me with his eyes as I entered the room. I had to work fucking hard to keep a lid on my emotions and remain impassive. I was on enemy turf for as long as this meeting lasted. I thought of my mother, and that helped to keep my feet planted. If not for her request, I'd be out the fucking door and back on the street where I could breathe again.

"Sit down, son."

I settled into one of his soft leather chairs and leaned back with an expression of relaxed comfort. An acting performance that should probably earn me an Academy Award because in reality, it felt like I was being ass-fucked on a bed of nails. I would probably walk out of here feeling the same way when this meeting was over.

"Thank you for coming today. I realize your mother had to persuade you."

I kept my eyes forward and ignored the calculated barb. "How is she?" I deflected by asking him a question.

"Your mother is very well as she always is." Undoubtedly he was lying, but I'd learned long ago that my parents' relationship was not my battle to fight. "I've asked you for a private meeting to share my news. You need to know what's coming."

I said nothing. There wasn't a thing on earth that could've compelled me to ask him for the information. I wasn't able to pretend that much with my father. All my energy was taken up by being present in the first place. I knew my silent disinterest rankled him. And I fucking loved that it did.

"Ted Robinson's recent cancer diagnosis has ended his political career."

"You know what they say about karma," I answered. All I could envision was the darkly beautiful goddess that was karma swooping in for her well-deserved due, because Ted Robinson shared space on the same list with my dad. Cut from exactly the same cloth. "Besides, he has *Mrs.* Robinson to care for his every need now, so he can certainly take some comfort in that."

Bitch, please.

The idea of my ex, Leah, nursing her sick husband back to health was so outrageous even I had to call bullshit on my own inner monologue. Robinson would abso-fucking-lutely have private in-home nursing care, because his *adoring* wife certainly wouldn't soil her hands cleaning up his piss and puke.

"It's time to let go of what happened in the past, James. It's done. Move on to the new."

Let go of what happened in the past?

My jaw twitched involuntarily, probably from how hard I was gritting my teeth. I *had* moved on to the new, as he put it. What the fuck did he think that was five years ago when I severed ties with this law firm and started my own? James R. Blakney & Associates, P.C. was something pretty fucking new. I shrugged and shook my head slowly. "So, what…you're running for public office now?"

"I've been approached by the party, yes." He unclasped his hands and placed both palms onto his desk. "I will accept their invitation to throw my hat into the proverbial ring. I have every intention of representing Massachusetts in the US Senate one year from now."

Of course you do.

I figured this day would come. My father's ego most definitely predestined a political career at some point. "Congratulations," I managed to ground out.

"The senate is just the first step in the overarching plan though."

"Overarching plan?" I loathed when he spoke in riddles like he was now. So arrogantly smug in his passive aggressiveness, it grated on my already stretched patience.

"Yes. The senate campaign announcement will come early February when everyone is breathing a collective sigh of relief the presidential race debacle has finally been put to bed. They'll use it to deflect some of the negative into a positive. Two years isn't a horribly long time to have to wait for a candidate they can really get behind and safely propel into the White House."

Whoa. Was he saying what I thought he was saying? "You're serious."

"Deadly serious."

"You're going to run for President of the United States." I didn't pose it as a question. I blinked at him, hoping to wake up from a really bad fucking dream—unable to accept the idea—grasping at straws of denial instead. "But aren't you getting ahead of things? The White House is a long way from a judgeship on the First Circuit."

He stone-faced me, taking me straight back to when I was a kid and about to get served my punishment for some irrationally perceived infraction. I had a lot of those moments in my childhood to draw from. A flicker of fear crept inside my heart.

"I-I m-mean, you have to win the senate seat before you can declare a run for President in two years." I wanted to cut out my tongue for stammering and showing weakness in front of him.

"The senate race is already done. All I need to make it stick is the cooperation of my beloved *family*." His lip curled up on one side in a definite sign of distaste as he spoke the last word. Jesus Christ, he must hate us all.

"How so?" I wouldn't have anything to do with his campaign. No fucking way. I held my palms up. "This has nothing to do with me. Your campaign is yours…as in, *not mine*."

"Oh, but it is in a way, *son*. You'll have to do your part to help present the right image to the voting public. Every aspect of our lives will be scrutinized. *Every* predilection…" He folded his hands and focused his dark eyes on mine, finally getting to the crux of the issue.

"Even I can't change who I am…*Dad*. You might think you can clean me up for your precious campaign, but you can't. You *are* responsible for my transformation, after all."

Maybe he was responsible.

But maybe not.

The darkness had always been there for as long as I could remember, just not acted on until rather recently. Now? I

11

needed it to survive. The control was essential for me. That my father had knowledge of my sexual proclivities was a far worse burden to bear on my part. That I liked to tie up women and spank them while fucking was going to be his.

"Don't be so dramatic. It's a simple solution. Your sister is already on the right path. She understands her duty to her family. The only loose end is you." He did the lip curl again. "You will also do your duty to this family, and you will do it quickly."

I shook my head at him. Denying what I knew he was asking of me. "I'm not hearing this."

"You *are* hearing this. I can't run a campaign for the highest office in the land with a thirty-something son unmarried and frequenting an underground sex club. Discreet you may be, but this upcoming level of scrutiny isn't what you've ever experienced. I might be able to get the past whitewashed somewhat, but my powers aren't infinite here. A pretty wife and young family will do a much more convincing job than a cover-up could ever manage. The Internet makes things goddamn complicated for all of us."

Ain't that the fuckin' truth.

"*Married* doesn't work for me. I mean, just look at what happened the last time I tried to put a ring on it. You orchestrated that catastrophe like a pro, I might add."

"Ancient history, James," he said with a dismissive wave of a hand.

Ancient history, perhaps to him.

"Knowing my own father arranged for my almost *marriage* to disintegrate at the fucking altar in front of a full church of wedding guests still grates."

"She wasn't the right wife for you…obviously, and beneath this family. Can you deny you're not better off without her now?"

That last part stung like a bitch because he was right on that one point. I *was* better off without Leah in my life. But even worse *was knowing* how I'd been played by the people who shouldn't have dreamed of playing me. At the time, it had been beneficial for Leah to leave.

Beneficial for him…and for Ted Robinson.

My father cared only about himself, and that wouldn't change until he took his last breath on this earth. Rage got the upper hand over my self-control and I jumped up from the chair. "Why do you feel entitled to dictate the who and the when I should marry?"

He shrugged. "Because I can, and because it behooves me to have both of my children happily settled with families of their own. Family values will be the impetus of my campaign. Family. Values." His frustration was beginning to show. "You are going to get some."

Happily married, my ass. He wouldn't even know what that is. "And how do you suggest I do this?"

He made a sound of disgust. "Do I really have to spell this out for you, son?"

"Since it's me you're asking to do this? Yeah, you do, *Dad*."

He settled back into the luxurious leather. "Marry a girl from a good family and get her pregnant. I *am* assuming you can figure that part of it—" He paused, his expression changing to one of interest. "Or get her pregnant *first*, and then marry her."

"I'm not doing any of—"

"In fact, a surprise pregnancy might work even better to endorse our support of traditional values with a thoroughly modern interpretation." He tapped his lips with an index finger and looked genuinely pleased for the first time since I'd entered his office.

"Have you lost your mind? I'm not *getting a girl pregnant* to benefit your fucking political ambitions."

"Careful now," he warned. "You *will* do exactly as I've outlined. And you *will* settle down and get to work on creating the picture-perfect family I need standing in support of the legacy I am building. It's not like I'm asking you to do anything you wouldn't do eventually, James. People grow up and get married. They have children. It's the only reason marriage exists. Why are you struggling with this?"

I had to fight off the urge to shudder out my revulsion. Of course he'd see the notion of marriage for reproduction only. It certainly wasn't there for love. The thought of standing on a podium somewhere forced to cheer on my father in support was just too much to have to stomach this early in the day. "Fuck you," I mumbled under my breath, hating that I didn't have the guts to spit it in his egotistical face.

"You will not fuck this up for me, James."

"What if I don't find someone?"

"I suggest you do if you want to be involved with the choice. If you can't manage to find a suitable bride on your own, then one will be found for you. A *suitable* bride, James. Not one of the whores from the club. Wealth is not as important as an upstanding family background for showing we can relate to solid middle class—"

"Just listen to yourself," I said disgustedly. "How in the hell do you—"

"Know that I *can*, and I *will* if you disregard my wishes. I am able to make just about anything happen to suit my needs, and I won't hesitate to follow through if you fail me."

"So you're just taking over my life to serve yourself?" I could hardly wrap my head around this conversation.

"You're thinking too hard, and I am weary of this conversation. I expect some forward movement on this issue by Thanksgiving. Your mother so looks forward to having her children home for the day."

Yeah, and she's the sole reason we go. "That's only three weeks from now."

"Bring your prospective bride to meet us so we can get to know this new daughter who will be mother to my future grandchildren." The smile he gave looked a bit maniacal. "Children, who will enjoy the honor and privilege of visiting their grandfather in the Oval Office someday."

Please, God, don't ever let that happen.

He then returned his attention to whatever document was in front of him and acted as if I wasn't in the room. My father had finished with me for the moment, so I was effectively dismissed.

I didn't remember leaving his office, but once I felt the warmth of the autumn sun seeping through the clouds, I knew I'd made it out somehow.

The fuck did my father think he could control my life in this way?

I stood among the foot traffic moving in both directions around me, and I felt…chilled. Cold with fear and worry. Cold like a winter fury.

Cold like winter.

Winter.

From the moment my father started dictating his sordid plans for me, I knew who I wanted. There was only one person. The only girl it could ever be for me—even though it would be something close to immoral for me to bring her into the shitfuckery that was my life.

It would be wrong…but it would feel so right.

Because Winter Blackstone was my kryptonite. This I knew. One small slip of indulging in my desires to be closer and there would be no turning back. With my father's edict burning a hole in my heart, I was being handed a reason to go there with her.

But I can't.

I was fucked and I knew it. I knew myself, and I knew how hard the struggle would be in resisting the temptation of her. For me, the allure of Winter Blackstone was something with which I was well familiar. Her unaffected beauty, her kind and generous heart, her gentle way of listening and knowing the right thing to say in any situation, made her approachable and easy for people to love.

Love?

Did I love her?

Of course I did. I'd known her since she was a toddler, and she'd become a dear and trusted friend. But, if I was honest…Winter was much more than that for me, and she had been for a long time. She possessed every quality I could want in a wife. In terms of promoting my father's political campaign, she couldn't be more perfect. YOUNG HEIRESS CHOOSES SOCIAL WORK OVER HIGH SOCIETY. The news agencies would eat her up and crown her their darling overnight. Yes, I loved Winter Blackstone, but loving someone and being *in love* with them were not one in the same. I couldn't say the latter was definitively true. Honestly, I wasn't sure if being in love was something I was even capable of.

You're still fucked because she's off limits.

This was my truth. Because I could *never* be with Winter the way I wanted to be. I could never have *her*. Not how I'd dreamed of having her when my innermost fantasies took over within my twisted headspace.

Winter was too good.

She was too sweet.

She was just too perfectly innocent…for the likes of me.

CHAPTER TWO

James

When the number eleven button lit up inside the elevator, my heart sped up. Winter's apartment was on the eleventh floor.

Directly under me.

Now, isn't that a beautiful picture? I tried to block the image of her spread out underneath me while I took my time fucking us both into oblivion.

I'd spent the last six months in torture, because she lived mere feet away from me. Caleb owned the building and could lease an apartment to anyone he chose. So, when Winter wanted to be out on her own, her brother eagerly made it happen. It made sense for siblings to stay close by when they'd just recently lost their father to cancer. I understood perfectly the reasoning behind Winter living here. I just agonized at the reality every time I imagined her naked in the shower or sleeping in her bed. Because I didn't just want to imagine her that way. I wanted to be right there with her. Naked. In bed.

How would I face her the next time I saw her? When all I'd be capable of seeing was the woman I craved above all others, it was a given I'd do or say something moronic, making us both uncomfortable. I was like a teenager around her as it was now. Getting hard at the sight of her—blurting out invitations to have dinner with me—being a fucking idiot. The familiar tightening of my dick reminded me that I could manage an erection just by thinking about her. I'd nearly outed myself a few weeks ago when our foursome for dinner ended up being just the two of us. How I kept from kissing her I would never know.

Fuck. Me. Forever.

Despite my father's directive, I couldn't entertain the idea of Winter in any capacity beyond a close friendship. Her brothers would probably put a hit out on me if I went there with her.

For very different reasons.

Caleb would freak that I was perving on his little sis, and Lucas would know precisely what perversions I wanted with his little sis. She had a third brother, but Wyatt wasn't around enough to be much of a concern.

But Lucas Blackstone knew what I was.

He knew, because he was one too.

Four years back, he'd showed up at Lurid as a new member. The cat was out of the bag for both of us, and marked the end of our anonymity as purveyors of kink. Lucas knew, but his older brother and my best friend, Caleb, did not. There was a hard and fast rule of keeping your mouth shut about other members. And so, as was expected of us, Lucas and I left our secrets right at Lurid where they belonged. I'd still lay odds he'd have a major problem with me touching his little sister though. Sisters were in the no-go zone.

I had a little sister, too. I understood exactly. Victoria was nine years younger than me, and she was getting married next summer. My parents were thrilled for my sister and her fiancé,

Clay, and if my father had been a normal person, the pressure to produce grandchildren would've been off me completely. But no, we couldn't possibly have normal where he was concerned. He had to set his sights on the motherfucking White House.

Dear God, please let me be asleep right now and in the middle of a nightmare.

As I made my way into my twelfth-floor apartment, I headed straight for my closet to undress. Two workouts were on my agenda for the night. First, my home gym would have my attention while I pounded out some of the physical stress until my body told me I'd had enough.

Then, I'd make my way to Lurid for an evening workout of a different nature. I'd satisfy that darkness of spirit inside me that fed my emotional soul. It was the only way I could exorcise my demons where Winter was concerned.

The only way.

DESPITE THE PUNISHING WORKOUT, my dick was still hard two hours later. The hot water and soap sluicing over my body did a good job of washing away the sweat easily enough. I wish it was as easy to wash away my filthy thoughts about Winter. Pretty much impossible now with my father's demands slung around my neck like an anchor. I closed my eyes, but all I could see was her beautiful face smiling at me in that quiet way she had perfected. So fucking sexy how she looked at me. And so undeserving.

I had, on more than one occasion, wondered if she felt anything similar for me. But I really didn't know. As much as I would have loved it, I knew I couldn't risk finding out. It would be cruel...for both of us.

Because I knew some of what happened to her last year. I only knew because Caleb had asked me to prepare the restraining order on her ex—a miserable excuse for a human who deserved far worse than what he'd got. Christopher Shelton was pond scum. He'd abused Winter. So, he was lucky to be breathing after what he'd done, in my opinion.

When JW Blackstone had been in the final months of his life, Shelton thought he'd secure himself an heiress the simple way—by marriage. According to Caleb, Shelton became very controlling of Winter in the time leading up to her dad's death, dropping hints that they were about to be engaged, while at the same time far too inquisitive about the terms of her father's will. He even approached me at one point for details, because he knew I would be handling the probate when the time came. I told him to back off. And when the whisperings of Shelton's "plan" to marry into Blackstone wealth via Winter made its way back to her? She dumped his fortune-hunting ass and sent him packing.

She broke up with him, and that should have been the end of it. But Shelton grossly overstepped himself, abducting Winter from her father's funeral under the guise of getting her out of town for a few days to process her great loss. He did it at a time when the whole family was deeply grieving and understandably distracted. Caleb told me Shelton took her to his parents' cabin in Vermont where he kept her drugged on Ambien for days on end, doing God knows what to coerce her into marrying him. He was too dumb and too greedy to avoid getting caught though. Once her family realized she was missing, running a check on Winter's Amex was all it took to find her. Shelton had been using her credit card to pay for his wife-acquisition adventure. The cocksucker had no brains whatsoever. Caleb gave him a choice: leave Massachusetts and don't ever come back, or face kidnapping charges. Shelton left the state.

Good fucking riddance.

But Shelton certainly left a lot of shit in his wake. I didn't know how much the incident had affected Winter. Was she afraid of intimacy now? Had he hurt her sexually or just emotionally? They had been in a relationship at one time, so I assumed it extended to fucking. Not a pleasant thought to dwell on, but it was there. I didn't know the answers, and I wouldn't ask Caleb. I wasn't sure if he even knew those details. It was the kind of thing you didn't talk about openly unless the person involved brought it up. Winter never had. And I worried how much he had broken her.

All I could do was chew on my theories until she wanted to talk about it with me. Regardless of my suspicions, her first experience with "marriage" had been traumatic.

As had mine.

My father was out of his fucking mind if he thought he could force me into marrying anybody. I wasn't getting married because he told me it would look good for him on the campaign trail.

I also wondered what my sister knew about our father's plotting. I'd broach the subject with her another time, though, because I definitely wasn't up for it tonight. Victoria lived across the hall from me in her own apartment. Her place and mine encompassed the entire twelfth floor. The setup gave us each the privacy of our own space, even though I leased both units. She lived there for now, but once she and Clay tied the knot she wouldn't. It was hard to imagine my little sister married and all grown up. She was young in years, but Vic was an old soul on the inside. Serious and smart and very mature. I had no doubts she would make a success of her marriage just as she did in all other areas of her life. Caleb had nothing but praise for how she managed his executive office. He said she was the best PA he'd ever had, and made it known he'd do whatever she needed to keep her happy and still working for him after she married Clay.

I refused to even think about my own wedding-day-from-hell. Five years hadn't done a lot to stem the bitterness I felt, but I honestly tried my best to keep the whole fucking mess buried in the past where it belonged.

So I thought about something good instead.

Something so beautifully perfect, my cock leapt in my palm as I wrapped my hand around the shaft painfully tight and started stroking up and down. I pictured her lips. Dark pink and fully stretched open for me to take. I imagined what had to be the sweetest lips on the planet wrapped around the crown of my cock while she knelt naked at my feet.

In my wicked vision, Winter allowed me to fuck her pretty little mouth with my rock-hard cock until I was ready to fill it with one spectacular orgasm.

It was her name I called when the jizz started spitting out of the tip, the earthy scent of semen mixing with the hot water and soap as it was washed away, draining into the sewers of the city.

The perfect metaphor of where my head was at whenever I thought of her.

ACCESS TO LURID was done by password, which changed nightly. I had to check in via my online account if I wanted entry. Management discouraged drop-in visits, and for good reason. Responsible people in the D/s scene weren't reactionary. Participation in whatever activities they chose was usually planned in advance, and with great detail. I didn't feel very responsible tonight, but then after what my dad had to say to me earlier today, I figured my membership here was on borrowed time anyway.

Maybe tonight would be the last time I'd ever need the password to gain entry into one of the very few places I could indulge in the expression of my desires without judgment. After Leah, I'd found dominating during sex was something I needed even more than when we'd been together. It was like my wiring had been permanently fused after she left me, and I didn't want to go back to how I'd been before.

Right now, I desperately needed to decompress for an hour or two, so I entered the code for the evening…S-I-L-K…into the keypad, waited for the green light, and turned the handle on the door. I signed in, left my keys and phone with the front desk attendant, and became officially off the grid for a bit. No texts or calls for me until I checked out later. The feeling of freedom was fucking wonderful, if only just for a couple hours. Real life wasn't going anywhere now, was it? It'd be right there waiting for me when I emerged.

Unfortunately.

Looking at the crowd filtering through the main area, I could see it was busier than usual for a weeknight. There were a few familiar faces to nod at before heading to the bar. A two-drink maximum was enforced at all times, because drunk play was a no-no. A clear head was necessary for the safety of everyone involved.

"What can I get you?" Bill asked as I took a seat at the bar.

"Ah, I think a shot of Lag will do me just right, Bill."

"You got it." He poured one for me and assessed my mental state no doubt. Bill Smith was a mountain of a man with enough muscles and tats to make the most badass biker take pause. He could handle himself no problem, but he wasn't an aggressor. He was a problem solver. Big difference. Besides tending bar, he was the security muscle for Lurid whenever he was needed in such a capacity, which was seldom, thank God. I wouldn't come here if the place wasn't quiet. Loud and noisy was never my thing. "Tough day?" Did I mention Bill could read people well?

I couldn't help the scoff that escaped. "You could say that." I took a sip of my drink and kept the rest of my thoughts to myself. If being told by your father that you'll be getting married and making a Hallmark-card-picture-perfect family in order to boost his political ambitions counts, then yeah, my day was shit. "Something unexpected landed on my plate today."

"Ah, man, you're supposed to leave that burdensome shit at the door with your phone." Bill wiped down the glossy wood of the bar and glanced to my right. I followed his line of vision.

I slung back another swallow of Lag and finished it off. A girl I'd seen in here before was making her way toward me. I held on to her eyes as she came forward, knowing precisely why I remembered her in the first place. She looked a lot like another long-legged beauty who tempted my dreams relentlessly. Thick brown hair I wanted in my hands. Pretty eyes that told me I could do a lot more than pull her hair. A lush body just aching for some properly dispensed attention at my hands. Fucking perfect.

"That's the plan, Bill," I answered, without taking my eyes off the girl. "That is my plan."

THE FEELING of calm I'd earned from my time at Lurid disintegrated as soon as I pulled into the basement parking garage two hours later. Because who pulled in just five seconds behind me? Yep, Winter's silver hybrid slid into her dedicated parking space just four spots away. I killed the engine and mentally willed her to go up without me.

Didn't work.

Because when she got out of her car, she headed to where I was parked, a half-smile on her beautiful face. A messenger bag slung over her shoulder and a backpack in her hand, she looked every inch the young university student she was. Wearing jeans and a jacket, her long brown hair pulled up into a loose knot, she appeared before me completely fresh-faced and innocent.

So beautiful.

Utterly perfect.

Fucking gorgeous.

But facing her right now—in my current state of mind, and from where I'd just come—was a disaster waiting to happen.

Unluckily for me, my sorry ass was out of options. So, I plastered what I hoped was a pleasant expression onto my face as I got out of the Lexus. "Hey you." I locked it and made my way to where she waited. I made a show of checking my watch. "It's almost midnight, young lady."

"Night class. Three hours once a week. It was the only time offered."

I didn't like the idea of her walking alone on campus so late at night. "What's the course?"

"Ethics with Dr. Drummond," she said, giving me another one of her half-smiles.

The irony wasn't lost on me. Did ethics even exist in the workplace anymore? My father certainly didn't have any. I held my hand out for her backpack so I could carry it for her.

"What's so funny?" she asked as she handed it over.

"Hmm?" I looked into her eyes, which were uniquely beautiful all on their own. A deep green and ringed with a gold band. Stunning even at the end of what had to be a very long day. I could only imagine how magnificent her eyes would be looking at me while I was deep inside her, and she was about to come. You can stop the fuck right now with those kinds of thoughts, because it's never happening with her.

"You laughed when I told you my class tonight was ethics."

"I did?"

"Yes, James, you did. What's wrong?" She tilted her head at me and waited.

"Nothing's wrong. Everything is fine. Good. Great." You can shut off the lame-ass babbling too, asshole.

"You're looking at me weird." She licked her lips and dragged her tongue over her teeth. "Do I have something stuck in my teeth? I had a granola bar for dinner during our break."

A granola bar for dinner? I didn't like what she'd had for dinner any more than I approved of her walking alone across a dark campus to get to her car. Next Wednesday night would go down much differently. No, I took the opportunity she'd just handed to me so neatly and used it to my advantage instead. I'm not a complete moron all the time.

"Let me look." I took her chin in my hand and tilted her mouth toward mine. "Don't move." I brought my finger to her mouth and tugged it along her bottom lip. I leaned closer and studied her pouty lips and the bottom row of her even, white teeth. I felt how she trembled slightly in my hold, and I heard her quick intake of breath. I even caught the flowery scent of her perfume all in the span of a precious moment. "There's something...I see a—"

"What?" she asked worriedly, her chin still held in my hand. I didn't think I could let go. I'd made a big mistake touching her. I realized it too late to stop the madness that tumbled from my godforsaken mouth in my next breath.

"All I can see is a very beautiful, lovely girl named Winter, and I think she should marry me."

Her eyes flared a little before she took a sharp breath and pulled out of my grasp. "You ass." She punched me playfully in the shoulder and then laughed, her face a little flushed.

I breathed a massive sigh of relief she'd taken my little confession as a joke.

Thank Christ.

As we walked toward the elevators, I diverted my mini-disaster and asked her about school and her volunteering job at the South Boston Youth Center—anything to take the focus off me, and why I was coming in at this late hour. She unhappily shared the story of a young brother and sister who were in a dismal situation with a mom who most likely prostituted herself to keep them fed. I could tell it broke her heart to have to send the kids home in the evenings when the center closed for the day. Winter was such a good person in her heart, and she would help a lot of people in her lifetime. I knew this without a shadow of a doubt.

"It was nice of you to carry my backpack and walk me to my door." She turned to face me as we got to her apartment and held her hand out for her backpack. I reluctantly gave it to her, wishing our short time together wasn't over so soon.

"My pleasure, Win. I like knowing you're right here beneath me all safe and sound."

Her eyes narrowed slightly, like she was trying to figure out my comment and what I was insinuating. Oh, I'd intended the double meaning all right. I was a dickhead for teasing her all the time. I said shit I shouldn't say to her. But still, I kept doing it. The kid in the third grade who relentlessly tormented the little girl he secretly had a crush on? That kid was me right now.

"Goodnight, James." She hurried to unlock her door, probably to get away from me.

"Night, Win. Get some rest."

"You too," she said with a sexy half laugh and gentle shake of her head—right before she shut the door in my face.

Yeah, Winter was one of a kind. A diamond amongst the rocks. She was fucking gorgeous with a heart I wished could be mine. But Winter Blackstone deserved someone much better than me. And always would.

As I headed for the stairwell, I knew something else, too.

All I can see is a very beautiful, lovely girl named Winter, and I think she should marry me.

Nothing in my comment had been a joke. I'd meant every word…even if it would always remain a fantasy.

CHAPTER THREE

Winter

Maybe James was trying to kill me. Because it was quite possible he was really a serial killer whose signature method was death-by-swoon. *All I can see is a beautiful, lovely girl named Winter, and I think she should marry me.*

Seriously, WTF just happened?

James Blakney said those words to me.

Right after telling me I was beautiful and lovely.

I snorted out a laugh in the foyer of my apartment, dropping my messenger bag and backpack where I stood. Yeah, I might be in good physical shape and have youth on my side, but any more talk like that from James and my heart would be at risk. For cardiac arrest as well as breaking.

What? Did he think I was made of stone or something? He's lucky I didn't climb him like a tree in the parking garage with the way he'd looked at me. And touched me. *Jesus...*

I brought my fingers to my lips and traced the path he'd used with his own fingers. Ever since I'd moved into this building six months ago, something had been different with James.

Ever since the mess with Chris.

It was James who prepared the restraining order against my ex because Caleb asked him. So James knew some of the story, but probably not all. I wished I knew exactly what Caleb had shared about the situation, but I suspected it wasn't much, because Caleb would keep it in the family. I knew my brother, and he spent a good portion of his time protecting our family. That's just the kind of person he was.

But...my God, James was in fine form tonight with the flirting.

That was flirting, right?

He'd always been a little flirty with me, but I knew he didn't mean anything by it. Unspoken logic had kept things pretty simple over the years. He teased, I laughed. Meaningless stuff between two friends.

But was it meaningless? *If it isn't spoken, then it isn't true.* Very shitty logic in my opinion, but oh how we all love to believe in miracles. And it would be a miracle if James Blakney really wanted me. It would be a miracle if James wanted me to answer his flirtation with a determined, "Yes, I'm yours for the taking."

In the past, I'd known exactly where I stood with James—basically a second little sister to him, as well as a close family friend. But now, I was so confused about what was really going on with us, and I'd lost some of my confidence around him. I had trouble knowing how to act or what to say. Where conversations between us had always felt easy, now there was tension. Straight-up sexual tension. There was no other way to describe it.

Any sort of attraction on my end would greatly complicate things. Maybe it could even destroy our friendship. Or possibly damage the close friendship between James and Caleb, something that went back decades to their time at St.

Damien's.

At the moment, Caleb was very busy running BGE, *and* enjoying his new girlfriend, Brooke.

Never had the mighty bachelor fallen so hard. My brother had done it in style for one very lovely British girl he'd met by accident, but who also turned out to be the granddaughter of our former housekeeper at Blackwater—Mrs. Casterley, who was now Mrs. Blackstone since marrying our uncle Herman last weekend. Fate can work in mysterious ways.

I'd watched the whole thing unfold before my eyes and still had trouble believing it. But Brooke was absolutely perfect for Caleb. They were so in love, and it was pure poetry seeing them together. If anyone should be getting engaged it was the two of them.

But why on earth would James say *I think you should marry me* just now?

Made no sense.

And really, it was kind of hurtful to tease when he so obviously meant it as a joke. And why was *he* coming in so late? It certainly looked like a booty call to me. He had to get it from somewhere, because since the whole Leah mess, I'd never known James to date anyone. He'd been single since the day he was to have married that bitch. Based on his past history with weddings and marriage, I *really* didn't understand where he could possibly be coming from with the sort of comment he made to me tonight.

He acted like I was a little sister one minute, but then in the next he didn't treat me like a sister at all. And lately, there had been something more in his attentions than what I'd consider brotherly. How he looked at me. The things he said often had me considering a double meaning. When he came to pick me up for dinner with Caleb and Brooke a few weeks ago, he checked me out from top to bottom, even requested I spin for him before declaring I looked good enough to *eat*. Then he brought my hands to his lips and kissed them both. He did it in a way that looked a little bit wicked and a lot hungry. Which had left me totally at his mercy as a jolt of sexy landed right between my legs—aaaaand forbidden images of him using his mouth on me flickered through my head.

Not good.

Very bad, in fact.

Brothers didn't say such things to girls they considered a little sister.

Sisters didn't imagine having filthy sex with the guy who had been like a brother to her, either.

No, they did not. I have three brothers and a lifetime of experience in the covert ways they operated. I didn't want or need any more "brothers" added to my collection. But I did love James, so I'd take him any way I could have him. If it were a platonic dinner between two friends, then I wouldn't turn him down. But the thing that confused me so much was how it didn't feel anything close to platonic anymore.

Honestly, things hadn't felt very platonic for weeks, ever since that night he ran into Sam and me in the elevator as we were heading to my apartment after dinner. He blew me off when I tried to introduce Sam, and barely acknowledged us when we got off at the eleventh floor. I turned back and met James eye to eye for a second before the elevator doors closed between us. He looked, for lack of a better term, *jealous* of seeing me with another man.

He had no reason to be jealous though, because Sam was *only* my advisor at the South Boston Youth Center where I was doing my clinical for my master's. I also considered Sam a friend. He was definitely not a booty call, but James didn't bother to find that part out. He just assumed Sam was going "back to my place" for some after-date sexy-time.

Not even close.

I wasn't sure of Sam's sexual orientation for one thing. And I wasn't about to ask him for clarification on that point for another. Our dinner was one hundred percent business oriented. Sam had wanted to bring a discussion about my options after I finished school to the table for the youth center. I did need to start thinking about what I wanted to do with a graduate degree in social work, one of which would have my name on it when the semester ended in another month. I was graduating mid-year because of the time I'd taken off when my dad was sick. I wouldn't go through commencement ceremonies until the spring, but classes would be over for me in a matter of weeks.

James was well aware of all of this. We saw each other often enough for him to know since I'd moved into the building. After Dad died, I'd asked Caleb if I could take one of the apartments in his building because I'd desperately needed a fresh start. Caleb lived at the top in the three-level penthouse, complete with a rooftop garden and a spectacular view of the Charles River Valley. He'd been happy to help me out, and now I enjoyed my independence living alone in an eleventh-floor apartment with a view almost as nice as my brother's.

We all knew what was going on in each other's lives for the most part. When Caleb met Brooke, the rest of us found out right away. It was impossible to keep secret the fact she stayed over with him constantly. So, when I witnessed a hostile James over my non-date with a colleague from work, I couldn't help pondering what he was thinking.

Why would James be jealous…does he feel more than I thought?

DR. DRUMMOND WAS WINDING down his lecture on ethics in governmental policy, when I saw a man pass by through the small window in the door on the far right of the classroom. He looked remarkably familiar when he came into view a moment later through the window in the door on the far left.

Why in the hell was James in the hallway outside of my ethics class at eight thirty on a Wednesday night?

"Let's be back here by eight fifty-five, please." Dr. Drummond announced it was break time and took off out the back exit while digging into his pocket for his cigarettes.

I stayed in my seat and texted James. **Why are you outside of my classroom right now?**

His reply was immediate. **Why don't you come out here and find out?**

When I made my way into the hallway, James was leaning against the wall looking far too sexy for his own good. Or mine for that matter. Gone was the impeccably tailored suit he wore so well for work, and in its place dark jeans paired with a white T-shirt and a leather jacket. James did casual just as well as the suits. Like that was a surprise. He always looked good.

"*What* are you doing here?" I asked as I came up to him.

He brought his arm up and dangled a white carry-out bag. "I brought you something more substantial than a granola bar for dinner." He pushed off from the wall and grinned one of his teasingly sexy signature James-smirks just a few inches from my face, before quickly dropping a kiss onto my cheek.

"You brought me dinner…to my night class on campus?" I mumbled the question, trying to process what he'd just said but clearly not doing such a great job.

"Uh-huh." He steered me forward with a palm burning into the skin of my lower back where my shirt had ridden up a little. It was only a few of his fingers touching me, but I felt every millimeter of contact in perfect clarity. "And we better quit standing here in the hallway and start eating before your professor smokes his last cigarette and comes back."

"Everything okay, Winter?" Ryan called from behind me. *Seriously?* Ryan was nice enough, but I wasn't interested in anything beyond a peer study group relationship, and I didn't think he'd understood that message yet. *Was he checking on me because a few of us usually headed for the vending machines at break, and I was changing up the routine?* Ryan depicted the man I was used to but hated as well with a seething passion—guys whose interest in me was first and foremost because of my trust fund. Sometimes it sucked being a rich girl, but I knew better than to ever voice that complaint out loud. It was something I had to accept and deal with silently, because it wasn't going away.

I sighed and turned to answer. "Everything's fine, Ryan. I'm with a friend."

"That's right, douchebag," James muttered just loud enough it was possible Ryan heard him as he continued to lead us farther away. I sighed again, dreading the dual inquisitions of "who is that guy" which would surely come from both James and Ryan before this night was over.

"Where are we going, and why are you here again?"

"This will do." James stopped in front of the next door into an empty classroom and tugged me inside. He flicked on the light and set his bag on the nearest table. "I already told you why I'm here, Win." He stuck an arm inside the bag and lifted his eyes up to mine. "To feed you."

Those three little words came out of his mouth laced with pure sex. *To feed you.* I think I might have moaned out loud. "Ahh…w-what did you bring m-me?" Screw that I was still confused. To render me captive, all James had to do was speak a three-word sentence in some kind of flirting sex-language…in which he was completely fluent.

He grinned as he took the lid off of a white Styrofoam bowl and stuck in a plastic spoon. "Clam chowder from Shorty's."

My stomach took the opportunity to remind me I was suddenly ravenously hungry by growling loud enough for him to probably hear.

"You know me well." It was no surprise he knew what I loved best at Shorty's, because we'd eaten from there a million times over the years. I took his offered bowl of my favorite soup in the world and thanked him before dropping into a chair. I busied myself with one of the hand-wipe packets he'd set out on the table before taking a spoonful. It tasted divine as usual, and I moaned on purpose.

"I most certainly do." He stretched his legs out and leaned back all relaxed while watching me eat.

"You do," I said after a full minute of silence. Then I stared him down as he lounged in his chair with his hands clasped behind his head. "But what *I* don't know is why you've brought this most delicious soup from Shorty's to me at the precise location of my night class on campus, and at the exact time we're ready to take our break. That all takes coordination and forward thinking, James, and I'd like an explanation for what in the hell is going on here."

"Well, it wasn't really that hard to find you on campus since you told me last week the professor was Drummond and the class was ethics. No, that part was easy." He unclasped his hands from behind his head and placed them on the table. "What freaked me the hell out was that you don't have your car here to take you home at ten when your class is over." The easy grin was now replaced with a touch of annoyance. "I'd planned to take you to get something to eat *before* class, but imagine my surprise when I found your car parked neatly in its spot. I said to myself, 'Winter wouldn't take the T to campus for an evening class. She's too smart to risk her safety like that.' But apparently I was wrong." He set his jaw forward…calling my bluff. "Please tell me you weren't planning to ride the T alone this late at night, Win."

Shit. I couldn't help squirming in my chair under his intense interrogation. "I…was…I didn't think it would be that big a deal. The T is safe enough," I offered lamely.

"The fuck it is," he barked. "What about the part where you're alone and walking that many blocks to get to the station and then to get home? That's not fucking safe, and you know it."

"I don't do it that often, only when I can't come directly from the center." Even I had to admit my excuse sounded stupidly weak. "I didn't work today."

"Even once is too often," he said sternly, the edge of his jaw set in a hard line. Still deadly handsome even while pissed at me. *Of course.*

"I'll drive from now on for the Wednesday night class. It's the only evening I have…and usually someone walks me to my car, so you really don't have to worry."

He snorted at that response. "You mean someone like Ryan the douchebag stalker?"

"Ryan's not that bad." He kind of was though.

"Trust me, *Ryan's* got his eye on you, and before you say no, please remember I'm a guy who recognizes exactly what that looks like. He definitely wants you." James was leaning back again, but now he had his fingers steepled as he flexed them back and forth while studying me.

"No, he really wants what's in my wallet," I snapped back. "All guys do once they find out my last name." And here I thought women were the only ones with dollar signs in their eyes when it came to a partner. *Chris certainly proved that wrong for me.*

He frowned at my comment and then checked his watch. "You have seven minutes left. Better finish your soup."

"Don't think I haven't noticed how you never answered

my question of why you brought it to me in the first place."

"Six minutes." His stern expression had me squirming again.

I took another few bites before popping the lid back on and settling my eyes on him. I waited for my explanation. I wasn't letting it go.

He stared right back at me, but his expression had softened to the point that the sternness had been replaced with another cocky smirk.

"James." I shook my head at him, exasperated.

"Winter." He blinked once with his slow sexy eyes raking over me as if I was naked.

"Why did you come?"

His eyes flared a tiny bit at the word "come" and just like that we were back to the Land of Innuendo with the comments being tossed around.

"So, you won't tell me." I waited while another beat of silence stretched out like an aeon of time, desperately wishing I could know what was really going on inside his head.

He finally spoke. "Because a granola bar for dinner is not acceptable for you."

I scoffed at that pitiful lie. "You expect me to believe that *you*, my very busy corporate lawyer friend, have time to be concerned about my lack of a proper dinner on one night of *my* week."

He nodded slowly from his lounging position in the chair, seemingly at ease with my question.

"Was that a yes?" I pushed for a little more, even though my heart felt like it might bust out of my chest.

"Mm-hmm."

"You care about what I eat for dinner," I said again, unbelieving.

"I care about *everything* that has to do with you." His eyes burned into mine as he said it.

HOW I MANAGED to stumble back into my seat for Dr. Drummond part *deux* I will never know. I certainly didn't hear one word or write down a single note. I ignored Ryan's curious glances and watched the clock instead. My heart was racing too fast to comprehend anything beyond what James had said to me during the break. *I care about everything that has to do with you.*

Was he telling me he was attracted to me? Tonight it was hard to justify his intentions merely as that of a concerned friend. He'd been nothing but clear when he'd made the comment. He'd also been clear about the fact he'd be waiting when class was over to take me home.

CHAPTER FOUR

James

Winter didn't say a whole lot on the drive home. She sat in the passenger seat of my car with her arms crossed looking beautiful…and mad. My traitorous cock loved the way she looked too.

A whole fucking lot.

The erotic Winter fantasies I often indulged in weren't even close to being contained anymore. While I'd waited for her class to finish in the empty classroom, all I'd been able to think about was how badly I wanted her bent over my knee. I'd spank that fine ass of hers until it was beautifully reddened by my hand, and all thoughts of wandering the streets alone at night were out of her pretty head for good.

I knew she was pissed at me for not saying why I'd come tonight, but I couldn't tell her the truth. What was I supposed to say? *I can't think of anything but you most of the time and worrying about you in a dangerous situation makes me fucking mental.* She didn't know how I felt about her. Not that I was very sure of how I felt, either. My headspace was so fucked up since my father's ultimatum, and I had no idea what I was doing with her anymore. My obsession had only grown with the urge to claim her as mine.

At least I didn't *think* she knew.

Maybe I'd revealed my hand tonight, because the shit that had tumbled out of my mouth in that classroom during her break was not so subtle. Time to dial it back again. I had to…for her sake.

I pulled into the underground structure of our building and parked in my spot. I made no move to get out of the car though, because first I needed to make sure we were okay. "Winter, I hope you're—"

"You won't have to do this next week," she blurted into the uncomfortable silence.

"Maybe I want to. I don't consider it a burden."

"No, you really don't have to, because Dr. Drummond has cancelled class due to Thanksgiving the next day. He said all we have is a paper to turn in and to sign the attendance sheet and then we can go." She was still mad at me, and that sucked.

"Ahh, makes sense."

"And next Wednesday I'm working, so I can drive myself to class from the center. I'll be busy getting ready for Thursday's big meal at the center anyway, so that will work better."

"Aren't you having Thanksgiving at your mom's?" I wondered what they were all doing since this was their first holiday since they'd lost their dad. It would be hard on all of them.

"Not this year. Mom will be in Charleston with her cousins. She said she couldn't bear to have it at home without Dad this f-first y-year," she stammered, as her voice grew shallow. *God, my beautiful girl, don't cry.*

"Right. I'm so sorry, Win. The holidays must make you all miss him even more."

"Yeah…" She dropped her head as a soft sob escaped.

The sounds of her crying pulled a visceral reaction out of me. I didn't think beyond another second of what I *should* do. I pulled her into my arms and held her with the console between us as she cried. I breathed in the scent of her, as I stroked the back of her head over and over. Holding her against me so close—offering her comfort—felt like heaven, even though the reason for it was horrible. She was hurting and missing her father, an honorable and beloved man she would never see for the rest of her life. It wasn't fair, but it was her reality.

I had no idea how long I held her, but eventually the sobs quieted. "If you feel like talking, I'd love to hear a story about your dad." I felt her press into me a bit harder as she comprehended what I'd said. I waited and kept on smoothing the back of her head with my hand. Letting go of her was not an option.

"On Th-thanksgiving every year, Dad had us all share what we were most thankful for that year. It's there with my earliest memories, so I know he had each of us doing it by the time we could talk. It was j-just p-p-part of the deal."

I could totally picture Winter as a small girl having her turn at the table. She'd always been sweet and caring. "Let me guess. You were so thankful for some new toy, that you wanted to give it to a poor kid who wasn't as lucky as you."

She burrowed deeper into me, and I did nothing to stop her. I wished we weren't in my car right now so I could really hold her…and see her. "Sometimes…" she sniffed. "Participation was compulsory, and we had to listen to everyone else share theirs without making fun."

"You're such a good person, Win." She couldn't even deny that as a child she gave away her toys to those less fortunate. What kid even thinks about doing that? My Winter, that's who.

43

She's not mine though, no matter how much I want her to be.

"What are your Thanksgiving plans?" she asked softly.

My father's demand that I take my chosen bride to him for turkey dinner waved in my face like red flag. I hadn't forgotten his deadline—which made this conversation even harder. I had nobody to take home, because I refused to do my father's ridiculous bidding.

In a perfect world, the beautiful woman in my arms would be with me because she wanted to be. Because it was right and good. Because she loved me and *we* were the right fit.

I spoke against hair that smelled like oranges, wishing she was tucked against me in my bed right now. Wishing I woke to this scent each day. "The usual command performance at my parents'. My mom really wants us there, and I can't say no to her. You?"

"Well, on Thanksgiving Day, I'll be serving at the center for the dinner they're putting on for the homeless and less-fortunate families in the area."

"You're not having Thanksgiving with the rest of your family?" Her answer surprised the hell out of me. *First time without JW and they won't be together?*

She shook her head against my chest. "Since Mom will be in Charleston, we decided to do our own thing this year. I'll be at the center serving food. Caleb and Brooke will be holed up in Brooke's cottage on the island most likely. Willow will go with Roger to his parents' in Connecticut. Wyatt is working on a film in L.A., and said he can't get away."

"That's not right, Win, for you to be alone on Thanksgiving."

"I'll be fine, because Lucas has invited us to his place on the day after. So, we're doing our Thanksgiving celebration on Friday instead of Thursday, sans parents. And one brother." She sighed into me. "It will be weird, but that's what we're doing this year. We'll cook a turkey and some pumpkin pies in Lucas's big gourmet kitchen, enjoy the spectacular view from his island beach house, and probably play drunk Scrabble and video games until we pass out." I could tell she was doing her best to sound cheerful, but fuck, she shouldn't have to. She shouldn't have to care that I wouldn't be upset by what she'd just told me.

"Family can be a difficult business sometimes," I told her, wishing I could take her with me to my parents' for Thanksgiving. My father would be motherfucking joyful. Which was just another really good reason why I shouldn't drag her into his insane plot.

"I know. I just wish it didn't have to be so difficult most of the time."

"Me too." God, how I wished the same thing about being with her.

"I think you are a good person, too," she said softly. *No, I'm really fucking not.* I could feel her lips moving through the fabric of my shirt as she spoke, and I nearly groaned out loud. Because I wanted those lips so badly I was in grave danger of losing my mind. All I could think about was kissing her breathless until her sadness had been pushed away.

"You're a saint, and I'm a sinner. There's a huge difference between us, and don't you ever forget it."

She shook her head against me. "Not so different. And I'm definitely no saint, James." Then she pulled out of my arms and looked me straight in the eye. "If you only knew what I really want, I think you wouldn't like it," she said carefully, her breathing picking up as she faced me.

Oh fuck. Here we go. The gloves were being thrown down for the first time, and Winter was the one brave enough to go there. My dick started throbbing as I took in her words. *Oh, baby, you are fucking awesome.*

"Why don't you tell me? I'm right here, and I'm listening."

She shook her head. "No. I can't."

"Yes, you can." I reached out and held her chin in my hand as I had earlier, watching her response carefully. "Tell me what you really want, Win," I demanded.

The rise and fall of her chest grew deeper, as did her breathing as I held her captive. I willed her to say the thing I wanted to hear most in the world. I didn't know what I'd do with it afterward, but at that moment, I didn't care. I needed to hear her say that she wanted me.

"James, I…I want—"

White lights flashed in our faces as my sister pulled into her spot opposite mine. I blinked my eyes to find Victoria waving at us cheerfully.

Winter pulled away and was out of my car in five seconds flat.

I didn't even try to stop her.

Instead, I watched as she greeted my sister with a hug, and then as they hooked their arms together, both waiting expectantly for me to get out and join them.

I slapped on a smile and went with that plan.

She didn't get to say what she wants.

No matter how much I wanted to hear Winter's answer, I shouldn't have pushed her. Even though I'd almost gotten it out of her didn't mean it was the right thing to do. I needed to remember why my future couldn't include Winter Blackstone, and remember it well.

Yeah, Victoria's timely interruption had been for the best.

But having to accept that it was for the best made my heart twist painfully as I escorted the two of them into the elevators.

"Why are you two out so late?" Victoria asked, her curious eyes moving between Winter and me. Her question was the politely worded version of: Why in the hell are the two of you *together* and out so late?

Winter answered but kept her eyes focused on the floor. "I had class—"

"And I picked her up, because she didn't drive her car. The T at night is out of the question for her." I finished Winter's sentence for her with my eyes on my sister and nowhere near the floor. Helping a good friend was nothing to be ashamed of.

"Ahh…" Victoria made a little "o" with her mouth as she took in my clipped response, her intelligent mind working through what might really be going on. I knew she would come straight out and ask me at some point. My sister didn't tolerate secrets and lies.

"What about you?" I asked pointedly.

"Clay's dad's birthday. We took him to dinner," she shot back.

The elevator dinged through the tension as it stopped at the eleventh floor.

Winter stepped forward, impatient for the doors to open. "Thanks again for the ride home, James, and good seeing you, Victoria. Goodnight, guys." Her long legs took her away quickly. Clearly, she felt she needed to escape.

And I made her feel that way—selfish asshole that I am. I wanted to follow her, so I could make sure she was okay. How did I fuck that up so badly? One moment I had her in my arms—exactly where I'd wanted her for a long time—the next she was a tigress. Seemed my Winter had a few secrets of her own, and fuck did I want to know what they were. I liked that. That there was a bit of naughty mixed in with the sweet. *A little fucking much…*

We called our goodbyes to her back as she headed toward the hallway, and then Victoria and I stared at each other. Silent scrutiny between siblings, communication without words—something we had done for years.

After the doors closed us in again, my sister wasted no time.

"James, you cannot hurt her. Caleb will kill you. And so will I…along with everyone else."

Fuck my life.

CHAPTER FIVE

Winter

S hane's big brown eyes held the power to render me helpless as we discussed the mysteries of the Thanksgiving dinner menu. The fact he was only six years old probably helped, but he'd captured my heart nonetheless. His jeans had holes in the knees, and his shoes were ready for the trash. He could use a long soak in a warm, soapy bath and a haircut for his unruly sandy locks, but still, my little Shane was a shot of adorableness on maximum overdrive.

He's not yours.

I would have loved it if he were, but the rules were clear on how much "help" we could give the kids who visited the South Boston Youth Center. No matter how much I wished I could take Shane and his twin sister, Brenna, home with me, it couldn't happen. I couldn't buy clothes especially for them, or shoes, or school supplies. I wasn't allowed to take them to Chuck E. Cheese's on their birthday or give them a present I'd bought myself. It wasn't right to give preference to one child over another. All donations had to be vetted through proper channels and distributed fairly. I understood how the system worked.

I also understood how the system was *very* fucked up.

I had money and would love to put some of it to good use. I'd love to be able to provide some security for my little friends, Shane and Brenna, so they didn't have to live in a scary apartment in Roxbury where there were drug dealers, sex traders, gang violence, and a myriad of other horrors children should never have to deal with in their young lives.

I'd been wracking my brain lately for ways to make this a possibility. The very best scenario would be to found a private shelter where I made the decisions about who could get assistance. If I was director, and had a governing board of like-minded individuals to help me, I knew I could make it viable. I had a huge trust fund sitting in the bank growing by the day. I also had connections to wealthy donors who'd love the big fat tax write-off that came as part of their generous donation.

There were some problems with my plan, though.

My trust fund couldn't be touched for six more years, and I didn't have my license yet. I could do something about my licensed status, but my trust fund…not so much. In another month I'd be qualified to apply for certification as a social worker within the state of Massachusetts, whereas I inherited my money when I turned thirty, or at the time of a legal marriage. The age requirement had been included to ensure maturity for the trustee (me) in regard to the financial decisions made in dispersing such a large amount of money. Getting funded when I was older also ensured the maximum potential for growth as the trust doubled every seven years.

The marriage clause was there to protect the trust should I find myself in a matrimonial disaster, or on my own with children to provide for. What Chris had never realized was, had we married, he wouldn't have had access to the trust fund anyway. It was protected under an enforced prenup, that could be dissolved after ten years of marriage. I appreciated the wisdom and understood the why.

But, it truly sucked that I was the only one who had to wait years for it. *Especially when I had goals…*

Caleb was already thirty-one. Lucas and Wyatt turned thirty in a few months. Willow and Roger would tie the knot in July. So that left me hanging in the breeze for another six years. It wasn't like I wanted to piss it away, either. I was ready...ready to make my dreams come true. Yes, I had money for school and to live comfortably, but it wasn't the kind of money I needed to fund a new shelter for mothers and children in need.

"Miss Winter, what does pumpkin pie taste like?" Sweet little Shane blasted away my worries for the moment and brought me back to the here and now.

"You will get to find out tomorrow at the feast," I told him with a little tweak to his nose.

"But what if I don't like it?" he asked worriedly.

"If you don't like it, then you don't have to eat it, but *maybe* you will love it. Did you ever think of that? Maybe pumpkin pie is your new most favorite food in the whole wide world and you just don't know it yet." I winked at him.

"You're funny, Miss Winter."

"Thanks, Shane. I'll take that as a compliment." He nodded at me but I got the feeling he didn't really understand. "I'm good at something else besides being funny," I offered.

"What is it?"

"Well, I make the very, very, *very* best chocolate-chip cookies in the whole world. I have a trophy to prove it." I didn't share with Shane that my trophy was from a bake-off competition at summer camp that earned me third place, but he didn't need those confusing details. The bottom line was simple: I made awesome chocolate-chip cookies.

"You do?" Shane asked in awe.

I nodded slowly for emphasis. "And I'm going to bring some of my world-famous chocolate-chip cookies to the Thanksgiving feast tomorrow. You know, in case the pumpkin pie isn't your new favorite."

My promise earned me a big smile from Shane. Something I didn't get from him very often, because sadly, things to smile about were few and far between in his young life.

Which only made this smile that much more precious.

A SOAK in the tub called to me the moment I stepped inside my apartment. I was exhausted. After my day at the center, a trip to campus to sign the attendance and turn in my paper for the ethics class, a dry-cleaners pickup, a mad dash around the market—jam-packed with last-minute shoppers emptying the store of its turkeys, pies, and cranberries—I was just about ready for bed.

But the warm water combined with the *Rockstar* energy drink I'd been sipping had thankfully revived me, because I still had some chocolate-chip cookies to bake before I could slip in between the sheets on my bed. I'd promised Shane, and I intended to deliver. Everything had been organized for the meal at the center tomorrow. Food ordered and places set for the droves of people who would show up for a traditional meal they'd never have the means nor inclination to prepare for themselves. When I thought about it too much it depressed me. The least I could do was bring a homemade treat for my little friends. I wondered if Shane and Brenna's mom had ever made cookies for them before they'd fallen on hard times. I knew there had been a husband or father at one point, but certainly didn't know their family history. Young children could only relay so much reliable information, and even then, you had to remember it came filtered through a six-year-old's view of the world. Very different from how an adult would see things. Yeah…depressing.

I finished the last of my drink and hauled myself out of the cooling water. As I reached for a towel to dry off I heard the clink of metal directly above me. I knew that sound.

James.

I could hear him moving around sometimes if I was in a quiet moment at my place like it was right now.

He was exercising in his home gym.

The weights or bars were clacking against each other on whatever piece of equipment he was using. I could also tell if he used the rowing machine, and when he ran on his treadmill. Each had its own distinct sound.

I hadn't seen him since my little meltdown in his car a week ago. Jesus, I'd almost confessed my feelings for him. He had a way of demanding things from me that I couldn't deny. At my core I was a pleaser. I wanted to please him, so when James demanded I tell him what I wanted—there was a really good chance I would've done it. Victoria's spectacularly timed interruption had saved me from embarrassing myself past the point of no return.

God bless Victoria forever and ever.

I can't imagine how James would have reacted if I'd actually gotten the words out. *I've loved you for years, and I still do.* Ha! He probably would have laughed, patted me on the head, and suggested I lay off the wine.

Or maybe he wouldn't have.

I didn't know, and it was definitely his fault I was confused. He kept sending me mixed signals lately, and I was getting tired of it. Screw him for making me mental.

I dried off to the sounds of him working out a mere twelve feet above me and applied my favorite orange citrus body lotion all over my skin—while trying very hard *not* to imagine how James might look with no shirt and his hard body glistening with sweat. Not the best distraction-free technique I'll admit. With a sigh, I brushed out my hair and twisted it up into a knot secured with a clip to keep it back while I baked.

Inside my closet, I glanced around until I found exactly what I wanted to put on. I was all about comfort at the moment, so my favorite robe was the easy choice. The floral silk felt divine sliding against my naked skin, which was one of the reasons I loved it so much. The fact it was an exquisite hand-painted work of art was another. My mother had given it to me, and if there was one area where she was really talented, it would be in choosing lovely clothes. The items she chose were usually extraordinarily expensive to boot. A present for my last birthday, I knew my beautiful robe had to have cost a fortune—a luxury I would never buy for myself—but since it had been a gift, I enjoyed it very much.

I was only staying up to bake cookies, and there was nobody to see me, but for some reason I headed back to my room for some underwear. Some little niggling voice told me I should be prepared in case James decided to show up at my door.

Weird.

I didn't know why the thought came to mind, but probably because we were both at home on a night when the others were gone. Caleb wasn't here. He was on the island with Brooke already. He'd called me earlier from her place to say they'd see me at Lucas's on Friday and to get myself to the helipad on Friday morning for my ride. By helicopter, the trip to Blackstone Island was fast. Fifteen minutes total from the top of the BGE building to Lucas's private helipad at his beach house. I'd also noticed Victoria's car wasn't in her parking spot when I'd come home, so I guessed she was away for the night. If for some reason James did drop by, I didn't want to be free-floatin' underneath my shorty robe.

Well, I might want to, but it definitely wouldn't be a good idea.

I spied my dead phone on the bedside table and plugged it in for recharging. Half the time I forgot, and endured regular complaints from my family about my slow response times because of it.

Less than an hour later, I had one batch of cookies cooling and a second baking in the oven as I finished up at the sink. I liked to clean as I went along. And especially tonight, I didn't want a massive mess to deal with after I was done. My recurring yawns pushed me to hurry as I wiped down the counter around the sink. The energy drink from earlier had worn off, and I really needed to get to bed. Tomorrow would start early and end late, and I knew some solid sleep was necessary, or I'd be a cranky zombie for Thanksgiving at the center. I also wanted to package up a few cookies for James and leave them on his doorstep with a note before I left in the morning. A peace offering after the "incident" from last week, especially since we hadn't spoken or seen each other since then.

James was probably avoiding me.

Strangely, his avoidance relieved me rather than hurt my feelings. Denial worked well most of the time, and James's friendship was far too precious to consciously take the risk of destroying it. I suspected he felt the same way. So, we'd both act like nothing had changed between us the next time we saw each other. And things would go along as they had been doing for the last six months.

It wasn't the best situation, but it was how it had to be unless I wanted to ruin a lifelong friendship with a person I loved and cared about. As if on cue, the timer went off. I turned off the timer and opened the oven to check on my cookies. They looked perfect, but the key to having them stay that way was to get them out on time and onto a cooling rack.

I reached for the hot pad where it had been sitting beside the sink and began pulling the cookies out of the oven.

The hot pad protecting my hand went utterly nuclear hot just as I had the cookie sheet halfway between the open oven and the cooling rack. Everything then turned to complete shit.

Hot as in a skin-scorching 350 degrees.

I dropped the pan the second I had it level with the countertop. I couldn't help it as the pan clattered down with a bang and cookies scattered everywhere. It happened so fast I didn't even feel my hand crash into the side of the dish cabinet.

My body's response to the burning of skin was reflex. I had zero control over direction of movement—only the instinct to put as much distance between the heat and what was being burned—*as quickly as possible.*

The fact that I kept a set of very sharp knives attached to a magnetic rack on the side of the dish cabinet in my kitchen?

Bad.

Bad luck.

Bad string of events.

Just REALLY BAD.

The blood didn't start gushing immediately, so I wasn't aware until I felt the tickling sensation of trails flowing down my arm, and the dripping of big, warm, plops onto my leg.

And saw some splash onto the floor.

I stared in horror. The sight of blood was nauseating to me. Always had been. I didn't know why, but I just couldn't handle *seeing* it. The pain wasn't the worst pain, and I could endure it. But the sight of gushing blood from my body?

Hell, no!

I needed help—and since I was incapable of even managing a simple glance at my hand to assess the damage—I needed help from another person.

My phone was charging in my bedroom. My brother was gone. The closest "help" I knew of was one floor above me working out in his home gym.

I didn't think about it, because if I did, it wouldn't matter when I was passed out still bleeding profusely, and hopefully not to death. I grabbed the first thing I could find to soak up blood. With the hot pad pressed against my hemorrhaging hand, I headed into the hallway and stairwell. *Only one flight of stairs.* I couldn't look at my hand, but I could climb a single flight of stairs. *What the hell have you done to yourself?*

When I stumbled out of the stairwell and to James's apartment, I'd just about exhausted my mental reserves. There wasn't a lot left inside me to combat the nausea. I felt myself slide to the floor to land on my ass.

I pushed my feet forward and kicked at the base of his door as hard as I could, and as many times as I could.

And screamed his name.

CHAPTER SIX

James

Tomorrow would suck because my dad would make it suck. This was a simple fact that I knew would play out with the upmost certainty. With AC/DC's *Thunderstruck* blasting through my headphones, and less than five minutes of treadmill time to go, I went through the possible scenarios of how he'd call me out on the ultimatum he threw at me three weeks ago.

I'd never do anything to hurt my mother. And ignoring my father wouldn't eradicate the problems there, either. Those would never go away. So, I'd go to Thanksgiving dinner tomorrow and put on a show that said he wasn't getting to me.

Maybe alcohol could help with that.

As the song ended, I thought I heard what sounded like a thump, but I dismissed it because I was pounding out the last bit of the incline portion of my run. A hot shower was going to feel so good in a few minutes. So would the whack job while I was in there—

Thump…thump…

Where the fuck was that noise coming from?

I ripped out my headphones, and that's when I heard screaming along with the vicious pounding. "James...James...Jaaaaames!"

I ran toward the screams.

The closer I got, the easier they were to identify.

But the sight of her just about killed me. I'm sure I lost a good five years off my life when I ripped open my front door to find Winter on the other side of it covered in blood.

Oh fuck, no!

"I've got you, baby. I've got you," I repeated as I gathered her from the floor and carried her trembling body inside my apartment. We went straight into the bathroom where the light was good and the first-aid supplies were kept. "Can you tell me what happened, sweetheart?"

I got a lot of words, but very little of what she told me came out coherently. I heard parts of explanations as I settled her onto the marble counter like: "baking cookies for Shane" and "so hot it burned" and "the knife rack on the cabinet" and "blood," so I got the gist of it. There *was* a shit-ton of blood and that scared me, but I also noticed she wasn't completely responsive to my questioning. Her eyes looked a little glazed, and I figured she was probably in shock.

"Whoa, can you sit up here okay? I don't want you falling off and hitting your head."

She focused on my face and nodded slowly. "I can't look. The blood...it makes me sick..." She trailed off weakly before her neck flopped to the side.

"Okay. It's okay, Win. I'm going to help you, but I want you to take some deep breaths and lean on me. Don't worry about a thing right now. Just breathe and try to relax. I've got you." I cradled her head in my hands and held her steady until she focused on me again. "You did the right thing, Win." *You came to me for help.*

Her beautiful green eyes with their distinctive rings of gold around the iris filled with tears as she looked at me. She was scared and emotional, but I could tell she was trying to be brave, and I felt her relax a bit. "I could h-h-hear you w-working out." She took in a few deep breaths as she tried to calm herself.

"That's it, sweetheart. Breathe for me. I've got you, and I'm going to take a look at your hand, okay?" She whimpered as I talked her through it. "I don't want you to look, though. I want you to keep your eyes on the wall. Just look over my shoulder and focus on the pattern in the tile. Can you do that for me, Win?"

"Y-yesss." Her voice was thready, but I could hear the determination in her one-word answer. I was so grateful she'd come to find me when she needed help. Thank God I heard those thumps on my door. I realized now the sound had been her feet kicking against it. Very resourceful considering she'd been unable to use her hands, with one injured and the other occupied to stem the bleeding.

"You are so brave right now. *Badass* is a good description for you." I rambled out more words of praise as I gently tugged her hand away from where she clutched it against her stomach. "Let me get a towel—"

"I'll get blood all over it."

I could hear panic settling in. "It's a towel, Win. Who cares?" I grabbed a clean towel off the rack and draped it over her lap and legs, which were also covered in blood. Jesus Christ, how bad was this going to be? Now I was nervous. "I want you to count the tiles on the wall and don't look at your hand. Can you do that for me, baby?"

"Y-y-yesss."

"Good girl," I said as I gently peeled off the kitchen mitt

she'd used to wrap her hand. I made a point not to react in any way that might upset her further, but fuuuuck. The cut was at least two inches long and sliced midway between her thumb and index finger on her right hand. Blood began seeping as soon as pressure was removed. It was difficult to see how deep the cut had gone, but judging from the amount of blood still coming out of the wound? Too fucking deep. There might be tendon or nerve damage that could impair her range of motion in that hand for all I knew. I wasn't a doctor, but I was smart enough to know she needed to be seen by one. "I'm going to take you to the ER so they can fix you up."

"Oh, God." Her whole body trembled mightily, but she kept her head facing the wall like I'd told her to. "How bad is it?"

"I think the cut isn't so wide as it is deep. You're going to need stitches, but the docs will know how to take care of it. Let me get it wrapped back up for now, and then I'll take you to the hospital."

She started sobbing again as I quickly washed my hands in the sink, but there was no protest about my plan. I could tell she was trying very hard to deal with the situation even though she was on the verge of falling apart. I needed to get her mind off her injury, and do it quickly.

"So, who is this Shane you were baking cookies for when you had your accident? Do I need to be worried about him taking my girl away from me?" I pulled open the drawer where I kept the first-aid shit and gathered some sterile gauze and a new ACE bandage still in the package.

She half laughed and groaned. "Well, it's true he's already stolen my heart."

"So, you're telling me I have some competition I didn't even know about?" I kept it light and teasing, as I packed the cut with gauze to absorb the seeping blood. I decided against cleaning or applying any kind of antibacterial because it was probably beyond that scope, especially if the wound was still bleeding, so I wrapped more gauze around the width of her whole hand to close the cut and keep it as stabilized as possible.

"But I told you about him last week," she said tightly, her head still facing the bathroom wall over my shoulder.

"Ahh, so he's a young guy then?" I took the ACE bandage and started wrapping, sealing over the sterile gauze until her hand was completely bound with her thumb flush against the side. It would do until a doctor could get to it.

"*Very* young." I detected a tiny hint of humor in her voice, and it relieved me.

"Are you cougaring these days, Win? Gosh, I had no idea."

"I don't think cougaring is quite it. That would get me into some trouble with the law considering I'm twenty-four and he's six," she said tiredly.

Shane was the little boy who came to the youth center. I'd be lying if knowing he was a kid didn't make me really fucking happy. I'd also be lying if I couldn't admit that the thought of Winter wanting another guy absolutely cut me off at the knees. I wanted her. I wanted her to be *mine*. "I must meet this Shane and set him straight. He needs to know that I've got my eyes on him," I joked.

She rested her forehead on my shoulder, and I felt her grow heavy against me as she leaned forward. "I don't feel very good…I think…I…I'm gonna be siiiiick—"

I moved quickly to get her off the countertop and leaned her over the toilet, so she could get it over with. There was nothing fucking worse than the feeling you got right before you're going to puke. Poor thing. I rubbed her back with one hand and turned on the hot water in the sink with the other. She gagged and retched but not a lot came out. When she was done, I flushed the toilet and closed the lid and helped her to sit on top of it. "You okay, sweetheart?" I handed her a wet washcloth.

She buried her face in the washcloth with her good hand and groaned. "Yeah…better. Thank you. I don't know what I would have done if you w-weren't"—a deep shuddering sob escaped—"h-here to help m-m-me."

"Shhhh." I put the washcloth back under the running water and then held her face to mine. "But I was here. And you came to get me, and everything is going to be fine. We need to clean you up a bit and get you dressed, and then we can go."

"Okay." She looked so sad and defeated as she stared at me with her tear-filled eyes and nodded her head a few times. I wanted to kiss her. Crazy lunatic that I was, I wanted to kiss her right now, while she was scared and hurt and upset. *What the fuck is wrong with you?*

What was wrong with me was I had it bad for a girl I should not have had it bad for.

I wet the washcloth a second time and wrung it out. I started with the blood on her arms first before moving to her legs. She glanced at me working a few times, now that her cut was out of sight. I caught a shudder or two from her as the blood was wiped away, and sympathized with her queasiness at the sight of it. Because there was a lot to clean off her. At least I could admire her gorgeous legs beneath my hands with nothing but the flimsy robe covering her. I'd gotten a peek of sexy pink panties when she'd been bent over and retching, so at least she wasn't totally naked underneath the thing, and we didn't have that awkwardness to deal with on top of everything else. What I wouldn't give to touch her like this without it being a fucking traumatic situation for her. Christ, it was hard to remain calm when my heart was pounding inside my chest from being so physically close I could smell her. *Oranges.* Her scent always reminded me of oranges.

When the last of the dried blood was wiped away, I was relieved. I wasn't made of stone, and touching her so intimately had given me an epic and totally inappropriate hard-on. A raging boner she would have noticed if she weren't so out of it.

"Listen, I'm gonna have you lie on my bed while I take a two-minute shower before I get dressed, because I *know* I stink." She could hardly sit up, and I definitely couldn't trust her not to fall and crack her head open, so bed was my only option.

She didn't even take the golden opportunity I'd handed her to joke about my stench. "That's a good idea," she weakly, closing her eyes the second she was prone on my bed. My Winter was a beautiful mess at the moment. My Winter *was in my bed…*

God.

"I'll be back in five minutes ready to go." She nodded at me without opening her eyes. "Just keep breathing deep and steady, and try to relax." I fought the urge to kiss her again.

I hit the bathroom and ditched my shorts for what had to be my speediest shower on record. I didn't even wait for the water to get all the way hot, but jumped under the spray, got wet, soaped myself, rinsed, and stepped out. The cool water gave the added advantage of tamping down my dick, so…bonus.

I dried off as I walked to my closet. Winter never even glanced my way and looked like she was asleep. Maybe that was another positive though. She didn't need the added complication of my cock on display and gunning for her.

God, what a clusterfuck.

Five minutes later I was dressed, but Winter wasn't. I couldn't take her into the ER in the flimsy—read, *sexy-as-fuck*—robe. Well, it could be sexy if not covered in blood. She needed clothes.

And that was a problem.

Because Winter was so wiped out physically—practically incoherent after the panicking and puking—and was no help whatsoever. I'd have to figure out how to get her dressed on my own.

THANK GOD her apartment door hadn't locked behind her when she'd left to find me, because we didn't share keys. Caleb probably had one, but he wasn't here to ask. Once I had a spare moment at the ER, I'd let him know what happened to his sister.

Winter mumbled something I couldn't decipher as I took her into her bedroom. To save time, I'd carried her out of my apartment, used the elevator to get us to her floor, and continued to carry her to her place rather than trying to help her walk. Despite the shitty circumstances, I loved the fact she was in my arms right now. *So close to me.* But Winter was in and out, and not fully in control by any stretch. "What you want to wear?" I asked against her ear, so she might hear me and actually comprehend my question.

She pointed to her walk-in. "Left side drawers has...y-y-yoga pants...Red S-s-sox sh-shirrrrt..."

"Okay, wait here and just keep breathing. Think about something nice and good to take your mind off everything," I said as I carefully lowered her onto her bed.

"You're nice and good, James. Soooo...good to me...alllll the time," she said in a lax voice with her eyes closed. I wondered what in the hell was going on in her mind to make her say those words to me right at this moment. In spite of her trauma, she was telling me that *I* was good and nice? Winter never ceased to amaze me with how big her heart was. It took every ounce of strength I had in me to leave her to go into her closet and search for yoga pants and a Sox shirt. I'd have to deal.

I found out the hard way that "dealing" sucked ass.

Undressing a woman was easier than putting clothes back on. This I discovered when said woman was barely able to stand. I felt myself breaking out in a sweat after dragging and yanking the gray yoga pants up her long sexy legs. At least the bottom half of her was covered, I reasoned after I'd finished.

But the top half of her was about to get uncovered, because I had to remove the robe to put a shirt on her. There was a twinge of guilt at seeing her bare breasts…but not that much. It was a clear case of *sorry, not sorry*.

Fuuuuck, she had beautiful tits.

Full and round, tipped with rosy nipples just begging for my mouth, and *other* things. Clamped, dappled in melted wax, artfully bound—I could picture everything—ready for my reawakening cock.

I remembered well the first and only time I'd seen them before tonight. Her fifteenth birthday party when Janice, Caleb's psycho ex, ripped off Winter's bathing suit top in the pool. God, I'd hated how much it had embarrassed her. I'd comforted her to the best I was able in a situation with people all around us, but I'd never forgotten how gorgeous she was even then. How *could* I ever forget?

The past nine years had only served to form her beauty into a more perfect version with maturity. She moaned and fluttered her eyes open as I struggled with the pink T-shirt. "You're looking at my boobs," she muttered at me.

"That couldn't be helped, sweetheart," I said right back. "And for the record, your *boobs* are spectacular, and I couldn't have *not* looked at them unless I had no pulse."

She giggled at me.

In fact, she didn't look in the least disturbed by our topic of conversation—that she'd caught me checking out her tits and ogling them.

Crazy shit kept happening here. There was no other way to describe this night.

"Okay, shoes," I commanded.

It appeared she'd come out of her fog a bit, to the point she was able to actually help me get shoes onto her feet. The difference between help*ing* vs. help*less* was nothing short of miraculous.

"My phone is there on the bedside table. Can you turn it on for me?"

"Sure thing." I finished tying her shoes and grabbed the phone. "We should bring your ID too."

"My wallet is in my backpack...I think in the hallway." She glanced at me and then frowned as if she'd remembered something. "Oh shit! I didn't turn the oven off. I just left it."

"Good call remembering that, Win. I'll take care of the oven on our way out." I helped her up from her bed to stand against me, all soft and rumpled from my less-than-efficient dressing techniques. She looked like an exquisite goddess to me. I held her face in both hands and brought us very close—close enough to kiss her.

I wanted to.

I almost did.

At the last moment I remembered why I shouldn't...and I was fucking frustrated. *God, I wish she was mine.* "Let's get you to a doc who can fix your hand," I said far too harshly.

Winter didn't flinch. She held on to my eyes with hers and said two small words that made my cock jump at the sharp jolt I felt all the way to my balls.

"Yes, sir."

Was I only imagining something I wanted to believe?

But, there was no sarcasm in her words. Just trust…*and* the desire to please me?

She chose—did I dare imagine it was possible—to be submissive to me?

Winter was allowing me to take over control of care for her. *Easily.* There was no resistance, only willingness.

Something I'd never considered before this moment was how Winter might feel about my little secret.

What if she wanted it with me?

I didn't know the answer to that question yet, but I did know something.

Finding out had absolutely jumped to the top of my list.

CHAPTER SEVEN

James

Closing in on five hours later, I had her back at the apartment with both of us in desperate need of sleep. The ER had been exhausting for her, but at least she'd been able to leave there with prognosis for a full recovery. She'd undergone a lot of tests to determine if there was any nerve damage, which would have necessitated immediate surgery to repair if the results had been classed at third-degree or above. Winter's injury was deemed second-degree, and would most likely recover slowly on its own.

Thank God, because she was right-handed.

Apparently, she'd sliced through the muscle that controlled movement of the thumb. She'd just barely nicked the sheath surrounding the medial nerve of her right hand. A close call, but not deep enough to sever the nerve, so she'd been able to receive layered stitches and antibiotics instead of surgery. Not surprisingly, the majority of her pain came from the superficial dermal burns to the inside of her fingers. We'd guessed that the hot pad she'd used to take the cookies from the oven had been wet on one side. As soon as the metal pan came in contact with the wet cloth, it had conducted searing steam straight onto the skin of her palm. No wonder she'd dropped everything and flailed her hand away. That she'd flailed it directly into the blade of a really sharp fucking knife? Goddamn unfortunate.

Still, watching her endure the endless probing into her open wound, the electric shocks, the shots, the scans, and the stitches hadn't been a walk in the park. Winter had a severe phobic reaction to the sight of blood and gore. So severe in fact, it had been really difficult for her to remain conscious throughout their procedures. I'd asked if they could give her something to calm her down, but they'd needed her awake to respond to the nerve-function testing. It had felt like an endless cycle of trauma for several tortuous hours: Winter withstanding the discomfort of whatever test they were conducting, and then her emotional breakdown as she had to mentally process each new thing, and was unable to manage much beyond lapsing in and out of awareness.

Watching her struggle had been fucking horrible.

The doctor, who looked to be barely of drinking age, seemed to know his job, at least. He'd assumed she was my girlfriend as he rattled off the instructions for wound care, prescription medications, and a follow-up appointment with her regular M.D and possibly an orthopedic specialist. I never once entertained the idea of correcting him. She should be my girlfriend—she *should* be more than my girlfriend actually.

Nobody else would touch her while she was hurting, unless they were in possession of a Mass Gen ID badge.

It should be my job to comfort her.

She should be mine to protect.

She should just be mine.

WINTER WAS asleep in my arms when I deposited her carefully onto her bed. God, how I wanted to climb in next to her and close my eyes too. I was fucking wrecked from this night—both emotionally and physically. I bent down and gently removed her shoes, deciding it wouldn't matter if she slept in her clothes. Some healing rest was what she needed more than anything else right now.

As I settled the comforter over her, I noticed the tight expression she wore, even while asleep. This night had been a grueling marathon, and I knew the very best thing I could do for Winter right now was leave her in peace. She should sleep for hours from the pain medication she'd been given. Whatever problems there were, we could deal with them in the morning. I set her phone on the bedside table and shot a quick text: **Let me know when you wake up, and I'll come down. You were so brave last night. J**

I glanced down to find her eyes wide open and watching me. "You're not leaving, are you?" So many times tonight I'd thought she'd been asleep when she hadn't been, as she'd done her best to bear through the whole nightmarish experience. Even in her exhausted state, there was residual panic. I could hear the fear, and it ripped into my heart like a red-hot blade.

"I thought you were out for the night, Win. It's two in the morning. Go back to sleep, babe," I said as gently as I could.

"But don't leave me." Her eyes filled with tears as she pleaded, reaching her good hand out to me before patting the side of the bed with the other bandaged one. "I won't be able to sleep if I'm alone. Please…"

She wants me to sleep in her bed—with her?

Fuck. Yes.

And just like that, I caved.

The whole thing was a no-contest situation, and again, shouldn't be a surprise. My sweet Winter was crying for me to stay. She needed *my* comfort so she could sleep. She begged me to get into her bed and sleep beside her.

But yeah, like I had even a shred of strength to resist by telling her no.

So, I kicked off my shoes and did what she asked of me.

I lifted the comforter and slid in beside her, careful of her bandaged hand. As I stretched out on my side facing her, I didn't say anything, because I couldn't form words. I was barely capable of believing where I was. I didn't know how I'd gotten here, but now I worried I wouldn't be able to step back like I *should* do when it was time for things to go back to how they'd been.

Back to normal.

Would tomorrow be normal?

You know it won't be.

I shouldn't be here, but I couldn't *be* anywhere else.

"Thank you, James," she said so softly it was almost inaudible, as she slid her body closer to mine, "for everything you do for me…all the time."

Her eyes were closed again, but she'd turned toward me so I could see every inch of her face clearly. Winter had always been gorgeous in my eyes, but at twenty-four, she was even more beautiful than ever. The bathroom light had been left on with the door open enough to illuminate the darkness should she need to make her way there in the middle of the night. I used that tiny bit of light to study every feature of her face. I was close enough to feel her body heat. The warm ivory of her complexion contrasted against the sooty darkness of her eyelashes as they lay atop sculpted cheekbones. The pouty, luscious lips I wanted to kiss so badly that I ached, parted as if she were going to say something more. I could tell she was still in a fitful state as she struggled to find the peace of sleep.

"Shhh, I'm here now. And I'll be here until you go to sleep," I whispered against her cheek before pressing my lips there. I breathed in the scent of oranges laced with the antiseptic smells of a five-hour hospital visit and couldn't pull away.

She nestled in closer, her lips nearly against mine. "Don't leave after I'm asleep. James. Stay…with me," she whispered sleepily.

"I'm always close if you—"

Suddenly my lips were busy.

Kissing her.

To be fair, she kissed me first. And once she put those precious lips to mine, all bets were off. I wouldn't stop this. I was finally doing what I'd wanted to do for the better part of a decade.

It didn't matter that she was still reeling from a traumatic event and dosed with pain meds. I didn't care that she was half asleep from exhaustion. I had no will to resist. None.

She might not even remember this tomorrow.

I'd never forget this for as long as I lived.

Because right fucking now she wanted me in her bed, and she wanted to kiss me. And as stupid as it was for me to indulge in my long-lived fantasy with Winter Blackstone, I wouldn't deny her either. I'd let her take whatever she wanted from me for as long as she wanted to take it.

Fuck. YES.

I felt Winter come alive the second our lips touched. It was like *she'd* been waiting for it, too. Once we started, there was no reeling it in. *Why the hell didn't I do this sooner?* It was everything and so much more.

I palmed the back of her neck and kissed down her jaw to

nip along her throat. I licked her skin, needing to know what that felt like. She gave me access by tilting her neck, and I understood her gesture for what it was. *Submission*. Winter was offering herself. All I had to do was take what she offered.

She felt so good.

So I took.

I found my way back to her lips with soft bites and nips trailing up her throat and across her jaw. *Sweet*. She tasted so sweet. When I pressed against her lips with my tongue, desperate to put any part of me inside her, she opened her mouth with a sexy moan that nearly undid me. With the wet warmth of her tongue tangling with mine, I had the first flash of worry of where this might go. The wild erotic creature in my arms didn't seem like she wanted to stop at kissing. She wanted more…

"James, please…I…I'm—"

"What do you want, beautiful?" I managed to whisper in her ear as I resumed my exploration of her lovely neck, unwilling to break our connection.

"I…I want you to touch…me."

My dick heard her words loud and clear, as did my embattled brain. "Where do I touch you?"

She moaned her answer. "Anywhere…everywhere…"

The princess had given me the keys to her tower with those two words. I would do what she wanted. I'd make her come and watch the whole amazing experience unfold as I did it.

I slipped my hand under the waist of the yoga pants and watched for her reaction. Her eyes were still closed, but she wasn't anywhere close to sleep. Winter needed something to take her mind off everything, so she could relax.

I needed to do this for her right *now*.

It was *on*.

She arched into my hand as I slid it down over the flat plane of her stomach, and kept right on going under the elastic of what I knew were lacy pink panties to find the prize. When my fingers met the soft wet heat enfolding her clit, she cried out and gripped my hand with thighs clenched so tightly I could feel them shaking.

"You are so fucking sexy like this," I told her, desperately wishing I could see where my fingers were buried. I felt slippery, hot flesh and couldn't resist going deeper. I dipped in one finger and then another, loving the tight grip of being inside her. "Is this what you wanted?" I asked.

Her answer was to ride my hand like a woman who knew how to get herself off.

But that was all I sensed coming from her. In her current state of mind, I realized Winter wasn't fully aware of me beyond being the source of a physical release she so desperately needed.

Still, I was at her service as I circled her clit and helped her get closer to it. I couldn't resist playing her body and controlling the delivery of the orgasms. Orgasms—*plural*. I would give them to her until she couldn't take anymore. The first came on very fast.

Far too fast for my liking.

She convulsed against me. I could feel her mouth working against my neck as she gasped out a few sharp shuddering breaths. Other than those small sounds, she was quiet when she came.

Very much to my liking.

The second orgasm arrived not far behind the first, as I fucked in and out of her with two fingers while working over her slick clit with my thumb.

Absolutely perfectly beautiful in the moment. This moment. *All moments.* I was so fucking lost to her already.

"Again," I told her. "Take it all."

I curled my fingers up and inward to find the rough patch of skin. From Winter's convulsive moan, I'd found her special spot and stroked her a little faster. I could have her coming for as long as I wanted to this way. The control was completely in my hands. Knowing she *wanted me* to do this to her?

Like nothing I'd ever known.

Somehow Winter turned everything around on me, and she did it in a split second.

"I love youuuuuu, Jaaaaaames."

She said it in a soft burst with her lips right against my neck as she orgasmed for what had to be the third time.

I heard her.

The words were spoken under the duress of dominant sexual manipulation by me, but they were said regardless.

"I…I…love   you…I-love-you-I-love-you-I-love-you-I-love-you-I-love-you-I-love—"

I found her lips and covered them with mine in an openmouthed kiss.

So I could feel the sweetest words coming from her.

And into me.

I LEFT her sleeping in her bed, and it was probably one of the hardest things I'd ever done, and it was only to clean up the mess in her kitchen so she wouldn't see it in the morning.

The cookies were a bigger mess than the blood actually. After putting the round ones into a plastic storage container, I gathered the deformed and broken ones scattered around the top of the stove and the counter and put them on a plate. I ate two of them. They still tasted great despite their odd shapes, as I knew they would. She made awesome cookies, something I'd known—and tasted—for years.

Why was I out here eating cookies after what had just happened in her bedroom?

I didn't know what else to do. If I thought my head was fucked up before, I should probably get a gun and let a bullet take care of my problems. My logical mind told me she wasn't fully aware of what she'd said to me. Winter was injured, exhausted, and medicated, so nothing she'd said could be taken as a conscious statement of truth. This was my lawyer brain speaking to me. My James brain had a different opinion.

My James brain argued that we didn't put thoughts into words if our minds didn't believe them. Winter could only say the things that were already inside her consciousness. She might be out of it, but she'd said and done things tonight that showed her feelings about me went deeper than I'd ever realized.

My James brain was a fucking goddamned asshole for dangling something in front of me that I wanted so badly.

I'd probably do anything to hear her say those three words to me again.

Those words changed everything.

Every-fucking-thing.

I turned off the light in the kitchen and went to check on her one last time.

She had rolled to her side, her long hair wildly strewn over the pillow like dark silk. Her expression looked peaceful now. The earlier tension had left her—finally—and I was grateful. I hated the idea of her suffering and in pain. I leaned over her, close enough to hear her breathing in a steady, calm pattern of in and out. She would get through this and be okay. Thank God, I'd been here to help her.

But things would be different now. For us and for our families. Because it couldn't go back to how it had been before between us. Not after this night.

And I didn't want things to go back to how they'd been before, either. Because even if I did want that, I was honest enough to admit I'd never be able to follow through on walking away from her. I'd have to make some changes—give up some of the things I craved but couldn't have with her—if I hoped for any chance at all.

I pressed my lips to her forehead gently so I wouldn't wake her.

"I love you too, beautiful."

For a split second she smiled.

She was dead asleep, but she heard me…and she smiled.

CHAPTER EIGHT

Winter

Sex dreams are totally conflicted. On the one hand, you wake up smiling and feeling like you were in on an amazing secret. That's the good part. The not-so-good part is feeling guilty for visualizing supremely filthy deeds with someone you are definitely not having sex with, but wish you were.

I peeked under the comforter and checked. I wasn't naked. The same pink Red Sox T-shirt and gray yoga pants were still in place. Clothes that James put on me so he could take me to the ER last night. I did remember him eying my boobs and saying they were spectacular when he was putting the shirt on me. Oddly, I felt no embarrassment about that. I didn't care that he'd seen me. Maybe it would help him to finally make a move—

"The princess awakens." The subject of my dirty dreams rose from the comfy chair in the corner of my bedroom and sauntered to the bed looking utterly delicious as always. He must have left at some point to shower and dress before coming back. "How are you this morning?" *He stayed after he brought me home.*

I lifted my right hand for inspection. Bandaged between

thumb and index finger with a stabilizer to keep me from moving it. There was a slight throbbing in the general area of the cut, but nothing I couldn't handle. My threshold for pain wasn't the problem. The sight of blood was what I couldn't stomach. "Hi." I smiled at him and wondered how I'd ever repay him for being so good to me. "I'm okay…really, I am fine. James, I don't know how I'll ever be able to thank you for all you did for me last night. God, I was so scared—"

"No need, Win. I was right where I wanted to be." To keep me from interrupting, he held up his palm. "I'm not saying you didn't scare the ever-lovin' shit out of me when you showed up at my apartment leaking blood all over, but I'm eternally grateful I was home." He carefully lowered himself to sit on my bed. "But don't *ever* do that again," he said sternly.

"Believe me, I won't. Jesus…" I dared to ask the question. "I was a mess, wasn't I?"

"Yeah." His stern look morphed into a wicked grin, letting me know there were a lot more details he could have shared to answer my question, but he was being nice instead.

"What?" I looked at him, supremely jealous he was showered and gorgeous in his worn jeans and soft white shirt, while I was full-scale call-in-the-National-Guard disaster. "Why are you looking at me like that?"

"How is *that*, exactly?" He made air quotes with his fingers and was adorably cute doing it.

I couldn't help staring at his lips as I sought any kind of comeback that would take the focus off me. "Never mind," I said finally, realizing there was no good answer to my original question. An image of us kissing flitted through my head, but the details were frustratingly missing. "James, last night—"

"How much do you remember from last night?" He hadn't lost the smirk on his face even a little, either.

"Umm…what do you mean?" Instant fear hit my gut.

"Did I do something…b-bad?" My muscles delivered me a swift and silent "fuck you" when I made the move to sit up. The aches and pains screamed at me, and I couldn't help the pathetic groan that escaped.

"Easy there," he scolded. "You need to take it slow, because your body has been through a helluva lot in the last twelve hours."

"Twelve hours. What time is it?" I tried to get a good look at the alarm clock on my bedside table but his frame blocked my view. "James, I…I have t-to be at the center by t-t-ten o'clock." I lost the small shred of composure I'd managed to bluff my way through. Hot tears fell as he drew me in with strong arms.

"Shhh, you're all right. I got you," he said reassuringly while caressing me up and down my back. "And you didn't do anything bad, Win."

Despite wallowing in my own personal ocean of self-pity, James was still here with me—helping me through the mess I'd made and taking care of me. I clung to him wildly, again feeling an odd sense of intimacy, or at least the flash of a memory of intimate acts between us. It was weird, and I had no proof that anything had happened, but my subconscious told me otherwise.

I pulled back from his embrace so I could look him in the eye, because seeing his reaction to what I was about to ask him was the only way I could get the truth. "But what did I do last night? You said something about wondering how much I remembered from last night. Well, the answer to that is nothing really after we left the hospital…so I need you to tell me," I pleaded.

His brown eyes with the green flecks—that made them so unique—flared enough for me to catch the surefire tell that there was more to the story of *us* and *last night* than I was currently aware.

"Was I…did I do something inappropriate, James?"

He shook his head back and forth slowly. "Not to me."

He answered every question like a lawyer, and it was starting to annoy me. "You mean I didn't do anything *to you*, or that you don't consider whatever it was inappropriate?"

"You don't remember at all?"

Now I was the one shaking my head at him. His careful hedging of the topic had me worrying more and more with each passing second. "I told you I don't remember anything after we left the ER. Look, I'm very sorry if I did some—"

"How about I just show you what you did?"

I swallowed hard. "What did I do?" I asked again, but this time the words came out of me in a fearful whisper…I might not really want him to tell me. *Please, God, don't let it have been sex.* It would be tragically cruel to have been with James and then have no memory of the experience.

He snaked a hand behind my neck and tugged me in toward him. "You did *this*," he said just before his lips found mine and took possession of any last scrap of resistance I might've still owned. Didn't matter, because I didn't want to resist him any more than I wanted him to stop.

James was kissing me, and it was real. It wasn't some sexy dream fantasy I'd feel guilty about later, but the real man. The same man who took possession of my heart years ago.

Soft lips framed with just enough stubble to make sure I felt every tiny prick as his mouth came demandingly alive against mine, caressing with a heat that shot straight between my legs. When I felt the press of his tongue at my lips, I opened for him. I *wanted* him inside me. He thrust past my lips with a forceful tongue that swirled and swept over every place he could reach with it. I loved it all.

James kissed me as if he'd done it before. I believed him,

even though I didn't remember what must have been a beautiful experience. My erotic dream made more sense now, but was still infuriatingly void of details.

None of that mattered though. I was lost the instant our mouths connected. Lost and so very busted, because this meant I'd kissed *him* last night—and not the other way around. Had I done more than kiss him? Did I say or do anything that'd let the genie out of the bottle? There was no putting her back in if I had. Could James know how I felt about him? There were so many questions I wanted to ask, but that time was not now. Right now, I wanted to be kissed by James, and let him take us wherever he might want to go. I wouldn't do a thing to stop him. I wanted this. I wanted him.

I heard myself moan in protest when he slowly pulled away with my bottom lip tugged between his teeth. "Open your eyes and look at me, beautiful," he said with his lips so close I could feel the tiny puffs of air against mine as he formed his words.

Our eyes met, and what I saw in those brown-green orbs told me he wanted this—every bit as much as me.

We stared at each other, both of us probably thinking about how we'd just crossed a line that separated a lifelong friendship from…something with the potential to be a lot more if we were both on the same page. All signs seemed to be pointing that we were indeed reading the same book. *Thank God. I didn't think I could take his rejection right now.*

I waited for him to make the first move toward talking about it, because that's how James operated. If he wanted to talk, he would.

But he didn't get the chance to say anything because one very distinctive ringtone—the Imperial March from Star Wars—crashed into our magical moment.

"My mom."

"I figured"—his beautiful mouth stretched into a cocky grin as he smirked at me—"and it's a nice ringtone, Win. And before you ask, I already spoke to Caleb about your accident this morning while you were sleeping. He knows, so there's a good chance your mom knows too."

I shut my eyes in frustration, prepping myself to endure my mother's interrogation. The fact she was miles away in Charleston wouldn't help smooth over her worry, either. "Awesome," I said sarcastically.

"They're just concerned about you, Win." He reached for my phone on my bedside table and handed it to me.

I took it from him and tapped the green button, steeling my voice with as much "everything is fine" as I could muster. My mood wasn't helped by James seeming to find the whole thing amusing as hell. *Bastard.*

"Hi, Mom. Happy Thanksgiving. How are things in Charleston?"

"Well, not very good when I've just been told my daughter has nearly cut her thumb from her hand," she replied with abundant tearful drama—just as I expected.

I counted to five before I said a word.

CALMING my mother down from her panic involved James speaking to her for clarification on everything the doctor had said about my injury—none of which I could remember. The idea that it was probably a good thing she wasn't around for the ER trip wasn't lost on either of us. My mom could bring the drama when she wanted to. Still, I knew she loved me and was understandably worried if I'd be okay, and have the full range of movement and nerve function restored. I *really* hoped

84

for that too when I listened to James's detailed explanations. I had done a number on myself, and the ramifications were startling when absorbing them with a clear head. I remembered virtually nothing of the treatment at the ER—not the diagnosis of the damage to the nerve that served my hand, or the suggested treatment. James had been my savior in so many ways.

"Yes, Madelaine. I'll take care of her today. You don't have to worry, it's already done." James and I shared eye contact as he patiently dealt with my mother. He was so good with people—confident and reassuring. If I didn't already love him after last night, and how he was gently controlling my mother, I would now. "And I was grateful to be here for her. Please don't worry, and enjoy your time in Charleston with your family," he said patiently before handing the phone back to me.

After a final goodbye with promises to speak again tomorrow from Lucas's in a group call, I ended it. There were texts from Caleb, Lucas, and Willow, and a missed call from Wyatt blowing up my phone, so I quickly dealt with those. I texted Wyatt to say it was sweet of him to call me when he was so far away, and that he'd better be home for Christmas or else. Then I sent a group text to the other three and told them I was fine and would see them all tomorrow morning like we'd planned.

Our eyes gravitated back to staring at each other after that. I was grateful he'd been able to deflect my mom so nicely. The alternative wouldn't have been easy or fun.

But my mother wasn't my biggest worry at the moment.

This *thing* going on between James and me needed to be addressed in some way at least. A kiss to the cheek or forehead is one thing—the kiss he'd just laid on me was entirely another. He'd given me an "I want you" kiss—a "let's get naked and make each other feel good" kiss.

"James, we need to talk about it—"

"But let's not just yet." His answer surprised me. He kept his eyes on me and brushed the back of his index finger up my cheek. I didn't sense any panic or urgency in him—just calm.

"You don't want to discuss that kiss we shared, or talk about whatever else I probably did to you last night and still don't remember?"

His grin widened a bit along with his eyes as he shook his head at me.

"You should just tell me, James." I had no intention of letting this go anymore.

"I know we need to talk about it, Win, I do. It's just that I don't think right now…today…is the right time for that discussion." He brought his thumb back to my cheekbone and caressed. "It was a long, traumatic night, and I was right there watching you struggle the whole time. There weren't that many hours for sleep by the time we got back here, and if I'm fucking drained, you have to be ready to drop." He looked at my bandaged hand and gently covered it with his own. "So, I'd like to propose how today will go instead of what you had planned, because your original one of dishing out Thanksgiving dinners for the homeless is definitely out. You know that, right?" The determined look he gave me was tempered with kindness, which oddly soothed me in spite of my disappointment.

My heart sank, but I was in no position to argue. I couldn't serve food. I wasn't totally confident I could shower and dress without some help. It was also an hour past the time I said I'd would be in. "I figured as much," I said with a heavy heart.

"Caleb and your mom already gave me full authority to make sure you take it very slow today."

I nodded and tried to get a grip on my emotions.

"It can't be that bad, Win. They must have plenty of volunteers today. Don't people with guilty consciences flock in for Thanksgiving in particular to help out? I've seen it in the news before."

"Yeah…it's not that. They'll have plenty of help today, you're right."

"Then why so sad?" He dipped his head to meet me face to face. "You look devastated."

"The cookies for Shane and Brenna…I promised them, and now I'll just be another asshole adult who let them down. I hate being *that* person more than I hate the sight of blood." I felt myself choke up. I could barely make sense of my emotions right now. Part of me wanted to fall into a deep sleep of denial, and the other part wanted to hear James's version of the two of us after he brought me back home.

"You've never been an asshole and you never will be," he said as he pulled me into his arms. I breathed in his spicy scent and realized nothing felt better than being against James. Nothing. I was quickly becoming addicted and didn't want him to pull away. I could be happy being held by him for as long as he wanted to do it.

"James, I…I hate to ask this, but will you take me to the center…just so I can drop off the cookies to Shane and Brenna?" My mouth was against the side of his neck, and I had the furious urge to lick him there.

His arms tightened their hold as he comprehended my question. "On one condition."

"What is it?" What could he possibly want from me in return? *James has never needed anything from me.*

"You're coming with me to my parents' for Thanksgiving after."

CHAPTER NINE

James

"I can do that," she agreed, maybe a little too quickly.

She surprised me by being so compliant, but her willingness only served as a turn-on for me. I wasn't complaining. Her eyes flicked over me as she studied my face, probably searching for answers about my motivations for asking her to join me at my parents'. I wasn't ready to do much beyond taking care of her right now, but the spark of an idea had taken root in my head anyway.

Something that would probably never fucking work.

But man, I wanted it to.

I didn't have the answers, but I sure as hell wasn't going to jinx everything by rushing in half-cocked. Which was never my problem around Winter. Ever. My dick was of the *fully cocked* variety if in the same room with her. Telling me she loved me last night wasn't helping in the sense of trying to keep everything cool and moving slowly. My heart was screaming one thing and my head another. Caution was a trait I'd adopted as a way to survive in my world, and I needed it now.

At least Thanksgiving dinner with my father, something

I'd dreaded for weeks, was now a meeting I actually looked forward to. Which was a novelty. I wanted to see the look on his face once he realized who I'd brought with me. I wouldn't offer a sliver of an explanation to him either. Let him try and figure out what was going on without benefit of the whole backstory for once. My father wasn't going to be allowed to control my future. As long as I had breath in my body, any decisions regarding my life were my own.

Winter didn't even hesitate in agreeing to go with me. In fact, she'd gone along with every one of my demands since I'd started handing them down this morning—which only made her all the more irresistible. I could no longer mistake her consistent signals for what they truly were: naturally submissive behaviors. My thoughts flashed to an image of her bound naked to my bed, her body splayed out for me to worship. I felt my mouth begin to water, and everything below the waist start to tighten.

Off-the-charts-fucking sexy was how she appeared in my fleeting fantasy. I had to keep reminding myself that's all it was. A glorious fantasy.

For now.

And I'd thought I was attracted to Winter *before* last night. My inner Dom was dying to meet her inner sub with a craving so intense I feared how things might eventually play out. I'd never felt this way about *any* other woman before. Not Leah. Not anyone.

My previous belief that Winter and I weren't suited was quickly going down in flames, and I was running out of reasons to keep a distance. Especially when she looked at me like she was doing right now with her sexy eyes melting through my resistance like a hot knife into butter.

I told my conscience to fuck off and leave me alone for the day.

"You're amazing, Winter Blackstone." It was the truth.

"I am?" She appeared genuinely surprised.

"Oh yes, you are."

"How am I amazing, James?" The corner of her mouth lifted in a tiny smile.

Mostly you're amazing because you love me. "Well, for you to be so happy and caring of others after the night you had is damn amazing," I told her. "You've never complained, not one time. You let me take care of you last night, and you're coming with me today so I can keep an eye on you. And you're doing it willingly." *And you love me.* I picked up her bandaged hand carefully and brought it to my lips for a gentle kiss. "I rest my case."

She blushed at the praise, which only served to bring my cock to full attention. Again, not a surprise, but it helped me understand something about Winter that I'd suspected all those years ago on the day of her fifteenth birthday party.

She wasn't acting.

There was no artifice or deceit in her behavior.

Winter was simply unaware of how beautiful she was.

And she loves me.

HOLDING on to any shred of self-control became my one and only goal when she needed help to get ready.

"This is making you uncomfortable, isn't it?" she asked in a small voice.

"Whatever gave you that idea?" I managed through gritted teeth as I did the hooks on the back of her bra.

When she'd called me into her bedroom, I really didn't know what I expected. I guess I wasn't thinking much at all beyond getting to have her with me today.

It shouldn't have surprised me, though. I'd showed her the surgical gloves she had to wear on her hand when she showered, because her cut needed to remain dry in order to heal. I knew her hand was sore, and her range of motion limited, so twisting fingers behind her back to fasten tiny hooks tightly into corresponding loops wasn't possible for her to manage alone. It wasn't rocket science to figure out her need for assistance was real, but my dumbass brain practically shorted out when I walked in there and got a good look at her in some sexy-as-fuck black lingerie.

Her silky hair flowed down her back and shoulders in soft waves, taking my line of sight directly to her legs in black thigh-high stockings topped with some kind of high-waist garment that did amazing things to her already amazing ass. She shyly looked over her shoulder at me and asked if I would fasten the hooks of her bra for her.

I was fairly sure I groaned out loud.

I could do this.

Yeah, asshole, keep telling yourself that.

Easier said than done when all that stood between my hands and her beautiful body was…nothing. I could smell her orangey scent again and fought the urge to put my lips to her shoulder and have a taste. I'd never be able to stop if I went that far, so I pushed those thoughts aside as best I could.

"I can just tell," she said. "I'm monopolizing your time, and now you're having to help me with everything and even watch over me at Thanksgiving, on a day when you should be with your own family." She sounded sad. *What the hell?*

"Hey"—I finished the last hook and turned her around to face me—"let's make one thing crystal clear right now. When I'm with you my time is *never* monopolized. I'm glad I was the one to help you last night. I *want* you with me today for Thanksgiving with my family. You know how things are between my dad and me, and this year will be a lot less torturous having you there to help defuse him." I smiled at her. "I might even be looking forward to today a lot more than I was yesterday."

She smiled back. "Really, James?"

"Really, Winter." If she only knew how true it was.

"Okay then," she said with another shy smile.

I should've walked out right then.

I should've done a lot of things differently in my life.

Instead, I looked her over from head to toe and tried to freeze-frame the image of her in my head. So fucking beautiful and sweet, standing serenely for me in sexy black silk and lace…

She cleared her throat softly, bringing my delectable little eye-fuck to a crashing halt.

Our eyes met and held. What did she think of me staring at her mostly naked? This girl told me she loved me several times last night. Did she really love me? Did the heat of some well-delivered orgasms she didn't even remember change that? Had she meant it when she said it?

God, I hoped so.

"I'll let you finish dressing while I run upstairs and get what I need to take today." Which was code for: *I really want to help you out of your sexy lingerie and spend the day giving you more orgasms, but I know I can't, so I'm leaving right now.*

She nodded once and asked, "What are you taking?"

"Flowers for my mom, a bottle of Bowmore 25 for my father, and…you." I kissed her on the forehead because I couldn't help myself.

She stilled when my lips touched her skin.

I inhaled the luscious scent of her, and got the fuck out of her bedroom before I did or said anything else.

THOSE TWO LITTLE kids loved her. Shane and Brenna. Winter loved them, too. Anyone could look at them together and see the mutual bond. When we arrived at the youth center, I held my tongue at the less-than desirable location in Roxbury. I knew Brooke volunteered once a week now Winter had brought her aboard, and Caleb made sure his girl came and went with his driver, Isaac, who had standing orders to stay and wait the whole time she was there. I wondered what Caleb thought of his sister being at the youth center on the other days all alone. If he wouldn't let his girlfriend do it, then why was he okay with Winter coming here? I wouldn't let Victoria come here alone. Mind you, she'd fight me on it, so I'd simply bring Clay into the fight.

I'd have to broach the subject with him in a way that didn't bring attention to my interest in her. Winter would not be happy with sanctions on her freedom, but if it wasn't safe for her to drive in on her own, then too fucking bad. Her safety was far more important to me than her displeasure.

"Did you hurt your hand, Miss Winter?" the little girl asked curiously with a gentle pat on the bandage. The boy, Shane, looked up at her expectantly from the other side. Both of them rushed toward her the moment we walked into the large room full of homeless and otherwise, people living out the not-so-great American dream and scarfing down free turkey and stuffing. The kids were cute, in a disheveled way. They appeared mostly clean, but there was definitely a look of neglect about them. They looked like children who didn't have anyone taking care of them, which was probably pretty accurate from what Winter had told me. *How do they get here? Safely? They're so…small.*

I watched as she gave them hugs, and then bustled them over to what looked like a classroom of sorts—probably where kids did their homework when they used the center after school. There was a poster of multiplication facts, and a few others with things like basic grammar rules and the periodic table stuck to the walls. Plastic tubs with pencils and crayons, and what I guessed were art supplies, were stacked neatly on a rolling cart. The whiteboard had a smiling turkey drawn on it with HAPPY THANKSGIVING written as a greeting. Despite the shabbiness of the space, it was comfortable, and probably a much more enticing place to be than wherever the kids "lived" with their train-wreck "families."

Winter seemed to be going for somewhere a little more private and away from where people were eating as she sat on a sofa and settled the kids on either side of her. She placed the container of cookies on the small table in front of the sofa but didn't open it.

"Yes, I had an accident in my kitchen last night, and that's why I'm late today. My friend helped me get here, because I promised to bring you something." The kids looked at me in acknowledgement as I gave them a smile and a clown wave. They turned their attention right back to Winter as if to say, *yeah, you brought her to us, and now your work is done, buddy.*

"What did you do?" Shane asked.

"I burned my hand on a hot pan and also cut myself with a sharp knife," Winter answered honestly. She censored her story enough to convey the facts without making it sound too terrifying. I was impressed with how good she was at communicating with six-year-old humans, if I remembered their age correctly.

Someday she will make an amazing mom.

My father's edict crashed into my peaceful observations unwanted, stealing the good thoughts away from me. I hated that he held the power to ruin something pure and good in an instant.

Don't let him.

"Your kitchen is a very dangerous place, Miss Winter," Brenna said, her brother nodding vigorously in agreement. *It certainly was last night, kid.* "Did your boyfriend put this on you?" she asked, touching the bandage with the tip of her finger.

"Oh, he's not—" Winter blushed as we shared brief eye contact. "My f-friend, Mr. James took me to the doctor who put it on me." She focused her attention back on the children and their questions, but I could tell she was flustered.

Winter flustered…another fucking turn-on. *God.*

I also had a craving for Brenna's innocent comment to be true.

If two little kids were making her nervous asking if we were a couple, then whatever shit my father might insinuate later on today might send her screaming for the hills. She would need reassuring. And I would give it to her.

"Well, he's a boy." Brenna gave me a sideways glance. "And you said he's your friend, so he's your boyfriend, right?" This small girl was not going to let it go apparently.

Winter still looked beautifully flustered, and my cock was still throbbing when I decided to take control of the situation. "That's right. I am her boyfriend."

"My mommy has boyfriends, but not a nice man like you."

Her comment delivered a blow that hit me right in the

heart. "How do you know I'm a nice man?" I asked.

"You don't yell, and you talk in a good way to Miss Winter." Winter and I shared a glance, both of us probably thinking about the reasons she would frame her evaluation of my "niceness" in such a way. Probably didn't have much experience with men speaking in a "good" way if what Winter suspected about the mom was true. I couldn't imagine Brenna and Shane, two innocent kids with their whole lives ahead of them, being subjected to such desperate conditions, but it was staring me right in the face regardless. Life was a shitty existence for more people than it was a good one.

"Is your mom here with you?" I wanted to get a look at this woman and make up my own mind.

"She brought us for the Thanksgiving but she had to go to her job. She'll come back when her job is over." Shane volunteered the information as if he'd already answered the question more than once today. It didn't take a genius to figure out what kind of "job" his mother was *doing* either. Selling herself to some degenerate pig...one fuck or blow job at a time. The whole situation was so wrong.

"Well, I'm glad I got the chance to meet you both today. Miss Winter really wanted to make sure you got your special gift she made for you guys."

"The chocolate-chip cookies?" he asked with a big smile.

"That's right," Winter answered as she opened the box and offered them each a cookie.

Their eyes lit up when they bit into the delicious treat. I knew how good Winter's cookies tasted, but it was almost sad seeing these two enjoying something as simple as a homemade cookie. Such a small thing, but so very important to Winter to do for two neglected children with a very dim future based on their current situation. I totally got where her drive to help came from now. She had such a big heart, and I was completely content to watch the three of them as they ate cookies and talked together. *She is such a beautiful sight.*

"Do either of you know how to use your mom's cell phone?" she asked nonchalantly.

"She showed us how to do 911 on it," Brenna offered.

"But she said only call it in a 'mergency." Shane nodded seriously as he chewed a mouthful of cookie.

"That's good you know how to use her phone. In the cookie box is an envelope with a card for your mom. I gave her my number in case you ever need some help, or if you get scared sometime, you can call me." She smiled gently. "Can you make sure your mom gets the envelope from me?"

The kids both said yes and continued focusing on their biggest priority—stuffing their faces with as many chocolate-chip cookies as possible.

"In the envelope is something else for your mom."

"What is it?" Brenna asked.

"It's grown-up stuff for her, but it's really important that you don't lose it…or show it to anyone else but your mom."

Both kids listened, watching intently as she drew out a small blue envelope from the side of the cookie box. She pointed to the phone number written in black marker across the front. "That's my phone number, and we're going to play a number game with it in a minute, but first I want to see who has the best pockets."

She made a big show of looking them both over before deciding that Brenna had a button pocket in the skirt of her dress. "We're going to have Brenna carry this important envelope in her dress pocket where it will be safe until your mom comes to get you. When you are home, you can give it to her and tell her it's from me, but keep it in Brenna's pocket until you're home with your mom, okay?"

"We will," they both answered in unison.

She smiled at both of them and asked, "Who wants to play the phone number game? First one to learn my phone number by heart gets to be Snack Assistant for a week."

The next minutes were spent watching Winter work her magic, teaching two six-year-olds her phone number. *Creatively.* In less than fifteen minutes, both could recite it from memory perfectly. My God, Winter had some serious skills. She was a true kid-whisperer. I dearly hoped neither of them would ever need to call her for help, but it was comforting to know they had a way to find her if they needed to. *Although*, that almost put the fear of God in my heart, because if they did call…Winter *would* go to them.

AFTER WE LEFT the youth center, it was a bit of a drive to Weston where my parents lived in a big fucking house that I tried to avoid as much as possible. Winter was quiet in the seat beside me, looking and smelling divine, but I sensed something was bothering her.

"Everything okay?"

"Yeeesss," she said slowly from where she was looking out of the window.

"Not very convincing, Win. You just told me a straight-up lie. Now you're going to tell me what's wrong."

She kept her eyes trained out the window at the autumn landscape as we flew along I-90 toward Weston.

"Winter?"

"I did something I wasn't supposed to do with Shane and Brenna." She sounded worried.

"What, giving out your phone number to a kid is a crime now?"

"No, giving them my phone number was fine."

"Then what was so wrong?"

She paused, her facial expression definitely etched with guilt and stress. "I gave them money. Inside the envelope was a gift card to Target and some money for their mom," she said in a small voice. "You know, so she could buy them some shoes that fit and don't have holes in the soles, and warm clothes…and new coats."

"Oh." On the surface it didn't seem like it was that big of an infraction, but in any business operating with government funds, the rules were hard and fast. "How much money did you put in the envelope?"

"All of the cash I had in my wallet."

"Which was *how* much, Win?" She didn't want to tell me…

She sighed heavily and then she answered. "Two hundred and some odd dollars."

"Shit."

"I know."

"And the gift card was for how much?" I asked.

She sighed heavily before answering. "Five."

"Please tell me you mean 'five' as in the number of fingers on one hand." I knew it wouldn't be as soon as the words left my mouth.

"Hundred." She wiped under her eye as if she might be brushing away a tear. "It's just…they need help so badly, and the rules make it next to impossible for me to do anything for them that might actually do some good. I have money, far more than one person could ever need, and I could put some of it to good use if my hands weren't tied working within the stupid system." She sighed heavily and threw her head back into the headrest of the seat. "I fucking hate it."

"So, if you had the opportunity to do your own thing, what would it be?" I asked the question, but I had a pretty good idea where this was going.

"I would start my own program for mothers and children—something like a private shelter where the decisions wouldn't be dictated by a governmental agency, but guided by a board of directors with the same vested interests as mine. Essentially, I'd be able to help whomever I wanted to help." *Which she would.*

"So, what do you need in order to start up something like that?"

"I'll be qualified with the state in a matter of months, and could therefore run the shelter, but the only thing I don't have is the money. I need my trust fund money, but I can't touch it for six more years."

I know how to get you your money. My heart started thumping hard in my chest as I connected the dots. "Have you spoken to Caleb about your idea?"

She shook her head. "I've thought about it, but I know he's really busy with running the bulk of everything, plus now he has Brooke. He's just been so happy for the first time in forever, so I've left him alone to enjoy it."

"I am sure he would be willing to help you get something started." *Or I could.*

"I know he would, but this is something I want to do on my own, you know? For once I'd like to be able to do some good without having to answer to some long list of policies and restrictions."

"You can get into your trust fund before you're thirty." I couldn't believe I was actually going there with her, but once I started speaking the words out loud, it was useless trying to rein them back in. "All you have to do is get married, preferably to someone who doesn't care about your fortune."

She scoffed as she looked over at me in annoyance. "That's a low blow, even for you, James."

"I'm not talking about someone like Shelton."

"Well, unfortunately I haven't found this hypothetical man who would marry me so *I* could tap into my hundred-million-dollar trust, but not want any of it for himself," she said sarcastically. "Like that guy even exists," she mumbled while shaking her head back and forth.

"Oh, he definitely exists, Win."

"And you know this how exactly?"

"Because that guy is me."

CHAPTER TEN

Winter

There was no way he just said that to me.

Just. No. Way.

I stared at James, certain my hearing was off from the late night-trip to the ER, and possibly some kind of latent trauma response confusing me.

"I'm sorry, James, but it sounded like you just offered to marry me so I could access my trust fund." I waited for him to say something but he didn't. He kept his eyes firmly on the road. "But I know that can't possibly be what you said...because...that's just crazy."

"*Is* it really that crazy, though?" he asked without looking at me.

I continued to stare at him for a moment, trying to make sense of the disbelief bouncing around inside my head like a pinball game—complete with sounds. "Yeah, it is totally freaking batshit crazy, James."

"Okay, you're right, it is a little crazy, but I'd still do it." He finally turned in my direction, nailing me with his gorgeous eyes, appearing completely at ease with his idea. I'd known

James a very long time—knew when he was teasing—but he was definitely sincere right now. I couldn't believe it.

I gulped. "But why would you?"

"Because there's nobody else in this whole world I want to help more than you." He didn't hesitate for even a second.

"Oh…" My heart gave me a jolt as I comprehended what he really meant. He wouldn't be doing it for any other reason than to help me get access to my money. "So just on paper for legal purposes," I said.

"Isn't that what you would want, Win, a paper marriage?"

"Want? Well, no…I definitely haven't dreamed of being married in name only, existing only as a couple on a piece of paper, but I certainly might consider it to be able to put my money to good use without having to wait six long years for it."

"I can draw up a prenup and have one of the partners present it—protecting your trust, of course—and I'd take no assets upon dissolution."

Dissolution?

He means temporary.

My weary brain finally caught up and figured out precisely what he was suggesting. James wasn't offering anything beyond a marriage on paper, which would grant me access to my trust fund, and then at a later date we would quietly dissolve the marriage. I tried to slow the pounding in my chest, but his actually stung a little. *It wouldn't be out of love.* "You would do that for me?"

"I would."

"What would you get out of it, though?"

"You," he said simply.

"What does that even mean, James? I am so confused, and just so you know, suggesting we get married isn't helping my confusion to lessen even a little." It was hard to be mad at him, but I seriously couldn't take any more of his mysterious crap.

"I know, Win. I realize we need to talk about a lot of things and figure shit out, but I've asked that we not do it today. I know I brought up the marriage thing, and I'm very sorry. My timing is really bad, but can we just put these ideas aside for a few hours and try and enjoy Thanksgiving dinner? We'll work everything out to where you're comfortable with the plan, or we won't do it at all." He reached for my good hand and squeezed it. "I promise. All you have to know right now is that you are very important to me, and I'd never hurt you. I want to spend Thanksgiving with you."

He pulled into the long private drive that led to the front of his parent's house, pausing in pleading his case so he could park the car. "We're here anyway, so it's a perfect stopping point for this discussion. We will pick it all up later, okay? Can we do that, sweetheart?"

Whenever he called me sweetheart I melted, so I did the only thing I was capable of doing. I nodded slowly, and gave him my agreement. I didn't know what to say to him anyway. What words could I possibly use that would clear up the fog that felt like it was growing thicker by the minute.

Thank you for offering to marry me, James?

You are the most generous friend ever?

I just might take you up on your proposal?

There was only one problem with agreeing to his plan.

Being married to James in name only would probably kill me.

VANESSA BLAKNEY HAD ALWAYS BEEN LOVELY and sweet to me. Judge Blakney, on the other hand, gave the impression he might be contemplating roasting you over an open spit and eating you one bite at a time. Seriously, the man gave me the creeps. How he'd fathered such beautiful children like James and Victoria remained a curious mystery. That, and how his wife had managed to stay married to him for thirty-plus years. She had the look of a woman who pretended, almost as if she was on autopilot with her conversations and behaviors. For example, while we were eating, she barely touched her food. It was weird, because it almost felt like she was present for ornamental purposes only, but not supposed to enjoy a meal. *Or participate.* Still, her love for her children was apparent, and I could tell she was happy to have them home for the day. Victoria's fiancé, Clay, was absent though, something about being away in Europe .

"I'm so sorry about your accident last night, but we're thrilled you were able to join us for Thanksgiving, dear."

"Thank you for welcoming me into your beautiful home, but really, James gave me no say in the matter. He colluded with my brother and my mother to keep tabs on me today." I hoped a little teasing might help lighten the mood.

I glanced at James beside me to find him grinning like a devil. "I know a thing or two about collusion," he said, "and I definitely know how to close a deal."

No doubt on that point. I think James could get me to do anything by merely asking. I was hopeless when it came to him.

I laughed him off and refocused my attention to his mother, because she was the one who had addressed me, but Judge Blakney inserted himself into our conversation. "Yes, *social work* is your focus at university, is it not?" He leveled his cold gray eyes at me in a way that made my spine tingle, and not in a good way. More like a bug under a magnifying glass with the sun burning a hole right through him.

"Yes…I'll have my master's in social work in another month. Then I'll apply for my license with the state so I can practice."

"Ah, a public servant. How noble. I must say it's very useful in its way…at least for the time being." James stiffened beside me, obviously annoyed by his dad's comment. He reached for my hand under the table and squeezed it. I assumed it was a signal to avoid taking the bait and responding defensively to the thinly veiled insult, so I took the high road instead.

"I hope I can be *useful* to those that need some help," I said firmly, meeting his callous eyes head-on. After my long night, I was in no mood for delving into another one of those conversations that started with: "Are you sure you want to surround yourself with poor people and their problems?" I'd heard it before, and I was sure I'd hear it again considering the world I came from, but the way in which James's father spoke to me sounded so archaically pompous, like he was of a higher class of human than the rest of us—even better than his own family.

What an incredibly heartless asshole.

Did he not have a shred of compassion for others in hard situations? And he was a fucking judge—the most revered "public" servant of all. God, pity the poor souls who had him assigned to their cases.

"I think you misunderstand me, Winter. I do approve of your endeavors to help the poor and disenfranchised. It will make for good press certainly." His eyes held no trace of insincerity.

What the hell? Now he was bestowing compliments? I didn't know what to make of that last comment he'd thrown at me about "good press" but I decided I wasn't going to engage him. If he could speak in riddles, then so could I.

"Actually, I am hoping to set up a private shelter facility that I will spearhead. That's my dream." I looked at James again and smiled at him, hoping he caught my appreciation for his offer to help me realize my dream. Even if it didn't work out, just the fact he was willing to do something as drastic as marry me so I could get to my money left me utterly speechless. Come to think of it, James was really good at rendering me speechless over a lot of things.

James gave me a wink back and said to his father, "I'm very proud of her and her altruistic ambitions."

"As you should be," Judge Blakney said with a thoroughly disturbing smile.

The tingle in my spine returned, and as it zapped me a second time I had to suppress a shudder. *What is his deal? I've known him for years and he's never been this weird.*

"PLEASE DON'T TAKE ANYTHING my father says to heart, okay?"

This was Victoria trying to smooth things over for her badly behaving parent while we set up the desserts to bring out later.

"It's okay, I'm used to it actually. What he said is nothing I haven't heard before, Victoria. Really, I can take it."

"Well, it's still rude as hell for him to even say one thing to you about what you choose to study in school, or what to do with your life. But I get it. He didn't even want me working for your brother as PA to the head of a billion-dollar corporation. He said that being a personal assistant was not a worthy occupation." She rolled her eyes as we both laughed at the ridiculousness of her statement.

"Yeah, well Caleb would probably give you a share in BGE to keep you as his PA. He's really worried you'll leave him after you get married."

"Caleb doesn't have anything to worry about, and I've told him that. I love my job, and *nobody* is going to dictate what I choose to do for a career." I sensed she might be referring to her fiancé, but I didn't want to be nosey and ask her outright. Clay Whitcomb was a charming guy, handsome and successful, but there was something just a little too shiny about him. A high-profile lawyer like James, but in a completely different way. Where James was serious and all business, Clay came off as arrogant with a little bit of snob thrown in. I didn't really see his attraction, but Victoria must see something in him that the rest of us didn't, because she'd agreed to marry him. Their wedding was planned for July.

"So, you want me to tell Caleb it'll be easier for you stay on as his PA if he doubles your salary? I'll be seeing him this weekend at Lucas's place on the island," I teased.

"Oh, please tell him hi for me," she said a little too quickly.

Why would she need to tell Caleb "hi" when she saw him every day? Weird. "Okay…I will?" I left the question dangling.

"I meant Lucas…tell *Lucas* I said hello." A flush appeared over her face, and I got the impression there was far more to this story than I was aware. Lucas and Victoria? I didn't know of the two of them having any kind of history, but then secrets are meant to stay secret, so it wasn't out of the realm of possibilities that I wasn't in the know. I kept pretty busy with school and work most of the time. *Interesting. Yet she's engaged to another man.*

"I will tell Lucas then," I promised. "He's going to pick

me up from the helipad at BGE in the morning. It's a good thing I trust his piloting skills, because I am not a fan of helicopter rides." I shook my head. "Have you ever flown with Lucas?" It was a calculated question on my part—I was curious to see her reaction—because I am a hopeless matchmaker. My sister would verify the "hopeless" part due to some disastrous dates I set her up with before she met Roger.

"Once."

I caught some regret in that one small word, and she didn't offer anything more to elaborate, so I let it go. Vanessa joined us then and asked if everything was ready, so it was time for a change of topic anyway.

But I'd noticed something important in my conversation with Victoria.

What had started out being about Caleb, quickly switched to Lucas the instant his name came up. She didn't acknowledge my offer to bribe Caleb into giving her a raise for agreeing to stay on as his PA—which was easily a joke, but seriously a viable option for her if she ever wanted to use it on him. Most people would at least laugh at the humor in the silly words rather than ignore them completely. *But not Victoria tonight. Hmmm.*

She also never mentioned her fiancé in the course of the entire afternoon. Not that she missed him, or that he might have arranged a phone call from wherever he was to wish her and her family a happy holiday—just nothing at all. It struck me as odd, because Victoria wasn't normally so quiet. Her silence was actually surprising.

"IS YOUR HAND HURTING, DEAR?" Mrs. Blakney asked kindly when she found me tossing back a couple of my prescription painkillers amidst dessert. Choosing between the exquisite-looking pumpkin cheesecake on my plate and pills would normally be a no-brainer. Dessert always won. But today, less than twenty-four hours since I'd sliced my hand open, I needed the pills more.

"It is starting to ache again actually."

"You must have been so frightened when it happened." She focused on the bandage covering my right hand. "Was it terribly painful?"

"It wasn't really. That's the ironic thing. The knife injury didn't hurt, in fact I didn't even feel it happen. It was the sight of all the blood that got me. I just can't tolerate looking at it. I basically passed out and don't remember very much about last night." I smiled at James and then leaned into him a bit. "If it wasn't for your son helping me, I don't know where I'd be right now."

Judge Blakney said, "You'll have to work on that when you start a family. Children bloody themselves all the time."

Excuse me, but what?

Where in the hell had that comment come from?

I gave the judge my best resting bitch face and shrugged. "It's a very good thing I intend to focus on my career for the moment, then."

Judge Blakney raised a challenging eyebrow, first at me and then at his son, but kept any comments to himself. Probably a smart move on his part based on the anger James was throwing off in tense waves. His whole body was stiff beside me yet again. Clearly, his father irritated the hell out of him. His dad was an ass.

I marveled at how the judge could effortlessly turn any topic into something weird and mysterious, while Mrs. Blakney did her best to defuse the awkwardness her husband's comments caused. *And she's had over thirty years to perfect it.* Definitely a saint. Jesus, how the heck did she put up with him?

"What color is your dress for *The Autumn Ball*?" she inquired in an attempt to change the subject. "Victoria and I just had our fittings earlier this week."

"Black," I answered. "I know it's not very festive, but I love the dress, and it just…works very well…for me this year."

She reached across the table and squeezed my undamaged hand in the sweetest gesture of comfort.

She understood. She totally got that I was still mourning the loss of my father and didn't feel particularly celebratory at attending this first major charity event since he'd passed. And I greatly appreciated her silent message to me.

"I have some stunning opera-length gloves I'd like to show you that would probably go nicely with your black gown. They are a beautiful dark coral. Nobody will ever know you've hurt your hand if you wear them."

"How kind of you, Mrs. Blakney. I would love to see them. That's a really good idea for accessorizing this year," I said, holding up my bandaged hand. "I'm going to need something pretty to cover up this ugly thing."

"Oh, please call me Vanessa, or even better just *Mom*…if you prefer," she said with another sweet smile.

Ohh-kay then. This whole afternoon just kept getting weirder by the hour.

I nodded and smiled back at her while squeezing James's hand under the table for some kind of reassurance.

He leaned in and whispered, "They all adore you, even my prick of a father thinks you're perfect."

Perfect for what, exactly? His father thought my career choice was substandard at best and would…*do* until I started a family. *Call me Mom?* They thought there was something between James and me? How ridiculous.

Yet.

He'd suggested we get married on the way over… Had he said something to his parents before I arrived to make them believe that? Like this was a test run, or something?

Was James truly serious about his offer to marry me?

CHAPTER ELEVEN

James

The reason I was happier than I could ever remember being—after spending an entire afternoon tolerating the company of my dickhead father—was sitting beside me in my car, smelling divine and looking beautiful.

I might have lost my mind during the course of the day, saying things I probably shouldn't have said, but I was actually happy for once.

And feeling very selfish—if I had to put a word to it—because even the limited discussion of a marriage of convenience didn't worry me. I already knew I wanted to keep her. I saw her face when I mentioned *dissolution* on the way over. I'd felt like such a bastard for using that word about our marriage. It was a lie.

My doubts and fears about bringing Winter into my life were being blown away bit by bit. The way she'd handled my dad today was nothing short of brilliant. Nobody pushed Winter Blackstone around and had an easy time of it. And I started toying with the idea that maybe it *could* work with us. My father's threat wasn't going away. I could see how ecstatic he was at the prospect of having a Blackstone in the family. Hell, he'd probably be calling me before Monday to ask the

113

date we'd chosen for our big day. *Not happening, Dad.*

Jesus...

No doubt he was eying campaign contributions from her extremely wealthy family. *Also not happening.* He would find—when and if he ever saw the terms of our prenup—that wouldn't be the case.

Because one thing was crystal clear.

Money was absolutely *not* on my list of reasons for marrying Winter.

Watching her earlier, charming my father speechless, had been a thing of triumph I suddenly had some hope for my future.

Why?

Because of the beautiful, sweet, smart, and compassionate girl beside me. Winter had a way of making the heaviest burdens feel lighter. She was responsible for the hopeless ache throbbing inside my heart feel as if it was disappearing. I hadn't felt this optimistic in years, so I knew it was all because of her.

I glanced over to find her studying me. She didn't seem upset or distressed, but if I had to guess, she was thinking about our day and processing everything that had been said. Winter was a thinker. Her emotions held weight in her decisions, yes, but she worked things through logically before acting on them.

"Thank you for agreeing to come with me today. It was the best Thanksgiving I can remember."

Her mouth curled into a half-smile and then fell away. "You're welcome. Thank you for inviting me to the strangest Thanksgiving I can remember."

I couldn't help the short laugh that escaped. "Like I said to you while we were there, they think you're perfect. My mother adores you, and my father was charmed into being polite, and even threw out a couple of compliments; what could possibly be strange about that?" We both knew I was joking, even though what I'd just said was the straight-up truth.

"Oh, I don't know," she said with a sexy tilt of her head. "How about why was I hit with the strangest impression…several times, mind you…that your parents think we're a couple and getting married. Oh, and starting a family of children who will bloody themselves from time to time." She folded her arms beneath her breasts and waited for me to start explaining.

Off-the-goddamn-charts gorgeous.

And if I wasn't driving us into the city right now, I'd have her arms pinned and my tongue down her throat. I'd be kissing her breathless until I had my fill…which would be a very long fucking time.

This was my girl, and she really *was* perfect in every way. I had to make this relationship work—for the both of us. If that meant giving up something I thought I had to have in order to be complete, then I'd give it up.

Winter superseded that need.

And it was that simple.

The time for putting her off was over, and she certainly deserved some sort of explanation after the shitshow she'd just put up with. "You're right, Win, my parents do think we are a couple…and furthermore, they fully believe we're about to announce an engagement."

"Yeah, that came through loud and clear, but what I *want* to know is why. Where is it coming from, James? I thought you came up with the idea while we were in the car on our way to their house. But they obviously knew before I did."

I forced the embarrassment and shame aside for the moment and remembered this was Winter I was confiding in.

She would never judge me based on the actions of my father. She wasn't that kind of person. "My father will soon announce his bid for a seat in the United States Senate. He gave me the task of *settling down*, in the best interests of his campaign, which will run on a platform of family based values. It's all bullshit, but he will find a way to force the issue somehow. Trust me, I've had firsthand experience."

She took a moment to absorb that bombshell before asking me a question that brought emotions to the surface that weren't welcome right now—or ever. The shit I kept locked up in a very dark place. "Like what happened with Leah… You mean your father had a hand in what she did to you?"

I stared at the road, forcing the words out of my mouth in order to answer her without subjecting her to the bitter poison of the truth. "Yes. To both questions."

The heat of her eyes on me burned, but I couldn't face her. I might be able to confide in her, but that didn't mean I was comfortable doing it. "And you're just going to go along with his plans for you?" Again, I felt the pull of her eyes willing me to look at her before she added, "That doesn't sound like you at all, James."

"You're right, it isn't me," I answered, grateful she seemed to have dropped Leah as a topic for discussion. I didn't want to talk about Leah with Winter. In fact, I didn't need to talk about or think about Leah ever again.

"So why are you even considering going along with your father's plan for you?"

Because…there's you.

"His demand that I choose someone got me thinking about you. For the last couple of weeks, I've thought about you a lot, but I didn't want to influence you in any way. That wouldn't be fair. And like I've told you before, I'd never consciously do something to hurt you, but I'm not going to marry just anybody in order to please my father."

"And you were thinking of…of m-me?"

"Winter, you're the *only* one I thought of."

"Oh," she said softly as she took in the idea. At least she wasn't screaming for me to let her out of the car so she could get away from me. Overall, she was taking this news well. *Is that because she does actually love me?*

"Look, I don't want to get married at all, but if I have to"—I let that sink in for a second—"and there's an additional bonus of being able to help you gain access to your trust, then yes, I would marry you."

"But you didn't even ask me to come along to your family's Thanksgiving until this morn"—she paused as she figured out the chain of events— "because you had already decided to defy him."

"You're very astute, but then I've always known that about you."

"You have?" Her shy question made my cock wake up. This marriage talk was sending the blood in my body straight southward. *If we were married?* I sure as fuck wouldn't be able to keep my hands off her. Not after where my hands were last night. Touching her, bringing her to a shattering orgasm, was something I wanted again, even if I didn't deserve it. Even if I had to do it all vanilla. *There.* Admitting it to myself wasn't as bad as I'd thought it would be.

"But yeah, I'd decided to defy my father. He gave me an ultimatum to bring my *choice* with me to Thanksgiving so they could meet her." I gripped the steering wheel and squeezed until the leather protested with a squeak. "I know that sounds so fucking archaic and absurd, but it's exactly what he said to me three weeks ago."

"Oh my God, your dad is using you for his own gain." She couldn't mask her revulsion, and honestly, I'd be worried if she wasn't fucking horrified.

"I know." I reached over and gave her hand a squeeze. "I would've gone alone today. I only go there for my mother's benefit anyway."

"And then I showed up bleeding last night, and you decided you could take me along and get your father off your back?" I could see her tilting her head at me in question from my peripheral vision. Evidently, Winter wasn't the only one needing some eye contact while we talked. I couldn't wait to get her home and in my arms close against me. More than anything, I wanted to kiss her. It was weird, but I wanted that—the freedom to kiss her and not have it be this undecided taboo between us.

"Not *exactly*, but you're in the general vicinity of the truth." This time I turned toward her, and even in the dim light inside the car...she took my breath away. Her pretty eyes glittered at me, so expressive and questioning. But not in a judgmental way. She wanted some answers as anyone would. "I hoped I could avoid a confrontation with my father over the stupid shit he pulls with me constantly, but you need to know that I have absolutely no problem telling my dad to leave me alone, and that I won't be getting married to support his political aspirations. That was my first plan anyway. He doesn't dictate to me."

I had to drag my eyes away from her and back onto the road.

She sighed and then whispered, "I thought we were just friends. That you only thought of me as your best friend's little sister. So what made you decide to lead him into thinking that we are together?"

Haven't thought of you like that for years, beautiful. But now's not the time...

"It was something *you did* actually...well, something you said to me last night that changed my mind." The gorgeous vision of her coming apart for me while saying she loved me had done things to my heart. Even now, nearly twenty-four hours later, the dull ache hadn't subsided.

"Oh no, James, what did I say?" There was panic in her voice.

"No. I'm not telling you while I'm driving. I need to be able to look at you when we talk about what happened last night."

"You're scaring me."

"Nothing to be scared of, Win. It's just me, remember? What did I tell you before we arrived at my parents' earlier?" I pegged her with a hard look.

"You'll never do anything to hurt me," she answered in a subdued voice along with the unmistakable signs of fighting off the urge to squirm in her seat. *Fuck.* That simple move of hers was all it took to send a spike of hot lust straight down the length of my cock. *Mine.* Everything she did—or didn't do—had the same effect on me, apparently. *And she has absolutely no idea.*

"That's right, beautiful one. Don't you forget it. If I make a decision that involves you, it will always be something meant in the spirit of your protection and with your happiness in mind."

She nodded easily. *Or maybe more of an act of submission.* "I will remember, James," she answered quietly before resting her hands gracefully in her lap and relaxing into the seat for the remainder of the drive home.

YEP. I could read the signs all right. By the time we'd made it back, I had a better understanding about her behaviors and body language. It led me into crazy fantasies of tying her to my bed and fucking her into the mattress, yes, but that attraction had been present for a while in me. This was something far more than mere attraction.

I'd bet it all on the idea that Winter was naturally submissive with me and would be when it came to sex. I'd seen it. After spending so much time with her in close contact, my mind was running rampant with filthy thoughts. And how in the holy hell was I supposed to subdue the images of us together rolling through my head like an 8mm porno? *Pointless to even try, asshole.*

Jesus fuck…

We hadn't even gotten out of the car before the plans changed yet again. I was just about to open my mouth and ask her if she'd like to come up to my place when her phone pinged. I watched her expression as she read it, and even predicted what it would be about.

"Lucas wants to pick me up tonight instead of in the morning," she said as she read his text aloud. "He says nine o'clock at BGE. That means I have less than two hours to get changed, pack a bag, and make it to the helipad." She looked at me and smiled one of her half-smiles I found so sexy.

"All right, I'll take you." I hated she was leaving, but the rational part of my brain knew it was wiser. What in the hell was I thinking anyway? That she would stay over at my place? Sleep in my bed? Let me have her any way I wanted? *You're a delusional fucking freak for even going there in your head.*

"Thank you, James," she answered as she texted him back to let him know she'd be there. Once she was done, she sunk into the heated leather and gave me her full attention. She appeared relaxed, but I knew she hadn't forgotten what I'd promised her earlier—that we would talk about *things*.

"You're welcome, but you know we don't have anywhere close to enough time for our *talk* like I promised you. I don't want to rush it, because it's important, and we need some time to process everything." I picked up her hand and held it. Lucas might have changed the plans for our quiet evening of soul-baring conversation, but in a way, I was relieved. Talking about what had happened the previous night would have to wait. The timing was way off for any kind of serious conversation about the future. Deciding if we were getting married any time soon certainly qualified as serious.

"I know that, but I really need to know what's going on here…between us. You kissed me earlier and it—"

"What about the kiss?" It was rude of me to ask her the question after cutting her off from answering, but suddenly I was desperate to know what she'd thought of it.

"It was good." I didn't miss the flush that crept up her neck to color her cheeks. Shy Winter did very dirty things to my imagination. Yet, I also saw trust in her expression. She wasn't submitting to me because she felt weakened by me. Less than me. *Unlike my mother with my father.* I now knew how attracted Winter was to me, and by the end of the night, she'd have no doubt how fucking gorgeous I saw her. She'd known me a long time, knew I was fairly serious for the most part, and knew I'd behaved differently with her today. But for now, I had to tease her a little more. I had to see her fire.

"Well, I should hope it was *good,* because you begged me to do it."

"Oh my God, I did not." She ripped her hand out of mine and glared at me.

I couldn't help laughing at her outraged expression. "Oh yes, you did, beautiful." I nodded slowly, allowing myself the luxury of taking my fill of looking at her. If I could, I'd take her upstairs and lock her inside my apartment and keep her with me until we'd hashed out every detail of how this would roll out—preferably naked or pretty fucking close to naked.

Her, me, us—*together*.

Because she was already mine, and if anyone was going to have Winter Blackstone, that man would be me.

It will be me.

CHAPTER TWELVE

Winter

At the elevator my phone pinged a text alert. Unknown number. **Thank you. Your generous gift helps so much...Shane & Brenna love Ms Winter! Alanna Markham** "Oh my God, James—Shane and Brenna's mom just texted me." I tossed my phone to him. "Read it." Unable to contain my joy, I jumped up and down. *She has a little help now*. The kids would get some winter clothes…and new jackets…and new shoes. This meant everything to me. Helping people, for whom even the smallest bit of extra help, could make such a huge difference to their daily life—

"Easy there, trampoline queen, we're in the elevator." He said it absently while studying my phone.

"Don't slow my roll, please. This is very good news to me, and it makes me incredibly happy to be able to help them just with this one small thing."

"It's not a small thing," he said distractedly while tapping into my phone.

I could tell he wasn't really paying attention to me. I doubted he even heard me. "James? What's wrong?"

He looked up and gave me an expression that was hard to read at first, but then it morphed into one of admiration. "You have no idea how good you are. You don't even realize it." James had been listening.

"But what I did today with the cash and the gift card was basically nothing. Just giving a tiny bit of something I have too much of, to Shane and Brenna who don't have enough. It won't change their situation long-term, but it helps them today. I want to do so much more, James. If I could help in a big way—"

"You will. I know it. And if I can help you make it happen sooner rather than later, then will you be my wife, Winter Blackstone? And also, you need to know I definitely won't be marrying you just to dissolve the marriage later. That's not part of the deal anymore."

My heart stopped beating for an instant as our eyes held. I felt the stutter deep inside my chest stab me with a jolt of pain before spreading warmth through my chest. As much as I wanted to scream YEEEESSSS from the rooftops, I knew he wasn't being literal in the moment, but simply reinforcing his incredible offer from earlier. *Oh, how I love you, James Blakney.*

I put one hand over my heart and moved toward him. I came right up underneath his chin very close and cocked my head sideways. The serious expression combined with the hard set of his jaw made him look a little dangerous and a lot beautiful as he waited for me to speak. I put my other hand up to his cheek and held it there, his beard stubble feeling so much softer against my palm than it had against my lips when he kissed me before. "Well, when you put it like that, then I want you to know that I will definitely consider it, Mr. Blakney. Thank you for the generous offer, sir."

He growled sexily, brought those beautiful lips of his to mine, and kissed me. Almost as if he couldn't help himself. James kissed the fuck out of me in the elevator of our building as we rode to the top. He owned my mouth with his tongue wildly at first, but then made slow passes and caresses. I have no idea how long we kissed—and would have happily made out with James for hours—but as I opened my eyes, the elevator door was clanging open and shut obnoxiously.

We had arrived on the eleventh floor far too soon...and the timing truly sucked. *Again.*

JAMES WAS the perfect gentleman while I got ready for Lucas to pick me up. He watched my every move though, like he was the hungry lion and I was the prey. There was no mistaking his intentions anymore. James wanted me. Something last night had definitely changed the way he behaved with me. He hadn't told me what it was. Maybe he didn't want to embarrass me by sharing it yet. It would be like James to spare my feelings.

But if I was completely honest with myself, I didn't care. If I wanted him, and he wanted me, then halle-fricking-lujah. I could live with whatever it was and wait to see where things went with us. Last night had been a traumatic situation that morphed into a what-the-hell-was-that-crazy-weirdness-with-his-parents showdown. *Parents who believe you are marrying their son.* However, I didn't feel pressured or pushed by him. He had my back, whatever the outcome, so I could trust in that. *I'd trust him with my life.* And hell, if it meant I got to kiss James more, I was so down for that

I TOOK A DEEP, steadying breath as James parked in the underground garage of the Blackstone Global building in my best effort to shake off my nerves. A couple days away to think

would be good for *me* right now. I needed some downtime to process everything, and James agreed, because he'd suggested we both do just that. I'd be back on Saturday afternoon to get ready for *The Autumn Ball*, which we were attending together since he'd invited me a few weeks ago. I never dreamed it would be us in any sense as other than friends, but now it would be. Waiting a couple days might actually help reconcile what James had said about marriage. To me. I should feel like a pawn, but I didn't. *"For the last couple of weeks, I've thought about you a lot… Winter, you're the only one I thought of."* Truthfully, James was the only man I could imagine in my life forever too. And marrying him? Well, I needed to know it wasn't just a paper deal, because I'd only fall more deeply in love with him. So, I knew I needed some time.

I also knew that when the time came, I wouldn't have to ask. He would be the one to initiate the discussion. Because I believed James when he'd said, in no uncertain terms, I was important to him and that he'd never hurt me. I had nothing else to compare those words against. He had always been there for me, and it was all I'd ever known with him. No reason to suspect anything different.

As he steered me toward the elevator that would take us to the helipad, his hand burned at the base of my spine. His touch felt different now. Like he was staking a claim. I shivered involuntarily as the doors closed us in together.

He promptly backed me into the corner, bracing his arms alongside my shoulders to pen me in. His big body crowded me, and his eyes did a lazy dance of staring before he spoke. "Thank you for today," he said simply in a low voice. He reached out a finger to trace my cheekbone and down to my jaw, his soft touch holding me spellbound.

I wished I wasn't going to Blackstone Island and leaving him behind in Boston.

"Thank you for last night…and today," I replied in a whisper, hoping like hell he'd kiss me in the elevator again.

Elevator kisses from James were my new favorite.

James was an incredibly beautiful man. A sculpted jaw shadowed with a few days of beard growth framed a face with the most expressive eyes I'd ever seen. I'd melt if I stared into his eyes for any period of time like I was right now. I took my offered chance and experienced the "melting" right on schedule, no problem whatsoever.

"Last night did have some very nice parts to it." He tipped his mouth down.

"I sure wish you'd let me in on that mysterious secret." I tilted my mouth toward his.

"Aren't all secrets mysterious?"

"Yes, but I still need to know."

"All in good time, sweetheart, and I'd much rather show you anyway."

Please show me.

My heart pounded crazily inside my chest.

"Oh, I plan on it," he said, just before touching his lips to mine. Clearly, I'd spoken my request out loud.

Dwelling on my mortification was a waste with James. He had a way of stripping down inhibitions and forcing them to take a back seat to the main issue. Which right now…was to kiss me.

He owned me with those magic lips of his. Magic lips. Magic tongue. He used both to press his way inside and proceeded to devour my mouth.

I welcomed every lick and swirl of him, offering myself to be devoured without hesitation. I lost any inhibitions the moment he put his mouth on me. I couldn't help it. Years of longing from afar finally had a place to land.

I felt his hand settle on my neck, his thumb moving slowly back and forth at the hollow of my throat, while his tongue pressed deeper inside, hot and hard. He had me trapped in the corner in such a way that I couldn't touch him back, and it was hot as hell. Held firmly and being mouth-fucked by James, it was all I could do to hang on for the ride of the best kiss I'd ever had.

Years of dreaming didn't even come close to doing his kiss—his passionate expertise—justice.

The flavors of whiskey and cinnamon met my tongue, delicious and seductive just like him. I felt him arch his hips inward, and I desperately sought to learn his taste. The feel of his body pressed hard against mine was sublime. My nipples pebbled into aching tips, and there was a luscious tingle where I was wet between my legs. Add one massive erection heating me further through our two layers of clothing, and I was blissfully lost in the kiss and the knowledge he was aroused as much as I was.

It all ended too soon though. When the ding of the elevator signaled we'd arrived at the top, he pulled away. I heard a moan of protest and realized it had come from me. The door opened as the thwack of helicopter rotors filled the silence. Lucas was coming in right on time. The doors swung closed again with a swoosh when we didn't move.

"Look at me," he said.

I met his eyes upon command and saw him smiling at me. It wasn't a smirk, and it wasn't smug. I hadn't seen a smiling James much in the last five years. *God, it's even worse knowing his own father was somehow involved as well.* If I made him smile like this, then what *did* that mean for me?

I was afraid to hope.

"I'm looking," I whispered.

"You're so beautiful to me…right now…right here…like

this."

I do feel beautiful. I feel beautiful because of the way you look at me. No one had ever looked at me as if I was their...as if I was their world.

"James, I...I want you to know—"

"Shhh, sweetheart, no words needed right now. Okay?" He'd put two fingers over my lips to hush me, but strangely it didn't bother me. If anything, it relieved me knowing he wasn't going to allow me to take this into awkward territory. *I trust this man implicitly. It's almost instinctive.*

I nodded and fought the urge to lick his fingers pressed against my freshly kissed lips.

"I'd like for you to think about what we talked about today and let that settle before we go any further. I'll be here waiting to take you to the ball on Saturday, and maybe you'll know more about what you want to do then." He slid his fingers away from my lips.

"All right. But, James, I want you to know that if you change your mind or have second thoughts about your offer, I will understand."

He lost the smile as he took hold of my face. "What makes you say that?"

"I don't want you to do anything you're not sure about."

"Oh, I won't change my mind, Winter. This is all about you and what you want." The intensity of his eyes seared right through me as I shouted out I DEFINITELY WANT YOU inside my head. I was left with no doubt that he read my mind, because he smiled again, his handsome face lighting up for me a second time. "Are you going to say anything to your family about what we've talked about?"

"No." I shook my head. I didn't want to share James with anyone yet. I needed him to be my secret for now. I couldn't justify any good reason for feeling that way, either. I only knew it was what I planned to do.

"I think that's probably best for now, but I do expect a text letting me know you made it to the island safely."

"I will."

He nodded once and stepped back, releasing me from my spot in the corner. Then he picked up my bag, punched the button to open the elevator doors, and led me to the helipad. I shivered, but I wondered if it was the chilly night air or that he was letting me go. I suddenly felt sad leaving him, even though I knew it was a completely irrational thought. I needed to sleep it off. Too much had happened in too few hours for me to even approach any sort of rational thinking.

The handover was quick and efficient, as he hustled me into the waiting helicopter.

"Thanks, man, for taking care of *my sister*," Lucas shouted over the noise.

"I was glad to do it," James fired back, as he helped get me strapped in and situated with the headset. I couldn't be sure, but I caught a vibe of tension between the two of them. James was close with Caleb, but I didn't recall him ever spending time with Lucas or Wyatt, so maybe they just didn't have enough history together. Our families had known each other for over two decades, but that didn't mean each one of us were close in the way of friendships.

Thank you, I mouthed to James silently as he finished with the straps.

I read his lips when he replied, "I'll see you Saturday." The added wink was just for me as he ignored Lucas altogether.

Then he stepped down and shut the door behind him. I watched as he headed away to stand in the safe zone, legs planted to brace himself against the windstorm about to blast him as Lucas brought the rotors roaring back to life.

Lucas busied himself with takeoff, and I stared out the window at James waiting for us to leave.

Our eyes met in spite of the distance between us, and I felt our connection—could still taste the cinnamon-flavored whiskey of his kiss on my tongue. I imagined he might be thinking similar thoughts as the helicopter began to rise, increasing the distance between us as the seconds passed.

James nodded at me deliberately, still holding me captive even as I drifted into the skies over Boston, his eyes telling me so much more than words ever could. *"Oh, I won't change my mind, Winter. This is all about you and what you want."*

Oh, I want you, James Blakney. Forever. But I need you to want it for yourself too. Because I love you.

"THANKS FOR LETTING me pick you up tonight instead of tomorrow morning. I'll get Willow and Roger in the morning, and it won't take me as long," Lucas said after we had gained altitude.

"Sure. I'll definitely appreciate it in the morning more than I do right now—when I'm sleeping and you're flying out to Providence to get them," I teased.

"How is your hand? Are you in pain?"

"Healing, and sometimes, yes. This is why I have excellent drugs prescribed by the fine doctors at Mass Gen, but it's only been twenty-four hours since I sliced it, so I'm feeling pretty good considering. I'm just really exhausted." I worked through the yawn that came on the instant I admitted my tiredness. The powers of suggestion to the mind were truly a thing.

"Good thing your neighbor was home instead of out last

night."

"Umm, yeah. James helped me through everything. I don't know how I'd have managed without him." I thought it was strange that Lucas didn't *sound* grateful for what James had done for me last night. Again, there was some sort of negative vibe coming off my brother toward James.

"So you went to Thanksgiving with his family today?"

I nodded ruefully. "The full Judge Blakney treatment was my special treat today," I said with as much sarcasm as I could manage through the headset.

"I've heard the judge is quite the beast."

"Quite," I answered flippantly. "I really can't figure out how that odious man ended up with such a lovely wife and children, because he is an asshole."

Lucas laughed at my less-than happy recollection of dinner with the Blakneys. "How is Victoria?" he asked carefully.

"She asked me to tell you hi."

"She did?"

"Mm-hmm."

My brother wasn't a cold person. Circumstances had changed the façade he presented to the world to make him appear that way, though. Not all the time, but sometimes. There was history I knew nothing about, because he dropped the subject of Victoria Blakney flat dead and focused on piloting his helicopter instead.

Which was now taking us over the dark waters of Massachusetts Bay toward Blackstone Island. Made me wonder if there were dark waters between Lucas and Victoria. Two of my favorite people, so it bothered me to think there might be any kind of grief there. Did James know what was up with his little sister and my big brother? Time would only tell.

I FELL asleep to the sounds of the ocean waves melding with the coastline where my brother's house perched just above it. Well, actually the sound of the ocean plus the memory of that last kiss from James before he let me go. The combination of the two must have been good medicine for me, because I woke up feeling wonderful and—for lack of a better word—hopeful.

Losing my father seven months ago had been devastating, and we all missed him terribly still, but we had known death would eventually claim him long before it finally did. The grieving had been present then. Coming out of the long period of illness that led to his passing went back nearly two years. So while it was hard being without him for holidays, I felt a peace within myself for the first time since he'd become sick. Dad was in a better place where he didn't suffer the pain of his cancer anymore, and I looked forward to celebrating him in memory now rather than focusing solely on the grief of being without him.

The opportunity to discuss with him my idea for founding a charitable organization would have been wonderful. Dad would've wanted every detail about my plans, and his interrogation would have been painfully—*but helpfully*—relentless. As a parent, he made sure we worked hard at whatever it was we wanted. *No slackers allowed in this family* he always said. We were taught to make goals and then to work toward achieving them. *Money can be lost far more easily than it can ever be earned* was another of his mantras, so I guess you could say we'd all been taught from birth that we needed to know where we were going—before it was ever possible to get there.

I felt like I finally knew where *I* wanted to go.

How fast I got there would depend on what I decided to do about the offer from James. Could I marry him to get access to my money? My heart wanted to, but I didn't know if my conscience could suffer through the guilt of doing something so selfish.

"What has you smiling this early in the morning?" Caleb asked wearily as he headed for the espresso machine, looking like he'd just rolled out of bed in a rumpled T-shirt and sweats. "I'm just the Starbucks stand-in for Brooke, because after I take her this coffee, I fully intend to go back to sleep."

The sight of my brother half-awake and up to get coffee for his beloved made me chuckle.

"Don't laugh," he grumbled.

"The two of you are adorable together. I'm just enjoying being witness to your transformation is all. Plus, you probably need some extra hours after all that mattress-dancing you two did last night. The ocean only drowns out so much."

He swung his head around and opened his mouth to say something, but then shut it, and perhaps even blushed a little.

"Kidding," I said, instantly feeling guilty for messing with him. "I was so exhausted, I heard nothing of your bedroom rodeo last night. I was busy sleep—"

"Going back to *bed* now, Winter," he said, stalking out of the kitchen, Brooke's espresso cradled carefully in his hands like it was precious cargo.

The simple encounter with my brother proved beyond a shadow of a doubt just how much he was in love with his Brooke. I sighed happily for the both of them and went back to prepping the turkey we'd eat later today.

The surgical gloves kept my incision from being exposed to any bacteria and kept it dry. So far it felt pretty normal other than a little achy in the vicinity of the cut, and I was grateful that it didn't appear I'd damaged anything permanently, like a nerve or tendon. It could have been so much worse.

Thank you, James Blakney.

As soon as the food for our feast was prepped, I headed to my room for a shower. I heard my phone chirp with a text notification the second I opened the door and stepped inside.

James: **Someone is in very big trouble for not texting me last night.**

Winter: **OMG! I am so sorry. I was just so tired I forgot.**

James: **Glad u r safe but still in so much trouble.**

Sweet Christ, it was hot when he turned all bossy and demanding with me. My hands shook as I decided how to reply.

Winter: **Oh really?**

James: **Oh yes, really.**

Winter: **Eeep! Is it bad I just wanted to see what would happen?**

James: **I guess u find out on Saturday night at the ball sweetheart.**

Winter: **<surprised emoticon>**

I waited a few minutes for another text from him but got nothing.

I had my shower and proceeded to prepare for the holiday with my family. I checked messages more than once over the course of the day and into the evening, but nothing more came from him.

James had gone silent.

And I was more confused than ever.

CHAPTER THIRTEEN

James

The last time I attended *The Autumn Ball* was five years ago. I remember the dress Winter wore. It was purple with silvery sparkles that had moved when we danced together. I also remembered thinking that someday soon she'd be snapped up by one lucky motherfucker, who by the grace of God, had somehow managed to make her fall in love with him. I'd hate the bastard on sight and would do a thorough check on him to make sure he deserved her, which of course, he wouldn't. That year was also the last time Leah and I were together at a formal function before our wedding in early December...just one week later. Funny how the mind chose what to remember and what to forget. Winter looked so radiant in her gorgeous dress, yet I had no earthly idea what Leah—the woman I was about to marry—had worn that night.

Since that time, I'd cared nothing for formal events. Until tonight that was. I'd asked Winter to go with me shortly after my father's summons to his office, because I couldn't stand the thought of her being anyone else's date, regardless of whether we attended as friends or as something more. The territorial feelings toward her had started the second my father opened his big mouth. The change was swift, and it didn't take long for me to make the decision that this year I'd be on the guest list.

Right now, there was a special someone smelling of beautiful woman beside me in the back of a limo. And she was the *only* reason for my sudden interest in putting on a tux and going to a thing where I'd have dinner and conversation with people I'd probably avoid at all costs the rest of the time.

I told my driver, Enzo, to take the scenic route and raised the partition to give me the privacy I'd been craving since I'd put Winter on that helicopter. Having her with me for those twenty-four hours had only made me want her more than I had before. Prior to that, I hadn't experienced what it was like to kiss her senseless to know what I'd been missing.

Fuck. I had definitely been missing out.

It was said that knowledge was power, but it could also be torture when you knew enough to realize you might break apart if the object of your desires was kept perpetually out of reach. But tonight I was lucky, because my desire was within reach. Dressed in a low-cut black gown that set off her tits in a mouthwatering display had me practically drooling, but I was enjoying the torture. I wanted nothing more than to tear the designer silk away and pleasure her into oblivion right here, right now in this limo.

But I couldn't do that no matter how obsessed I was with making her come again.

She held herself stiffly, giving off a vibe meant to keep me at distance. I wasn't sure why but was in no great hurry to change her mind about it.

Yet.

I could practice patience when needed, and right now I sensed that my lovely obsession wouldn't tolerate being pushed very far. Best to keep things neutral until I had a better read on her mood. And preferably when I had her to myself for hours not minutes. Then, she'd give me her all.

Reading people was something I'd learned from being a lawyer. Knowing if a client was lying or telling the truth came in very handy in deciding if I wanted to represent them or not. Winter was so much more important to me than a potential client, though, and I didn't want to fuck things up any more than I had already. I'd purposefully kept my distance since Thanksgiving, because I'd wanted to give her a solid few days to really think about what she wanted to do…with us. If she wanted to explore the idea of an *us* at all.

She wants me. She loves me. She wants to be with me. I needed to keep believing, because I had plenty of doubts too.

"Are those the gloves my mother wanted you to have?" The need to touch her nearly overpowered me, so I took her hand firmly into mine. A hand encased in dark pink silk, embellished with flowers made of the same, and covered from the tips of her fingers all the way to well past her elbow. Fucking sexy.

My inner fantasy decided it wanted another date with her wearing those gloves and not a scrap of anything else—except for the shoes. She could keep on the heels that matched the gloves.

Annnnd looked sexy as fuck strapped around her ankles with little bowties at the toes. They'd look even better draped over my shoulders.

"Yes." Her eyes burned green fire at me for an instant before flicking down to study the gloves. "They really are one of a kind: the dark pink color—the silk flowers—the opera length. Your mom gave them to me, saying she would never wear them, and that they were far too beautiful to sit in a box wrapped in tissue." She lifted her eyes back to meet mine. "I would say I have to agree with her."

"Beautiful gloves on beautiful hands." I drew her hand to my lips and kissed the back of it, my lips regrettably touching silk instead of skin. "To go with a beautiful dress…worn by a very beautiful woman."

"What are you doing?" she asked on a soft breath, her eyes moving incrementally as she studied me.

"Just paying you a compliment that you very much deserve. I am a lucky man tonight."

"Anything else you'd like to tell me before we get in there and start pretending, James?"

"Nothing other than how happy I am to be taking you to the ball tonight. No pretending on my part."

She closed her eyes just a fraction and...shivered? It looked like she had.

But I didn't have a chance to ask her, because Enzo pulled up to the security checkpoint and gave our names to the attendant. "James Blakney and Winter Blackstone."

I squeezed her hand and sent her a smile. "It's showtime, sweetheart."

WINTER'S MOOD didn't improve as the evening progressed. She seemed to enjoy the company of her friends and family, but whenever I got too close, she grew stiff and quiet. Apparently, someone else caught on to her mood as well.

"The happy couple might try looking a bit...happier, don't you think?" my father asked as he strolled up with a practiced bow for Winter, and what appeared to be an affectionate slap to my shoulder. Both gestures were an act of a narcissistic asshole.

"I have no idea what you're talking about," I replied before turning to Winter and pressing a kiss to her cheek.

"Sweetheart, do you have any reason to be unhappy tonight?"

She ignored my father completely and stared at me for a moment before shaking her head slowly back and forth.

Silently simmering.

Okay, so Winter was definitely not happy with me, my father, this whole public farce apparently, but she wouldn't say so. No, she'd been trained at the same charm school we'd all had to suffer through as children. *Never let them know how you really feel.* Smile, and put on a front that everything's wonderful, even when life is shit.

I needed to get her alone, somewhere quiet where we could talk, and I could reassure her that she didn't have to do anything she didn't want to do.

"If you gentlemen will excuse me, I see a friend I want to say hello to." She turned heel and left us both watching the back of her as she went, the skirt of her black gown swaying gracefully with each step of her sexy pink shoes. I could almost see the anger radiating off her in waves.

Ouch.

"Trouble in paradise so soon?" He raised a brow as if entitled to the information, making my blood boil.

"You need to back the fuck off if you want this to happen. I already told you her family doesn't know about us yet."

"Why don't they know? What are you waiting for? Get this situation nailed down and settled, or I'll settle it for you. Do your job and get her pregnant. It shouldn't be this hard, *son.*" He got a little gleam in his eye and laughed. "But maybe that's the problem for you. Your cock's not hard enough to get the job done. Do you need some help from another cock perhaps?" he scoffed, finding humor in his own fucking joke.

I had to choke out my next words because all I wanted

was to get away from him. "Are you even human, because sometimes I wonder."

"Are you even my son, because sometimes I wonder. Be a man and fuck your baby into that Blackstone bitch and be done with it." He narrowed his eyes at me like a snake about to strike. "My God, the senate announcement is in less than two months."

"You know, *Dad*, if you want to fool the voters into thinking you're a loving family man, you're gonna need to work on your game and have an ounce of patience. Winter is already mine and you'll stay the fuck away from her."

I slapped him hard on the back in a fake show of affection before leaving him standing alone. I did it to let him know he wouldn't have an easy time pushing me around. And most certainly not Winter, either. To anyone who witnessed our exchange, it probably looked typically normal. Just a father and a son having a conversation, happy to be in each other's company.

If they only knew…

But it had felt so good. The surprised look on his face was worth any retribution I'd just earned for myself down the road, because my father had a memory like a steel trap. He forgot nothing. Still wouldn't trade it, even though I knew it would come back to haunt me at some point.

I needed to find Winter and see if I could repair whatever the damage between us was.

Annnnd then Jan Thorndike appeared. *Fuck.*

I hadn't made it ten steps before she accosted me. She had something seriously wrong in the head and was so far off the rails I didn't think anything less than a straitjacket and a padded room would do her any good at this point. The girl was obsessed with Caleb. She'd called me a few times begging me to be messenger, because he wouldn't take her calls.

141

Bitch, he's blocked your number, and so have I. I still hadn't forgotten how she'd shown up at my door and offered to blow me five minutes after breaking up with her boyfriend—who just happened to be *my best friend.* I even called him that night to let him know she'd stopped at my place. She sent Caleb a picture of herself with her lips around some random dude's cock five minutes after that. At the time, Caleb believed the picture was of me, but I set him straight. Janice Thorndike has never had access to my dick, and she certainly didn't get near it that night, so she had to have already taken the picture from her phone *before* Caleb broke it off with her. She probably had a whole album of porno selfies saved on the thing. God.

I stared at my forearm where she'd sunk her claws in to stop me. I wanted to bust out in a fuckin' sprint to get away from her. She looked crazed. "James, I need to talk to Caleb alone. Go get him and bring him to me. You have to make him listen to—"

"I am not his keeper."

"Well, you're his best friend and he listens to you." Her eyes appeared strangely vacant, as if she was on something.

"So? He's done. Even if you hadn't cheated, he'd be done."

The crocodile tears started flowing in a desperate attempt to gain sympathy. "That was a mistake—a one-time thing," she cried, fisting handfuls of her hair and creating a mess. This girl had always been pure drama.

"For Christ's sake, stop embarrassing yourself with this shit!"

"But I can't help it, James. I'm so in love with him."

"Right." She was fucking certifiable. Not happy with cracking him in the eye with her shoe, she ran to me hoping to make him jealous by fucking me. Who does that? "Because all the sick shit you did to Caleb just screamed love, didn't it?"

"James, please, I didn't mean any of that. I was very upset."

"Well, *Caleb* sure as fuck meant it when he broke up with you. And *I* was fucking pissed when I found out you sent him that stupid dick pic." I jerked my arm out of her grip.

"You're not listening to me. James. I want him back and I'll do whatever I have to do—"

"Don't you get it, Janice? My brother is with Brooke now and he's in love with *her*," Winter said angrily from over my left shoulder. I hadn't even noticed her approach I was so busy trying to detach myself from all the crazy I'd stumbled into headfirst. How the fuck did I get tangled in with this shitshow tonight? All I wanted was to spend a nice evening with Winter. It was time to leave.

Jan's face twisted into an ugly mask of meanness as she directed her rage onto Winter. "Is James finally fucking you? It must be the trust fund he's after, because it's been years since you flashed him your baby tits in the pool."

"They aren't baby tits anymore." *Nope. Definitely not.* Winter held her composure like a pro, spine straight, her confident posture setting her tantalizing cleavage off to perfection. Her tits were an undisputable, straight-up ten—to anybody who wasn't blind...or insane.

Jan tilted her head to one side and rolled her eyes. "Oh my God, you mean he's never stuck his dick in you before now," she said, throwing her head back and laughing like a psychopath. "Better strap in, little girl, because he likes all the kinky, deviant shit from what I've heard—"

"We're done here," I said, grabbing Winter's hand and pulling her with me. "Jan, take your crazy out on someone else, and leave us all the fuck alone."

I didn't look back or wait for Jan to finish whatever she was going to say about me. I just moved us both away—and left the lunatic bitch standing in a roomful of Boston's high society mumbling some unintelligible bullshit about making everyone sorry.

What I needed was to put as much distance between her and us as quickly as fucking possible. I wouldn't ponder how she knew about me. Although the knowledge of my kink could have come to her from anywhere, it didn't make me any less mental about Winter finding out.

I forced myself to block out everything.

Even to the point that I didn't realize that Winter wasn't following along with my plan. In fact, she was doing the opposite, pulling back, and trying to get away from me.

"Let go of me."

I tightened my grip on her hand and then panicked for a second that maybe I was hurting her injured one.

I wasn't.

"What's wrong?"

She tried tugging her hand out of mine again, but I wasn't having it.

"I'm leaving. I'm going home," she said, flashing me an angry glare.

"Correction, sweetheart. *We* are leaving, and *we* are going home."

HER ANGER hadn't lessened since I'd bustled her out of the goddamn ball and into Enzo's heated limousine, where she now sat as far away from me as possible. I studied her fuming quietly in the seat, arms folded beneath luscious breasts as she stared moodily out the window. In profile, she made a stunning picture against the city lights reflecting off the tiny raindrops currently drifting from the night sky.

It had taken a few minutes to get away without arousing the suspicions of the eagle-eyed gossips, who lived for the soap-opera drama like what had unfolded inside with Jan Thorndike. It spiced up their otherwise very boring lives. But was "boring" such a terrible thing? Sometimes I wished for my own life to be a lot more boring than it was at present.

After placing my bid in the silent auction, I'd gone and made excuses to my mother. I lied and told her Winter had a bad headache. Mom didn't blink an eye at my lame explanation. She just offered her cheek for me to kiss and told me to take good care of her, and that she hoped Winter felt better soon.

I fished out my phone and took a picture of her staring out the window. She might be angry, but it was still a beautiful image I selfishly wanted to keep for myself.

"What the hell, James," she shouted when she noticed the flash.

"It's just a picture of you looking furiously beautiful. I wanted to capture the moment."

"Instead of stealing pictures and dropping compliments, you might start by being honest."

"I am always honest with you, Win."

She scoffed angrily toward the window but said nothing.

"Are you planning on explaining what you mean?"

She shook her head, still staring out the window.

"Okay, then tell me what the fuck I did tonight that was so wrong." No response. "How about you look at me when we are talking," I bit out, my frustration growing with each passing second of this stupid motherfucking argument.

She turned to face me, eyes blazing across the distance between us. "I *know*, James."

"What do you know?"

"I know what happened between us after you brought me back from the ER. I know what you did. I know what I said to you." Her eyes welled up. "I remembered…everything… today while I…I…was getting ready for the ball."

A single tear spilled down her cheek and made me want to lick it away, even as my heart pounded out erratic beats.

"Sweetheart, no. I wanted to help you, that's all I was trying—"

"Just…how…could you keep that from me? For all these days without saying something…anything," she hissed. "Why would you use me like that, James?"

Fuck.

No.

CHAPTER FOURTEEN

Winter

Four hours earlier.

Since *The Autumn Ball* was one of the better attended charity events of the year, and because the funds raised went to a variety of good causes, I couldn't fault the intent, and truly hoped each of the beneficiaries came away from the event with generous checks.

Working in the field of social work with the ludicrous trust fund I had must be an offensive irony to probably ninety-nine-point-nine percent of the population who wouldn't hesitate to call bullshit on it being true—even though it was. The other point-one percent of the population—of which my mother was at the top of the list—knew it was true and thought me a stupid fool for wanting to use my money for something other than a Tesla or a rainbow of designer handbags in every hue anyone ever decided was a good idea.

Please. Did anyone really need a purse in pumpkin-orange leopard with purple croc embellishments? Even if the whole bag were environmentally constructed from top to bottom, I'd still say no.

I had more important, long-term things on my mind.

Like being nervous as hell about going out with James

tonight. Our friendship had definitely changed, but his hot and cold mixed messages had really started to mess with my head. I hadn't heard a peep out of him since his text on Thanksgiving telling me I was in trouble for not messaging him. Over the last weeks, he'd made gestures and said things that gave me hope he actually might see me as more than a friend. And then, even going so far as to offer to marry me to benefit the both of us, but I already knew that a "pretend" marriage wasn't in the cards for me.

I was unable to *pretend* anything with James.

Therefore, my decision was made.

I'd thank him again for offering, but there was no way I'd take him up on it. I'd find a different pathway to making my career dreams materialize. I belonged to a very generous family who were charitably minded. Maybe I would go to work for BGE and head up their philanthropic development as Caleb had suggested to me before. There were other roads I could take than torturing myself with a fake marriage to James. *I hope I don't lose his friendship in the process.*

And I still couldn't get over the fact that an offer of marriage was a major thing to just give away to a friend. Why on earth would James do that for *me*? But as soon as I started to believe he felt something more than friendship, his walls would go up and he'd back away again, putting a distance between us that left me frustrated and confused as to whether I'd dreamed up the whole thing in the first place. *But that kiss he gave you in the elevator says different.*

My point exactly.

Even Brooke had noticed. Earlier, when the two of us were getting hair and makeup ready for tonight, she'd asked if James and I were seeing each other. I lied and told her we were just very good friends, but I'm not sure if she believed me. She's an intuitive one, that girl. She's also the best thing to ever happen to my big brother. I hope when Caleb and

Brooke are married someday, that they'll have lots of nephews and nieces for me to spoil. Caleb will be such a great father. He was so much like our own father it was scary. Caleb was pretty much our dad's clone.

It hurt my heart to be reminded again that he was gone. I missed my father so much, and I knew the rest of my family did too. He would've been here tonight, supporting the charities and enjoying himself immensely. My dad was altruistic to his core. When I announced I'd be majoring in social work, my mother said I'd been bitten by the same bug. Dad was proud of my choice, and he told me on his deathbed to follow my heart and never compromise my dreams for anyone. He made me promise to trust my instincts and not be influenced by any disapproval I might encounter from others. In particular, my mother. To be fair, she wasn't disapproving so much as unenthusiastic. Her reaction was half-hearted, and I could tell she believed I'd be wasting my life on public service when I could just support a few chosen charitable endeavors with a fat check while still spending the bulk of my time shopping and lunching with other girls who'd also inherited excessive trust funds.

But that sort of life was not me.

I wanted more—for myself, and for my life's work. I was grateful my brothers and my sister felt the same way I did. Just sitting around spending our father's money and wasting time wasn't how any of us rolled. Willow was a super successful author, and my brothers had each found their niches in different areas of business. We were all making our way in the world, as we should be.

I sighed, thinking that all this ruminating was depressing as hell, and totally pointless. Only time would tell how things would turn out. I just needed to have some faith, and believe that James really meant it when he promised to never hurt me. And I trusted James completely.

I really do.

I dropped onto the bed to put on my shoes—coral-pink peep toes with ankle straps. The shoes were just a shade darker than the gloves from Vanessa Blakney, and luckily, already lived in my closet. I had *not* inherited the shopping gene from my mother, much to her great dismay. So, whenever I could manage to pull together an outfit without having to traipse through multiple shops to do it, was cause for a celebration. This year my gown was black, but its hi-low hem softened the look. Paired with the gloves and shoes, it came off feeling flirty and festive. It suited me. I felt a nervous shiver roll through my body at the thought of James and me spending the upcoming evening together. Like being out on a date "together." I would be lying if I said I hadn't thought about what might happen *after* the ball was over. He'd said we would finally be able to talk about everything that had happened since my accident, and that made me a little nervous.

But it's James, and I have no reason to ever be nervous with him. Aroused, most definitely.

My mind wandered as I buckled up the straps, when I realized I was sitting precisely where James kissed me for the first time.

The morning after my accident. I'd woken up to find him in my bedroom watching me. Hungrily watching.

If I closed my eyes I could recall his lips touching mine. The perfect mixture of firm and soft. James definitely knew how to kiss—

Suddenly another memory pushed to the front. I was kissing James, and not the other way around.

Wait.

Had I had kissed him first?

In my bed?

But that wasn't right. I shook my head as a flash of us lying in this bed together—we were kissing—and his fingers were—

Inside me.

Kiss me.

Orgasms. Intimate touches.

Touch me.

Words spoken.

I love you, James. I love you…I love you…I love you.

I remembered every mortifying thing I'd done and said to him that night. And now his comment made sense to me when he kissed me in the car after returning from Thanksgiving with his parents. *"Well, I should hope it was good, because you begged me to do it,"* he'd said.

Oh my God, no.

"It was something you did actually…well, something you said to me last night that changed my mind."

No, no, no, no, no…

NO.

I sat there stunned. Shocked. Of what we'd done together. Of what I'd revealed to James that night.

I had no idea how much time passed before I was able to move my ass off the bed and finish getting ready for the ball. It could have been five seconds or five hours. I couldn't say. My mind was on a repeating loop of something too intimate and too important for me not to have known about it until right now.

James knew, and he hadn't said anything.

I felt humiliation to the depths of my soul. Beyond

expressible words. Why he didn't tell me?

He didn't tell you because he didn't want *to tell you.*

The fact that James had pushed aside my request to know more made me wonder if he was incredibly embarrassed at how I'd virtually attacked him. He could be with any woman he wanted. Now I wondered if he was offering to marry me to give me access to my trust fund simply because *he got me*—but it wouldn't mean anything more than perhaps stolen kisses for him. He probably intended to keep the booty calls on the side too. *God. I'm such a fool.* No wonder…

That James hadn't wanted to talk about the things we'd done and the things I'd said to him—once he realized I had no memory of it—crushed me terribly.

Crushed. Me.

But what do I do with that now?

"WINTER, SWEETHEART, I wasn't using you." He reached for me and dragged me against his chest. I was unable to resist him whenever he touched me, even now when I was seething with enough anger to inflict bodily harm. Upon his body. I stared at those sludgy-green eyes of his, immobile, captured like a fly in a web. "I was letting you use me," he said clearly.

"You were *letting me use you*?" I felt my eyes sting with more tears. *It's even worse than I thought. Pity orgasms. Fuck.* "What does that even mean?"

He held my face in his palms and used his thumbs to brush my tears aside before he answered. "It means that I wanted to help you and give you whatever you needed to feel better."

"Orgasms aren't included in the patient care handbook." I couldn't look anywhere but into his eyes since he held me like he wasn't planning to let me go anytime soon. I was burning with embarrassment, wishing I could look away, but he wouldn't allow it. I felt heat settle low between my legs.

"They should be, because an orgasm was exactly what you needed at the time. You slept like a baby after the third one."

Three orgasms? *Jesus.*

"You're an evil bastard for not telling me what happened between us that night, James, and don't you even try to deny it."

"I try very hard to never be bastardly with you." He had the nerve to smirk at me. "You're one of the few people on the planet I actually make a concerted effort of being polite."

"Oh, you were definitely *bastardly.*" I squirmed to pull out of his grip. "And trying to make light of it isn't helping your case, Mr. Slick Attorney."

He laughed at my comment and held me firm, as if I my struggles were mere amusement for him.

"The next morning when I was coherent, I even asked you if we could talk about the kissing and whatever went down after the ER visit. You said no."

I feel sick. I can't believe this.

I still hadn't given up on trying to free myself, because I knew if he got any closer to me I'd be doomed. I could barely think as the weight of his body pressed into me. The scent of spice with a swirl of his own unique flavor added into the mix of him crowding me onto the leather seat, and I was about done for.

"Fuck. Would you stop fighting me for a goddamn minute," he snapped, giving me a small shake for emphasis. "I'm not letting you go." And he meant it, because he didn't loosen his hold. "If you had recalled it the next morning, we would have talked, but when you didn't remember anything from the previous night, *I* made the decision to wait things out. That's on me, yes, but I didn't do it to use you or to hurt you in any way, Win. I wanted us both to be on equal footing, and we weren't that night with you as high as a kite on meds. I never planned to seduce you and keep it a secret."

"But that's basically what happened. You seduced me and kept it a secret," I managed to whisper, even though he did have a valid point. I had been incapacitated from the drugs they gave me.

"No." He shook his head sharply. "I did not. That's the God's honest truth. You asked me to touch you after—*you kissed me.* So, I asked you where you wanted to be touched. You answered 'anywhere…everywhere' and went wild when I followed your instructions. I would do anything for you, Win. There was no denying you. And there's no fucking way when I was given the opportunity to touch you, serve you, that I would turn it down. Do you think I'm made of stone or something?"

I opened my mouth to speak, but no words came out. Instead, a wave of red-hot shame cloaked me like a blanket.

He wasn't lying.

Every word of what he said was true.

As he explained how the events of that night unfolded, I pieced it back together with him. It had happened just like he said. I came on to him. I begged him to touch me.

Oh. Please. Let me die now.

"M-m-my in-structions?" I stuttered weakly.

"It was the sexiest fuckin' thing I've ever seen, and I want to do it again," he replied just before his lips crashed into mine.

My resistance ended the moment I felt him on me.

I melted beneath the demanding kiss, as he set me straight about what he wanted.

Me.

He thought what I'd done was…sexy? *There was no denying you. And there's no fucking way when I was given the opportunity to touch you, serve you, that I would turn it down.* And here I thought I knew so much about this man.

Years of living with my feelings only cemented what I knew. I was so lost in him. I always had been, and I knew that I'd accept whatever he offered and deal with the consequences later.

My face was held in the grip of both hands as he plundered my mouth, taking me further under his spell with each slide of his tongue. I savored the taste and the feel of him against me, the rough abrasion of beard stubble covering my lips, the scent of his spicy-sweet cologne tantalizing my nose, and the press of his thumbs caressing my neck. He held me completely under his spell, as he pulled me deeper into a place I'd wanted to go for so long, that I couldn't remember a time when I hadn't desired him. I'd never felt more cherished, or more wanted than right now. The way he held on to me made me believe he really did feel more for me than I'd ever dared to imagine. No other man had ever compared to James.

I knew no man ever would.

Every person had self-truths—and this understanding of my feelings for James was one of mine.

When he stopped the kiss, I wanted to protest the loss of his lips against mine, but I summoned my self-control and stared into his beautifully mysterious eyes and waited for him to speak. I had a pretty good idea where this might go if he allowed it.

"Tell me right now what you want, Winter." The question wasn't asked softly. The words were delivered with a harsh edge. I sensed he was on the verge of losing his tightly held control, and for some reason it only made me hotter.

"I want you."

"Tell me exactly what that means," he commanded without pause, his eyes boring into mine.

"It means I-I-want…I want to be with you, James." The truth. It was simple, not much more than what I'd just said. I wanted to be with the man I'd been in love with for years. I wouldn't make the mistake of saying those words out loud a second time, but I was totally fine with the fact that the cat was finally out of the bag. Weirdly, I simply didn't care if James now knew how I felt about him. It took the pressure off me somehow. I didn't have to pretend anymore—and I wouldn't. He could do what he wanted with it. I was well past caring.

His eyes flared when I answered him. I could feel the heat behind the gaze, and realized I was taking us into uncharted territory by giving him the green light. "You're sure you want to do this?" His jaw flexed slightly along with the press of his hips against me, where I felt the whole hard length of one impressive erection hitting me right where it counted.

I let his hardness sink into me and rolled with the sensation of pure pleasure that came with it. I nodded slowly. "Yes, I'm very sure. Even if it's just for tonight, I want this with you."

James released me abruptly before leaning over to speak into the intercom with the driver. "Enzo, change of plans. Take us to the Sherborn address, please."

"Of course, sir."

James then turned his attention toward me and helped me back into a sitting position. He took my left hand and intertwined our fingers, mine encased in silk gloves that contrasted sharply with his long, tanned ones. The sight was sexy to me. His grip on me secure and firm, as if he had no intention of letting me go now I'd made my decision to be with him. Read "be" to mean sex.

I had no idea where he was taking me, either. Somewhere in Sherborn. Did he have a home there I knew nothing about?

"Give me your phone." Again, his request was more than a little abrupt, but it didn't bother me. Experiencing this very dominant side of James was a major turn-on to me.

I reached into my silk clutch with my other hand and drew out my phone. He took it and turned it off before handing it back to me. Then he did the same to his own phone. I tilted my head at him, asking my question silently instead of out loud.

"No interruptions of any kind are happening tonight, Winter. Just you and me." I saw the hard edge of his jaw flex. "We are off the grid…and we fucking deserve that."

I swallowed air and nodded at him, my heart pounding furiously.

"Phones don't get turned back on again until tomorrow morning, when we're ready," he added.

"Tomorrow morning?" I whispered weakly.

"Tomorrow. You didn't think I'd let you get away with less than an entire night, did you?" He gave me a dark smile that could only be described as wicked. "You're *all* mine for the next twelve hours, beautiful."

A shiver rolled through my whole body as the words left his lips.

CHAPTER FIFTEEN

James

I *want to be with you, James.*

Those words were all I'd needed to hear from her—all that really mattered. She wanted me. I wanted her. The truth was out. No more pretending nothing had changed between the two of us. For better or for worse the path had been set. That was the good part in all of this. But there was no disputing the fact I was still fucked.

So very fucked.

Winter presenting herself like a perfect sub with downcast eyes as Enzo drove us to the house was the problem. Scratch that. It was *my* problem, not hers. My inner craving to dominate was on high alert, screaming at me to go for broke with her. To act on every filthy thing I'd fantasized doing to her, for her...*with* her. What if I overstepped when we were deep into it and said or did something that scared her, or worse, repulsed her? A flash of the demise of my relationship with Leah shuttered in the back of my mind for an instant like a reminder of exactly where this could lead with Winter if I wasn't careful, or if I revealed too much. I wasn't one hundred percent sure I could rein it in, but my training should make it possible. You didn't become a Dom without learning boundaries, limits, and control. I'd wanted Winter for a long time, and I knew I had to take things very slowly tonight, as if I was training a new sub. *But I've never trained someone I love.* Winter was *my* ultimate endgame, but if I wasn't hers? She was young and focused on her career. And I was considering actually following my father's insane orders...but *only* if I could do it with her.

She'll tell me what she wants. Because that was the kind of person Winter Blackstone was. She was honest to a fault. All I could do was show her who I was and go from there. It was a risk. It could end badly. She could be hurt. I would be ruined—worse than I already was—if I lost her in the process.

I couldn't go through that again. I wouldn't.

Why did something so simple have to be so fucking complicated? Two people who felt something good for each other being together because they wanted to.

She also told you she loves you.

I had to keep reminding myself of that, because I'd never known she felt that way about me. In fact, I'd been shocked hearing those three small words leave her sweet lips. Winter and I had been easy friends for as long as I could remember. We'd always clicked. As she grew up and transformed into the gorgeous woman she was today, I'd noticed...of course. I would've had to be dead not to notice her over the years. But I'd only admired Winter from afar, accepting she my best friend's little sister and wouldn't ever be on the menu for me. But thank fuck...she was.

Because we're barreling down the Freeway of Fucking at high speed with no brakes.

I was a careful person by nature. It was necessary to survive growing up with the manipulative and conceited father I had. Life experiences had made me into the man I was, and Winter would get a partial view into that tonight. It's impossible to hide your true self when you had your cock buried in someone who wanted it there, and the only thing on your mind was when and how hard you'd come. And how many times you made her scream your name through the multiple orgasms you made sure she had. And after that, how many times you could do it all again before you're satisfied, because you knew instinctively you'd never get enough of her.

More. I'd want more than this one night. I wanted all of her all the time. I wanted to be out in public with her on my arm. I wanted to come home to her after a long day. I wanted her as the mother of my future children. I wanted so fucking much...*and all of it is with her.*

The time for pondering this pointless shit was over, though.

She was right beside me—and she was waiting.

An ambulance screamed past us in the opposite direction, the shrill siren cutting through the tension with a jolt. Someone somewhere was probably dying on this cold wet night, while I was about to cross boundaries a lifetime in the making with my best friend's little sister.

I turned toward her and put my index finger to her chin. She didn't say a word, just looked at me with those gorgeous eyes of hers that spoke volumes in the silence. She was fucking beautiful with her lips still wet from my kiss. Her lips were going to stay wet from my kisses all night long.

"If at any point you change your mind about this, you need to tell me. Talk to me, and I'll hear you." I'd probably combust if she shut me down now.

It would hurt, but I'd live.

"I...I'm not going to change my mind, but maybe you will." She looked at where our other hands were still entwined. I never wanted to let go of her. Not ever.

"Why would you even say that?"

"I'm just not that—"

She shook her head in frustration as she continued to look at our hands.

"You're just not that…what?" I tipped her chin back up. "I need to see your eyes when you tell me why you think I'd change my mind about being with you." She didn't flinch, but I could tell her confidence was being tested. "I've wanted you for a long time. This is my fantasy moment," I added, trying to lighten the mood. It was the truth. The shocked surprise on her face? So worth it. *Yes, beautiful. You are my fantasy.*

"James, I'm…I'm not very…sexually experienced," she finally blurted.

She tugged her hand against my hold, which only made me grip tighter. I wouldn't let her pull away from me after that bombshell she'd just dropped. "Okay," I said calmly. "What does 'not sexually experienced' mean for you?" I couldn't quite wrap my head around the idea, and wasn't sure I should even ask, but of course I did, because it was sort of fucking vital that I knew the answer. "Are you trying to say you're a virgin?"

Holy fuck.

"Holy fuck" indeed, even though I couldn't imagine how it was possible. Shelton had hatched a plan to marry her. Surely the two of them had been intimate…

"Not a virgin." She shook her head again, but this time she kept her eyes on me. She was watching for my reaction, wanting to know if her news made a difference to me. It didn't, and I was careful not to show any surprise.

"Elaborate, darling. I need more information," I said as my heart started beating again.

In total relief.

She wasn't a virgin, and that helped. I was already doubting how far I could take her—take whatever the hell *this* was between us. But I also realized that if she "wasn't very experienced" as she put it, then her expectations would be right in line with that inexperience. Better for me. Better for us. I didn't want to fuck up and ruin what could be my only chance to show her what we could have together. Before she could answer, I rearranged our positions, effectively sitting her across my lap with her back supported by the corner area of the seat where I could see her eyes as we talked.

"Comfortable?"

She nodded slowly, her expression subtly mysterious. It felt like a reward to be able to look at her with no imposed time limit. *For once. I don't have to hide anything from her. She can see the full force of how much I adore her. Love…her…*

"Good, because I like having you in this position." And wasn't that the motherfucking truth? Having her over my lap felt like heaven.

"Why?" she asked softly.

"Why do I like you in this position?"

She nodded once.

I hesitated, needing to find the right words to answer without outright lying. She definitely wasn't ready to hear about my need for control during sex. Baby steps. Maybe we'd get there, maybe not. Worrying about it was pointless right now though.

"Because I like holding you and knowing you aren't going anywhere, that I've got you," I offered, the truth told the best I could. Telling her about the vision I really wanted to see—her tied to my bed where I could keep her pleasured for as long as I deemed it—wasn't exactly possible, so I focused on other points instead. "In this position, I can see your face right before I kiss you."

Her eyes flared just enough to show me what I wanted to see. *Desire.* Winter was turned on by my words. So responsive. So sensual. *Completely mine.*

"And be able to read your emotions if I'm lucky. You are so beautiful across my lap right now. I need to enjoy my view for a moment."

"Me too," she said, settling her head and neck to a comfortable position, probably because being situated directly above my hardening cock was requiring an adjustment on her part. "I love my view." She stared at me, her pretty green eyes studying me as intently as I was studying her.

Every time the word "love" came out of her mouth, my heart zinged me with a jolt that bordered on pain. Jesus, I was so lost already, and all we'd done was some eye-fucking in the back seat of a limo. Time to up the ante, though, because I'd go crazy if I didn't know more. "So, you want to tell me about *not* being a virgin?" I asked carefully, not wanting to make her uncomfortable.

She blushed, but didn't hedge my question. "Only a few times, and only ever with Chris. He wasn't all about the sex in the beginning and said we should wait until it felt right. Later on, after Dad got sick and our relationship started to suffer, he changed."

HOW the fuck she'd never been with anyone but that moron was a true mystery. "Changed how?"

"He began pressing me for sex all of a sudden, but only at certain times. It took me a minute to figure it out, but I caught on to what he was trying to do."

"Which was?" I asked. Oh, I had a very good idea exactly what that piece of shit was trying to do.

"Hoping to get me pregnant so I would agree to marry him."

Not a surprise, but it made me furious to imagine him attempting to impregnate a grieving girl at a horribly vulnerable time. The cocksucker figured out early on about her trust fund and its requirements for an early release. "Shelton was lucky he didn't get jail time with what he pulled taking you away after your father's funeral. Did he hurt you when he took you to that cabin in Vermont?" *If the answer is yes, then his miserable excuse for a life is over.*

"Hurt me? No." She shook her head quickly. "We were together at the cabin, which I am sure he thought might get him to his goal, but I'd ditched birth control pills in favor of a Depo shot after my pills were lost a *second* time." She frowned in annoyance and closed her eyes. "I don't want to talk about him anymore. Chris was just another guy in a long line of guys whose interest in me was financial over personal. The sex was barely memorable and the reason for my inexperience. I've never been with anyone who just wants me for who I am." *I should have stepped up a long time ago.*

"And who are you?" I asked, curious for her answer.

"Just a girl whose last name is Blackstone…who doesn't want her name to be what matters most to someone." I heard sadness in her answer, and it made me even more determined to get this right with her.

"Open your eyes, beautiful."

They fluttered open, finding mine.

"That's all about to change tonight," I said, bringing a hand between us to settle behind her neck. "I want you, and I'd never try to trap you into marriage with a pregnancy or anything you didn't want. Was done to me and it's fucked up."

"Leah did that to you?"

"Yeah, she pulled the whole 'I'm pregnant' bullshit, but neglected to tell me the father was someone else. I mean, I wanted to legitimize my child of course, but her betrayal left me blindsided so badly I…I needed a reset. I couldn't go back to my life how it had been when I was with her." It still burned now to even talk about it, but with Winter I didn't feel the need for keeping secrets. Anyone else I'd happily lie to, saying whatever to make him or her think I came out of my relationship with Leah unscathed, which I definitely hadn't. But I had absolutely no desire to lie to Winter. We weren't about lies and never had been.

"What she did to you was horrible, James. It bothered me so fucking much. I hated how she treated you, but I didn't know what to say or do at the time that could've possibly helped." She brought a gloved finger to my lips and traced them top to bottom slowly, the silk threads catching on my beard stubble as her finger moved. "I wished so badly I could help you then."

"I'm so glad you didn't try." *Fuck.* I hated to think of what really stupid shit I might have done five years ago when I was out of my mind with anger and rage.

"Why are you glad?"

"Because back then I wasn't fit to be in the same company as your sweet, nineteen-year-old, innocent self. I wouldn't have brought you into my hell for anything. Truly. I let darkness rule me for a while until I found a path of least destruction. At least it felt a lot like it at the time. Changes were made in my life, I left my dad's firm, started my own, and eventually settled into a…*situation*… that worked for me."

I studied her expression for any signs that she'd caught my small reveal about the "darkness ruling me" but she didn't react as if she did. Winter listened to me in her typical nonjudgmental fashion, a skill she'd perfected in the course of being a social worker I imagine. She had always been a good listener now that I thought about it. Mostly she was just a good person. So much better than me.

"Until about six months ago," I added, trying to move our conversation along to something more pleasant.

"Oh? What changed six months ago?" Her grin gave away she knew the answer. *Little tease. How I'd love to paddle her ass for that sass.*

"This gorgeous girl moved into my building, and I started to spend a lot of time thinking about her in her apartment, which just happens to be right below mine."

Her whole face lit up as her grin became a full-on smile. She looked like she had a lot to say, but whatever was on her mind remained a mystery as I cradled her in my lap.

I wanted—no, needed to kiss her again. I mostly wanted her spread out naked, so I could take my time with kissing every inch of her. And I did mean every single inch.

Anticipation and worry engaged in an epic warfare inside my brain. I wasn't used to feeling this out of control—something I never experienced while hooking-up with—

With whom? Those random subs you find at Lurid? The ones you choose because they remind you of Winter? Don't put her in the same category as those other women, asshole.

And this was most definitely not just another hookup for me. That much was a given, but from what she'd just told me, this wouldn't be a random hookup for her either, and that changed things. But *everything* was different with Winter, and it always had been. I needed to start being truthful with my feelings.

As I battled my demonic conscience, reconsidering just how many lines I would be crossing tonight with her, Winter brought me back into the moment by touching me again. This time her finger just pressed between my lips, suspending my runaway fears in a split second. "What kind of thoughts do you have about this girl?" she asked in a demure whisper.

"Filthy ones," I blurted. I pulled her off my lap and up onto the seat, where I could have her lips close to mine. "So very filthy, but right now I'm keeping a promise I made to myself earlier."

"What promise, James?"

"The one where your lips stay wet from my kisses all night long."

Touching my lips with her finger was Winter's way to ask me to kiss her without saying the words. Without a shadow of a doubt—and it was fucking hot. Beautiful perfect submission, and she wasn't even aware of it, which made it that much better. She'd given me so many clues in our recent interactions, and my theory was being confirmed bit by bit.

I closed the distance between our mouths and gave her what she wanted. It wasn't a crash of lips and tongues though, not at first. I needed to kiss her without time racing us forward impatiently. There was no rush. Just the two of us alone, and as much time as needed to get it right for once.

And I was determined to get it right for the rest of our trip to the Sherborn house. I could feel the warmth of her body heat, and the softness of her breasts shaping into my chest. All I wanted was to get closer to her.

I moved my lips away from hers to kiss her jaw and then her neck. I had so much skin to kiss before this night was over. So much more than just her pretty lips I realized, as I moved to the other side of her neck and licked a path back to her bottom lip. I took it between my teeth and bit down just enough for her to feel it. The moan that came out of her as she arched her body in my arms shot straight to my cock—she not only felt it…but she wanted it.

She wanted more, and I was going to give it to her. *Fuck. Yes.*

I HADN'T BEEN to my house in almost three months. Before tonight, I hadn't given the place much thought beyond questioning why I still paid caretaking services when I hardly ever used it. Mostly I pondered selling the fucking thing.

I bought it five years ago as a *surprise* for my fiancée. A place in the suburbs where we could start a family and do the grown-up shit people did when they got married.

Turned out I didn't need the big house in a private equestrian community with an empty barn waiting for a pony or two. Or situated within easy distance to the best schools. Providing for a family was no longer my concern. That ship had sailed to the benefit of all parties involved—fuck you very much.

So why *had* I held on to the house?

Not completely sure, except that I'd craved the idea of having a place nobody knew about, a sanctuary for whenever I needed one. I'd never told Leah or anyone in my family about this house. The deed wasn't even in my name, so it was completely off the grid, with the sole exception of my driver, Enzo. He knew about it because he lived in the guesthouse on the property and kept an eye on things for me.

My house was finally useful. It couldn't be more perfect for tonight with Winter.

"James, whose house is this?" she finally asked as I opened the front door and led her inside, grateful for the timed heating and lighting that kept it from feeling cold and dark.

"Mine."

"I didn't know you owned a house." She looked around at the mostly empty space, her eyes taking in the wood and stone and glass without comment. I so wished I knew what her thoughts were right now. Was she curious? Nervous? Scared to death of screwing this up between us like I was?

"Nobody knows, because I haven't told anyone before."

"When do you come here?" she asked, turning back toward me with the serious expression on her beautiful face.

"When I need a break."

"Is it often that you need a break?" she asked quietly.

"I haven't been to this house for months." Only the truth for her. "But I'm really happy that you're here now. I finally have you all to myself."

I backed her against the wall and settled my body against hers. Soft and quiet, and smelling so fucking wonderful with her whole body aligned with mine, I took a moment to breathe her in before I went insane. I could tell she was anticipating what I'd do next, but I had no intentions of rushing it. Not this first time anyway. Being with Winter was something I'd wanted for so damn long I ached. I couldn't even remember when my feelings had started. The wanting was something I recognized as a familiar companion. Always with me. Very well understood and accepted. I'd lived with it for years.

I never expected we might ever get to this point together.

I took her jaw in the palm of my hand and tilted it toward my lips. I smelled flowers mixed with oranges. The scent filtered into my senses where it would stay, because I was committing her to memory.

"Do you trust me?" I asked with my lips just out of reach of hers, so close but achingly much too far away.

"Yesss...always." I heard frustration loud and clear in her whispered words, and so did my cock. Painfully hard—and loving every second of the sweet torture of being so close to her.

"Good girl." I brushed over her pouty lips lightly with my thumb. "I need to tell you the rules before I take you upstairs."

"You have rules?" Her lips parted as she drew in a heavy

breath and shaped them around pad of my thumb for a second before I took it away.

"Just two," I paused before adding, "but two very important ones."

The tip of her tongue wet her bottom lip before disappearing into her mouth. I'm sure I groaned audibly, when all I could imagine was that pretty pink tongue licking up the length of my rock-hard dick.

"Complete honesty from you is the first rule. You tell me we need to stop? We stop. You tell me to give you more? I will give you more. If I ask you a question, you give me a truthful answer. I'll hear you, as long as you tell me. I'll always listen to whatever you say."

She stilled as my words sunk in. I sensed a rapidly beating pulse against my lips as I kissed up her neck, but still she asked, "And rule number two?"

"I'm in charge in the bedroom. It's the only way I can do this with you. I'll make it so good, and give you exactly what you want, but I'll be taking the lead the whole way." I pulled back from her neck reluctantly. I had to read her face so I knew. It was a risk for me to even voice my second rule out loud, but I knew I had to do it, if not for me, then for her.

The breath left her in the softest way, in a quiet rush that almost masked the intensity of it. Almost. Her eyes were directed down but I could clearly see the pulse at her throat fluttering as she contemplated my conditions. *What is she thinking?*

"What if I say no to your rules?" Her chin lifted but her eyes stayed down. Such a tantalizing contradiction of gestures she presented while pinned against the wall by my crowding her. It was fucking hot. She wasn't even doing anything beyond standing before me waiting for an answer to her question. Winter didn't need to *do* anything for me to want her.

"Then we don't fuck. Not tonight…or ever."

Her eyes flickered up and held mine. "Then I…I agree to the rules, James," she replied without a trace of fear. "I want to fu…I want to do everything with you."

Probably the wrong thing for her to tell me when I was nearly out of my mind in crazy fucking lust. I knew she didn't have any idea what she was saying or the meaning behind it. Winter's idea of "everything" was a far cry from mine when discussing sex, but that didn't matter right now. She'd agreed to my rules. We were done with waiting.

I kissed her deeply, my tongue as far into her as I could get it. I kept her pinned to my wall and kissed the fuck out of her, pleasured myself on her mouth until the raging need burning me from the inside settled into something more familiar.

The darker edge of control I was used to took over as I learned her: the softness of her lips and tongue dancing along with mine; the way she moved her body against mine; the little sounds she made when aroused.

Which she fucking was. Her pussy was no doubt already wet, and soon I'd know when she was spread out naked in my bed ready to be fucked. Hell, she was ready right now just from kissing.

Her response was fucking perfect. Soft and accepting, she let me go to work on her. Before this night was through, Winter would be on the receiving end of more orgasms than she'd ever known. And I was going to enjoy giving every one of them to her.

I ended our kiss abruptly and took a step back.

Slowly she opened her eyes, her body resting against the wall as she took in deep breaths, waiting for me.

I obliged her.

"Take off the dress."

CHAPTER SIXTEEN

Winter

My mind went blank for a moment as I tried to remember where the zipper was situated on my dress. Back? Side? I had no idea. I considered telling him the truth, but I didn't want to break the spell of our sensual dance. It felt too good being in the moment with James. Obviously. He had me so turned on I couldn't even recall how my own dress worked.

"Turn." One sharp word, but it was plenty. James had figured out my dilemma and was taking charge. Oddly, a wave of pure relief crashed over me as the decision was lifted away from my sphere of responsibility. The heat of his fingers finding the zipper and dragging it down seared into my skin despite the layers of silk in between.

Now opened at the waist, my dress allowed the cool night air to dance over my exposed skin. I could feel his eyes staring at my back. "Sorry," he whispered into my ear as he turned me around to face him once more. "I forgot about this." He drew my injured hand to his lips and kissed the back of it through the silk. "It won't happen again."

Why was he apologizing?

I was the one so stupefied by the sensual, dangerous man before me.

He stared at me; so serious, and even slightly harsh, but with a predatory gleam. I was about to be devoured.

Fear of the unknown mixing with desire twisted low in my belly and reminded me to take a breath. Depriving my body of oxygen was just as involuntary as the air I was forced to swallow in response. I waited.

"Now the dress. Off." His words—so precise—were a definite command.

Determined, I gripped the bodice of the dress where he'd unzipped me, worked the fabric over my hips, and let go. Gravity took hold, pulling it into a satiny heap around my calves. I stepped out carefully one shoe at a time, the chill of the night air sweeping over my skin. Designer ball gowns came with built-in bras and underlying slips, so once it was off my body, there wasn't much left to remove. Panties, stockings, gloves, shoes—was all that remained.

Slowly I lifted my eyes to his, meeting his stare. The harsh look on his face would've startled me if I wasn't so aroused. I could hardly breathe. The cool autumn air swept over my skin tightening my nipples to nearly painful peaks. James noticed. He stared leisurely before meeting my eyes again with a slow shake of his head.

"I used to imagine you like this—what you'd look like standing before me, waiting for me to tell you what to do next."

I took in a shuddering breath, unwilling to speak. I was too far into the exchange to even think about forming any words of my own. *The look in his eyes.*

"The reality is so much better, beautiful. You're perfect in every way."

I wished he would touch me. The longer I stood on

display the more desperate I felt. Surely I would combust soon.

"Are you afraid?"

I nodded my head.

"Answer me with words, baby. I need to hear you," he scolded gently.

"Yes, I am afraid," I answered honestly.

"Afraid of me?" He raised an eyebrow in surprise.

"Never of you."

"What then?"

"That I might burn up if you don't touch me." Even I could hear the frustration in my voice.

He gave me a wicked grin. "You want to be touched?"

"Yes."

"What else do you want?"

"I…I want…I want you to kiss me again."

"And?"

"I want to feel your hands on me." I wanted more than just his hands, and he knew it. I waited for him to command that I say how much I wanted his cock, but it didn't come. He kept staring at my body hungrily as if he couldn't decide where to start.

"We need a bed for the many things I want to do to you before this night is over."

"D-don't you have a bed?"

He laughed. "Oh, I have one. And I'm going to fuck you in it just as soon as you walk that very fine ass of yours up the stairs."

A bolt of heat hit me so hard my knees nearly buckled.

James saying the words, "I'm going to fuck you," in any context related to me would certainly do it. I sucked in a breath and looked toward the staircase, wondering how on earth my legs would manage to carry me up so many steps when they could barely hold me up. *I'll never make it on my wobbly ass legs.*

"You'll make it because I'll be right behind you enjoying the view. If you stumble, I'll catch you, and for the record, your legs are sheer perfection," he said, jerking his head the direction of the stairs.

Mortified to realize I was speaking the thoughts in my head out loud for him to hear, I closed my eyes tightly in frustration.

"You're going to have to open your eyes before you start walking, though," he said, clearly amused by my dilemma. "Go upstairs to my bedroom, Winter. We're not doing this anywhere but in my bed tonight. At least the first time."

The promise of something I'd desired for so long staring me right in the face was so different than how I'd imagined it would be. James was different. He was so demanding…and dominant.

I loved everything about this new, bossy James.

From the stern look on his handsome face, to the piercing eyes raking over my mostly naked body, along with the promise of something I'd always believed forbidden with him.

Some really hot, filthy, dirty, amazing sex.

But James must have similar thoughts about the "forbidden" aspect of being together. Both of us were in uncharted territory. We'd always been friends. And right now we were friends who were about to fuck. How would things be after the hot sex was over? Would James still care about me in the same way? Would I?

"If you're having second thoughts, you tell me now. Remember my rules, Winter," he warned.

"I remember."

"Repeat them." Another command delivered with the darkness of tone I'd quickly come to appreciate, because I had made an important discovery. Bossy James was hotter than hell and slapped every sexual button. Hard.

I licked my bottom lip and dragged it under my top teeth before answering. "First rule, complete honesty. I'm to tell you if I want you to stop, or if I need more. Second, is that you are in charge." His second rule had me on the verge of incineration already, and I was beginning to recognize why. My years'-long attraction to him, the hot blushes that consumed me whenever I found myself on the receiving end of one of his penetrating stares, the flash of understanding how powerfully those penetrating stares had affected me. My submission was as natural as my attraction. I wanted it.

Needed it. *From James only.*

"Very good." He pointed in the direction of the stairs. "After you, beautiful."

Feeling strangely detached from the insanity of exactly where I was, and what I was about to do, I took a first faltering step toward the stairs. And then another. I focused only on taking steps; moving my body through the motions of climbing the winding staircase that would take me to James's bedroom. His determined footsteps from behind pushed me forward. The delicious scent of his spicy cologne intoxicated me. The heat from his eyes staring at my ass framed in nothing but a little bit of skimpy lace burned my skin. I couldn't see him staring, but I felt him.

I wanted James Blakney, and he wanted me.

This might be my only experience of knowing what it felt like having his hot stare on my ass. *Supremely sexy and strangely empowering.* I hoped not, but I'd learned early on that what we *wanted* and what we actually got were often very different. *Not far apart right now, though.* I pushed my doubts aside and embraced the moment instead, found strength in knowing my time for wondering was over.

The closed door at the end of the hallway loomed before me. The final barrier to what would happen between us. I realized that we'd pass our point of no return.

James must have had similar thoughts.

"Last chance to change your mind," he said softly against my ear, his lips nearly brushing the shell, "because once I have you behind that door, you'll definitely feel my touch." He pinned me to the door, crowding me with solid arms that boxed me in. "For hours," he added as he pressed his body against mine. Those last two words pulled a desperate shuddering moan out of me, especially combined with the purposeful press of his very hard body behind me. Sandwiched between a cold wooden door and the heat of his erection that stole the breath right out of me.

He must have turned the doorknob because I felt the coldness of the wood fall away from the front of my body as he pushed me forward. I tried to register my surroundings, because I was being led into his inner sanctum of sorts. He might not come here often, but it was still his private, intimate space. For a split second I thought about the others he must have brought here over the years, but I couldn't deal with imagining it. I had no patience for doubt. *Forget everything else.*

James broke through the pounding silence of my indecision with a clear directive. "Get on the bed and lie back. I want to look at you."

Somehow, I moved my body and did as he asked. I lowered myself onto the black covered bed that looked like a huge industrial modern sculpture. Tall bedposts at the four corners with metalwork incorporated into the head and footboards dominated the entire space of the room. I shivered against the coolness of the fabric as it met my back. I was so very exposed, but it felt completely right, as if this was the only way for us to ever do this act together.

I watched James as he looked his fill with fiery eyes that roved hungrily over my body. As he moved closer to the edge of the bed, I could feel the heat coming off his stare. And then he grinned...and licked his lips. "Arms up over your head, hold on to the headboard, and let me *take* care of you, beautiful. That's what I want from you."

The ache at my core grew stronger, as did the tightening of my nipples as I drew my arms upward to find a place to grip the headboard. My body yearned for his touch, but I knew instinctively he'd deny it altogether if I voiced it. *I'm in charge in the bedroom. It's the only way I can do this with you.*

I wanted his mouth. His tongue. Some part of him. Any part of him.

Before I died a slow, agonizing death due to sexual frustration.

"I'm taking a picture of you in my head. I don't ever want to forget how you looked in this moment." He'd taken off his tuxedo jacket and removed his tie at some point. His shirt was half-way unbuttoned. I appreciated the glimpse of his chest where his shirt gaped open. I wished he'd strip for me right now. Now that would be an added sweet torture I'd love to experience.

"And how do I look in this moment?" I asked.

"Flawless." He toed off his shoes, tore open his shirt, and pulled it off. The sounds of threads ripping and buttons scattering pulled a wave of anticipation that hit me so hard between my thighs I arched my back and rolled through the sweet ache. "Like you're meant to be here." The bed dipped from his weight as he put one knee on the mattress, and then the other. Straddling me, his arms and legs boxed me in underneath him. "Ready for me to take you," he added darkly.

I moaned at his last comment. I wished he would *take* me. I needed him to. Desperate and unable to wait patiently for even another second, I begged, "Please, take me."

"Do you know how long I've wanted to have you just like this? Naked in my bed and dying for me to make you come? Desperate for my cock?"

"Too fucking long, James."

"I know," he said as his mouth came down onto mine, pushing in hard and deep with his tongue—owning me.

Finally.

I welcomed the surge of primal energy that bolted through me the instant I gave myself over to him.

The very instant of the act of him taking what I wanted to give.

His mouth moved down to my neck and then to my shoulder as he trailed kisses and gentle bites with his teeth. I felt each mark as he made them, each pinch soothed by soft caresses of his tongue to temper the cruel heat of want and desire. As his lips moved over my breasts, so did firm hands, cupping and lifting each peak in turns to his mouth to suck. He took as much as he was able into his mouth and sucked hard before drawing back until just my nipple was left between his teeth. He teased me relentlessly with more soft bites and sucks and kisses. I knew he was marking me.

The marks he made were the visual evidence of the crossing over in my head to my body, to the understanding where I knew if he stopped...I would most certainly die.

I felt determined fingers at my hips digging under the sides of my panties to slide them down my legs. Panties were tossed and then his hands slid roughly up my legs to my knees where they stopped. I knew what was coming next.

A firm grip to the insides of my knees pushed them apart, placing me on full display for his hot stare. A hot stare I could feel burning the flesh of the most intimate part of me. I was so grateful for the spa treatment I'd done earlier in the day with Brooke—at her insistence. *Bless you, sweet Brooke.* Because of her resolve, things were as tidy as they could possibly be where he was looking.

"You are so fucking beautiful," he said with his eyes glued to my very wet and aching pussy. But I had to look away. The sight of him staring so hungrily at me was far too much to take in. So, I closed my eyes and embraced the anticipation instead, focusing on the fact that this was always going to happen. Fate had decided for us a long time ago. We were always going to find our way to this point.

And we had. We were here.

His busy fingers found me first. Tracing around my clit slowly, teasing me with careful touches just shy of where I really needed him to be touching me. Delaying sexual gratification was definitely amongst the skill set of James Blakney. *Bastard.*

"So pretty…so soft…and so very wet," he said admiringly, just before he put his whole mouth on me and licked me from bottom to top. My entire lower body came up off the bed as a lightning strike of pure pleasure commenced at my clit. I heard a shrill cry from somewhere in the room and was forced to accept that it could only have come from me.

With my thighs pinned open by firm hands gripping hard enough to leave marks, James devoured me. I reveled in what he did. Every melting lick, each teasing flick, each delicious tap of his magical tongue brought me closer to nirvana. I didn't need to be told it was going to be bigger and better than any orgasm I'd had before tonight. It was happening whether I was ready for it or not.

"Give me all of it. Give me everything," he grunted in between licks and sucks with the power to detonate me into the next galaxy. I moaned in protest when he pulled his mouth off, thrusting my hips upward to try to reclaim contact. "You want more."

It wasn't a question.

"Yeeess, more, *please* give me more." Speech seemed impossible, but yet words still tumbled from my lips.

James flicked his eyes up to meet mine, flaring wide in frustration. "There's so much more I want to give you…and I can't—I can't do it all at once."

"I don't want you to do it all at once," I insisted, hoping he understood me. And since I figured his good judgment was heavily clouded by what he was doing with me, I was honest. "I need you to do it over and over and over again. I need you to never stop."

My words seemed to please him. "I won't stop. Not until I feel your tight little cunt clamp down around my tongue when I'm fucking you with it."

The things that came out of his mouth only made me burn hotter as he went back to work at licking my pussy. *Thank Christ's heavenly angels.* The heat that had been building low in my belly flared white-hot as the convulsions took hold of me…and catapulted me into sweet ecstasy. I let out a long, low cry as the climax seized me, incoherent to everything but the pleasure. I felt myself fall away as I rode his mouth. There was no way to describe having James inside me, even if only his tongue. The intimacy so much greater than the act of touching mouths in a kiss. It was James revealing himself to me. An epiphany in understanding, that for the first time in my life I didn't have to do anything other than *take* from him.

Pure bliss. Relief. Love. I felt all of those things. I also discovered something else after the mind-blowing climax from his tongue doing very dirty and lovely things to me.

FILTHY *Lies*

I am ruined for any man on this earth that isn't James Blakney.

THE OPERA GLOVES needed to come off, so I could touch him and feel him without anything in between. But James wasn't having any of it, as he shrugged my hands away from where I'd buried them in his hair.

Bossy James was still new to me, but I loved *him* a lot.

As if he were reading my thoughts, my arms were firmly pushed back above my head and returned to the headboard. I didn't remember letting go of it, but I must've during the sheet-clawing orgasm I still felt coursing deliciously through my body. From head to toe.

James loomed over me, his eyes questioning, looking for answers. "Are you okay?"

"I'm fi—"

His lips dropped down to kiss me, taking away my ability to answer. I didn't mind, because I didn't need to talk. I wasn't sure if I was capable of anything beyond accepting what he was doing to me right this second. Which was kissing me ravenously while devouring my mouth and lips. I could taste myself on his tongue, and it all felt so filthy and wicked...and divine.

His hands were all over me. No part of me was left untouched. He feasted on my breasts, sucked them, pinched them, teased my nipples with teeth that knew just how hard to bite. His long beautiful fingers pressed their way inside me, fucking in and out of my pussy while his thumb teased my asshole. He would have all of me. Everything was relentless in forcing me into a tailspin of sensation and pleasure. Every kiss and bite and penetration of my fevered flesh was demanded wildly but done in a way that gave me everything in return. I had no idea how, but it was as if my body had been waiting for him. For him to pleasure, cherish…consume. As if he'd known my body forever. *Because my body already knew him.*

The second orgasm incinerated me into another realm as hot tears slid from my eyes squeezed tightly shut. I tasted the sex in the air that I drew in for my next breath. I heard him say, "You're coming for me. *Only* for me."

I did what he asked.

Almost brutally hard with fingers stroking deep and relentless in their purpose, with no censure of any kind. He took what he wanted from me…and then demanded more as he owned my second climax. I lost track of…all things, understanding only that I was utterly in *his* care.

James taking care of me.

This I knew without explanation of any kind. And so, I drifted away to a place I'd never been before, but where I wanted to stay forever.

I wasn't ever coming back.

CHAPTER SEVENTEEN

James

I held Winter against the length of my body with a hand at her throat, taking her breaths along with the kisses I stole from her. I wasn't even a little bit sorry. Making her come was my new favorite obsession. Still amazed that she hadn't backed down from any of what I'd done to her, I waited for my beautiful girl to recover from her orgasm.

Because the night was young, and she wasn't finished yet.

And also because I now knew I'd never be finished with her. That was on me, not her. I couldn't change what I was, but what I'd just discovered in the course of her two orgasms had changed my future. Changed *our* future.

"Winter...my Winter," I whispered against her mouth.

She moaned beneath me, needy and fitful.

"I want to fuck you...and make you come again...this time with your perfect pussy wrapped around my big hard cock."

"Please, please, James, please," she begged.

She shouldn't have to beg. Not ever. She shouldn't have to, but it was a thing of exquisite beauty to witness, and I knew

I'd make her beg me again and again and again. She was too fuckin' sexy...I wouldn't resist the temptation.

I left her on the bed and stripped off my pants first, and then my socks. As I got naked I leisurely admired her, stretched out waiting for me to fuck her. In my house. In my bed. In my life. Mine, all mine, all mine.

But she's not just waiting to be fucked.

It didn't feel like that at all. In fact, nothing had felt familiar tonight. Because it wasn't. I had never done this before with any other woman.

You aren't fucking her. You're making love to the woman who owns your heart.

I stepped out of my boxers and stroked myself from root to tip. It felt so good to do it with her seeing my body for the first time. Her eyes were greedy, watching my every move as I fisted up and down the length. And then they grew wide in surprise when she noticed exactly what I had on the underside of my dick. Two silver balls at each end of a bar pierced horizontally through the skin just below the head of my cock—a frenum piercing.

"You're smiling, Winter baby."

"You are pierced on your very big, beautiful cock, James Blakney." Her grip on the headboard was abandoned for a second time as she sat up and stripped off the gloves while leaning forward to get a better look. She didn't follow directions very well, but I forgave her. What she lacked in discipline she more than made up for in enthusiasm. She also said amazing things for my ego. *Yes, she is a keeper.*

"Do you mean this?" I asked, stepping forward to show her.

"Yes...I want it," —she reached out with her left hand, wrapping her fingers around the base— "Does it feel good when you fuck?" The combination of her touch and the directly worded question nearly sent me to my knees. I bowed my back and thrust forward into her grip, hoping like hell I could hold off long enough to have it inside her…somewhere.

"It does. And it'll feel good for you too…when I'm in you." I thrust into her tight grip a few times…and then she opened her mouth and flattened her tongue out wide.

Oh, mother-FUCK. I steered my cock right inside her beautiful mouth and pushed it to the back of her throat.

Where she took me all the way down in one swallow.

"Fuuuuck—feels so good." I sounded like an animal growling out the words I spoke even to my own ears. In my mind I realized I was probably too rough with her, but I rationalized it by watching her carefully for any signs of needing me to slow down or back off.

She gave me not a single one.

Her mouth. God. I could die a happy man with my cock bottoming out at the back of her throat. I thought I might die when I gripped the sides of her face and began to fuck her mouth in earnest. My strokes hard and fast, almost painful in the sensation of pleasure as she took me in, her hot, wet tongue caressing against the bar of my metal with of each rough thrust of my cock. She sucked me like it was her new favorite thing to do. *This girl…mine forever.*

I felt my balls tighten up, ready to unload down her throat, but I didn't want it like that. Not for our first time together. I knew how I wanted the sex to go…even if it was wrong of me not to ask first.

And so, I made my decision.

I pulled out of her mouth on a harsh groan and replaced cock with tongue, kissing and licking thoroughly over her abused lips, hoping she could know what I felt.

I love you.

187

I pushed her down on the bed and moved her up to the middle where I had some room. I arranged her arms above her head and jerked her wrists together sharply, letting her know I expected her to keep them there.

Her eyes flared as she looked at me in silence, waiting for whatever I'd give her next. *Flawless.* Winter was a quiet lover—another thing about her I'd discovered. I don't know why it turned me on so much, but her silent acceptance of every way I'd commanded her so far tonight was dangerously addicting.

I spread her open with bent knees and took my cock in hand. I penetrated just the tip between her slippery folds before pulling back out to rub over her clit drenched in the wet from earlier orgasms. Her mouth fell open and her head rolled back in a kind of perfect, silent submission, her sweet cunt on offer...to me.

I fucking love you so much.

So, I teased the tip of my cock inside her again, just to see her give me that same beautiful response one more time. *FUCK yeah.* And like a true addiction, I had to repeat the whole act several more times, because I couldn't get enough of seeing her like this with me—couldn't have stopped myself even if I'd wanted to. I worked her over until she became a writhing erotic creature beneath me. Both of us slick with her juices and aching to fuck. She was more than ready for me to take her and I was way past ready to have her.

So, I buried my cock all the way to my balls in one hard, deep thrust that sent me to heaven. Then I pushed in deeper still, needing to be as far in her as I could be. *Never far enough.* And in true form, she took my cock in silence, the only audible sound being a sharp gasp as her heat surrounded me in a tight clasp. I had to close my eyes for a moment and revel in the feel of being inside my Winter...because now I had finally and truly claimed her.

"Okay?" Worried she might not tell me if she wasn't, I needed to ask.

"Yes..." she answered on a soft whisper with the sweetest answer she could ever give me.

I pulled out on a hot slide and then back in with one continuous stroke. "I don't have any condoms." Another deep delicious slide in and out of her tight heat. "I didn't know we were coming here and I wasn't prepared." My cock sank into her again, moving on its own now. "Are you protected?" I started to fuck faster. "Do I need to pull out or can I come in you, because I'm fucking you bare here," I barked, unable to slow down as the madness took over.

She arched into my thrusts, rocking against me with every stroke, squeezing her tight little cunt even harder around my cock. I wasn't going to last much longer at this rate and she still hadn't answered me.

"WINTER?" I roared, on the verge of losing it.

"Come inside me...it's okay if you do. I am—I'm protected." She said the words softly, but my brain heard her as if she'd yelled it at me.

As I got busy with the fucking, I knew it wouldn't be long before I erupted in her. But it was necessary for her to come with me. The friction of my metal dragging through her tight pussy was a pureness of pleasure to the point that I got lost in the sensation of being inside her. I wasn't completely sure of everything I said...or did to her.

The tightening down low where our bodies connected surged upward and took over, superseding even my need to breathe. My fingers strummed her clit with precision, watching for her to fall over the edge with me. The first pulse arrived with a single low cry from deep from within her chest. She arched into me and convulsed around my cock, the shuddering movement making her beautiful tits quiver below me.

The sight of her climaxing set me off like a volcano. Hot cum from down in my balls, spurted out of me and into her with every deep surge of my cock. Within the act itself, I knew I was marking her in my very essence from the inside out as belonging to me. My seed was in her now, therefore she was mine. Ancient caveman *DNA* residing deep within my lawyer's brain was very fucking certain of this most basic truth.

I know I kissed her many times, and also said things I can't remember saying throughout the course of our night together. I made love to her again after we slept for an hour or two. The second time was not so frantic. The third time was in the shower and turned into a sweet and slow exploration for the both of us.

After we were done with all of the sex, and I had her tucked in bed beside me for sleep, she told me something important before she drifted away in my arms.

The words she spoke—they terrified me because I knew then that I'd played my hand to her.

My heart now served at the mercy of another person for the second time in my life. And with that unfortunately came the knowledge of just how vulnerable my heart was of being crushed into nothingness again. If things ever went wrong with Winter Blackstone, it could happen. *It would happen* if I was not careful. So, I wouldn't take the risk of ever losing her. My ability to exist with a functioning heartbeat would depend upon that never happening.

And as they fell from her soft, beautiful lips, her words also meant…everything…that was good and joyful, and full of hope.

She said, "I love you too, James."

CHAPTER EIGHTEEN

Winter

I woke to find his head between my legs and his tongue moving over my clit in the most delicious way imaginable. My first thought? *This is the best James-dream I've EVER had.*

But it wasn't a dream. I could feel the grip of his hands pinning my thighs open down to the bed. And feel the pricks of his beard stubble to the *very* sensitive places up and down my sex. And smell the heady scent of James, mixed with the essence left behind from hours spent filthily and lovingly fucking. Because *none* of those things would happen in a dream even if it was good.

So…no dream.

All of those beautiful, wonderful things had happened…to me…last night—and were still happening to me right now. I was *Sleeping Beauty* awakened with a kiss from her prince. But my prince had done a lot more than kiss me last night. He'd claimed me in so many ways…and not only sexually. It had gone so much further in our hours together, and I was definitely a new woman this morning, feeling completely changed from how I'd lived before.

As I started to fall over the edge into another climax,

James knew. He could tell when it was happening, and he ramped up the intensity of his tongue action to make it so good for me. *So GOOD.* For me. I seized onto the burning heat that blasted my core, then rode the waves that flowed through my extremities as his mouth made sweet love to my clit. James knew how to do everything so right. *I love him.*

After a time, I felt him moving me, my limbs slack as he pushed me into place, arranging my body how he wanted me—on my hands and knees with my ass in the air. I guessed how the sex was going to go this time. There had been a lot of sex with him last night. I lost track of the orgasms he forced on me. I wasn't complaining though, even if I wasn't at all used to so much pleasure. I could get used to it pretty quickly though, because the person I loved was giving it to me. I also knew now that he loved me too. He'd told me many, many times already. *And all this time, I've had no clue how much he cared about me and for how long.* Part of me mourned the time we could have had together. But the other part knew our waiting had a purpose, and that was okay. *Now was good.*

My prince of pleasure greeted my ass with an affectionate slap to one of my butt cheeks. He used his hands at my hips roughly, jerking me backward to probe against my asshole with the wide head of his very hard cock. "Soon," he growled low, a single quiet word sending an uncontrollable shiver down the back of my neck. "I'll be taking *this*—and it'll feel *so fuckin' good* when I do, baby." I shuddered at the thought, wondering if "soon" meant in the next few minutes. I wasn't at all opposed to trying it for the first time. Saying no to anything James wanted wouldn't be something I'd be capable of.

I pushed back into him, the hard tip of his cock meeting my sensitive hole with a sharp sting that drew a sudden gasp out of me.

"Not right now. I don't have everything I need to do it right, and not hurt you. I need lube to take you here"—he pressed in with just the tip of his finger—"because my cock is big, and you'll be so tight when it's buried inside you, fucking your gorgeous ass."

Oh God, the things he said to me when we were deep into the sex made me wild. All I could envision was his beautiful, pierced cock wildly claiming my virgin ass and fucking me into another orgasmic meltdown. A girl could fantasize. James would keep his promise to me...I had no doubt.

He positioned himself and sank his cock hard into my pussy, instead, filling me so full I couldn't hold back the cry from my lips. I felt the metal balls of his piercing dragging along the walls of my sex, making my eyes roll back in my head. All I could do was take it from him as he pounded into me from behind—a wild, lusty beast with nothing on his mind than fucking me.

But then there was more.

Another thing James was good at was giving me more...which he did by wetting his thumb with the slickness at my core and pushing inside my ass with it.

"But right now, I'll do this," he said roughly, "and you can decide if you like me inside you this way." Penetrated by him in two places, his thumb acting like a barb to hold me steady for his thrusting cock, he told me how much he loved me while he used my body fiercely.

"Do you like me in your ass?" he grunted as he fucked. If there was any pain, I didn't feel it, because I was too far gone in the pleasure of being taken by James. Gone from this earth to somewhere else. "Answer me," he scolded with a yank to my hair fisted in his other hand.

"Yes...yes...yes...yes...I like it, James—everything you do...is what I like."

As my answer came, I felt him do the same. The hot flood of his orgasm filled me. And then his very beautiful words. Words I could never grow tired of hearing as they fell from his lips. "My Winter, I love you."

And so, falling under the spell of his dominating treatment was an easy thing for me. So easy to take his harsh kisses as he bestowed them. So easy to take the sting of his teeth as they claimed lips and breasts and shoulders. So easy to take the bite of fingers and hands as they held me down or moved me wherever he wanted me. So easy to take anything at all that he would give me.

So very easy to become addicted to being…*his*.

It was as though my body had been waiting for *him*. As though, despite or because of my lack of sexual history, my body and soul and mind had been primed, ready to accept everything about him. About us. *He's wanted me for years as well, yet he never took any chances…until now.* And now? In his bed, in his house that he'd kept from everyone…

James was making up for all of the years we'd both had to wait to get here.

THE SECOND TIME I opened my eyes he was watching me, his expression one of peace and contentment as he lay on his side facing me. Neither of us spoke for a long time, instead we just looked into each other's eyes…thinking…probably about the same things—what we'd done together, the words we'd said to each other, and where we went from here.

James broke the spell first. "How is my woman this morning?" The adorable smirk added to his question just about killed me. The fact he was far too handsome for his own good, as well as naked in bed with me also probably helped shorten my lifespan. But I rationalized that I could still appreciate my good fortune in having such a magnificent man to call my own. I was fixated. James was *my man* now. Any other females out there who might want a piece of him could just back right-the-hell-off.

"Well, my love, since you're asking me in such a lovingly and romantic way, I'll tell you." I lifted the sheet, threw my leg over and straddled him—sitting my ass down right on top of where it counted—his beautiful, pierced, and very talented penis lying flat on his stomach. I couldn't resist the little shimmy I did over the impressive morning wood he was growing as I settled into place on top of him. His eyes laughed up at me for my naughty behavior and then went right back down to lust after my boobs. James loved staring at them almost as much as he liked touching and sucking on them. "Up here, big guy, eyes are right up here."

"Sorry," he said without ever taking his eyes off my tits, "I'm admiring my woman's incredible and splendid rack as I prepare to start my day. It's very important to begin each day with positive thoughts and a healthy appreciation of your many blessings."

"I guess I should accept it as a compliment that my breasts are counted among your life's blessings," I teased.

"Without a fucking doubt."

I laughed. "Okay, well, then you should know that *your woman* is very well this morning. Oh, and about last night, and how she spent it…with you? Her whole life has changed because of it." I shook my head for emphasis. "I don't think the happiness will ever stop spilling out of *your woman*."

He got a wicked little gleam in his eye just before he tossed me onto my back, rolling over on top of me, and caging me beneath his hard body. He brought his lips down to mine and gave me the best good morning kiss I'd ever had, and I knew then that James didn't have any regrets, either.

"Just one thing I need to know. Are you sure I wasn't too rough with you?" he asked with real concern in his voice. "I don't ever want to do anything to make you feel uncomfortable or to scare you in any way. I only want to make you happy like you make me." He kissed me sweetly and then pulled back to say, "Last night with you was really fucking beautiful."

I shook my head slowly up at him, feeling suddenly a tiny bit shy. Which was stupid really, because we'd been as intimate as it was possible to be together—all night long and again this morning—so feeling shy with him was ridiculous and pointless? "James, you were not too rough with me. I loved everything we did—that you did. Don't you know that by now?"

"Certainly in regards to the sex, yeah, but there's still so much that we haven't talked about." He held my face framed in his two palms with so much gentleness as he looked down at me. "We never had our discussion about everything that's happened already, and what you want to do about accessing your trust fund...and...getting married." He stared at my lips. "When *are* you going to marry me, Winter Blackstone?"

I smiled up at him and bit the inside of my bottom lip in a feeble effort to brush it off as teasing. If James knew how easily I'd agree, I'm pretty sure he'd stop bringing it up.

"What does the lip biting mean, huh? Am I wearing you down at all?"

"If I believed for one minute you wanted to marry me right away I'd say *yes* and then where would you be?" Let him digest that little tidbit and see how it felt. Tempting me with it was only making me frustrated.

James nailed me with his eyes. "Oh, I know exactly where I'd be, Win." His voice was low, but deadly serious. "I'd be inside you...taking my time to do everything I want to do to you, spread out underneath me in my bed. All. The. Fucking. Time."

A shiver rolled through me and landed right between my legs.

I could tell he still wanted to hear what I wanted from him. I think mostly he just needed some reassurance. "But I think we really solved a lot of our problems last night, don't you? I mean…I know my feelings and so do you."

"Yes, I concur, Miss Blackstone, because we both said things last night…and it pretty much changed everything for us."

The I love yous.

"I know. And that's why I'm so ecstatic this morning."

"I'm going to remember last night for the rest of my life, and how it felt to hear you say you *love me*." He looked so solemn, gorgeous as always, especially with his just-fucked-bed-head and naked-man-chest on view for me to admire, but still so very solemn.

"I do love you, James. But most importantly, you have to *believe* that I love you—and I trust you when you say the same." I cupped his cheek in my hand and nodded. "If we have that much love for each other, then I don't think there's much of anything for us to worry about right now. We can figure it out in time, together. I am so relieved that I didn't have to tell you no to your offer of a paper marriage. I wouldn't have been able to fake it with you for even five-minutes."

"Yeah, me either. Everything you've just said sounds right. You're always very smart about what matters most." He gave me a peck on the lips. "Very practical and beautiful at the same time, too. Have I mentioned this lately?"

Yes, you call me "beautiful" all the time.

But he never gave me a chance to answer him because he was too busy kissing me.

And because I was too busy being kissed by my loving, gorgeous man.

CHAPTER NINETEEN

James

Enjoying our new relationship status lasted about as long as it took to power our phones back on. After our morning "talk", we decided to go back to the city without anything more important to decide than where we would be sleeping tonight—her place or mine. Although, having Winter in the shower with me had been very fucking nice. I'd loved that part of our day so far.

Enzo had just pulled out from the Starbucks with our breakfast sandwiches and coffees, had us on the road back to the city, when Winter decided we should check in with the rest of the world after our night away of love-fucking. She was probably right, but man, I was not keen.

"I wonder how many texts are on here about why I left early with you last night," she said with a sigh.

"I wonder if I have any from Caleb or my sister about why I wasn't home last night."

"Oh, I'm gonna go out on a limb and guess yes."

Wearing our formal clothes from last night made us look really guilty of doing exactly what we'd done. Winter looked amazing after a night in my bed being loved up by me, her elegant ball gown back on her delicious body once more. I was counting the minutes until I took it off her again. The low cut of her dress didn't cover the hickey I'd made between her neck and shoulder, either. Seeing her marked by me? *Off the chain.* I checked my watch again; grateful for Enzo being efficient at his job, so I'd know how long I had to wait. So, I watched Winter eat instead. She took a bite from her ham and cheese croissant and moaned in appreciation as she enjoyed the food. *Fucking sexy even when she eats.*

"You know there'll be comments and teasing from all of them. Honestly, I would just love to blow everybody off and deal with it at a later time. Or maybe never."

"Are you saying that you don't want anyone to know about us yet? Because I'm fine with keeping it between us for now. I'm also feeling a lot selfish with you at the moment. I'd love nothing more than to keep you all to myself for days, without people being nosy assholes about us." I took a gulp of my coffee and realized what a fantasy that was. "But who am I kidding?"

"Right?" She sighed and took another bite of her sandwich, snuggling in beside me on the seat and putting her head on my shoulder. "I'd happily stay here like this eating a croissant and drinking coffee with you in the backseat of a car, and I'll be content."

I couldn't resist kissing her, cheese and ham and all. She tasted delicious every time my tongue touched her, so I didn't mind. "You took the words right out of my mouth, beautiful. I just want to be with you. That is all I need."

And then we turned on our phones.

Motherfucking hellstorm. The implosion of text alerts, voicemails, and urgent tags were almost comical at first as we watched the phones blowup. We looked at each other. We stared at our phones again as if they must be demonically possessed. I was hesitant to pick up the fuckin' thing.

Winter was the brave one.

She went first to a string of texts from her sister. Her voice grew shallow and her skin became pale as she read. Something was terribly wrong.

"What the fuck has happ—"

"Oh, no…no…no. Willow says Janice attacked Brooke at the ball with a champagne glass. She cut Caleb too—oh my God—that crazy fucking bitch went psycho killer on my brother and Brooke. They're at Mass Gen. Brooke's had surgery…and oh my, James"–she made a wide O with her mouth–"Brooke is seven weeks pregnant."

What the fuck?!

AND SO ENZO DROVE us to the hospital where we made a big fucking entrance—still wearing our finery from the ball of course—for nearly every single person we hoped to avoid for a few more hours.

Even so, it was a non-issue, because we were still in shock about Janice. After Winter and I left the party, apparently Janice got into it with Caleb and Brooke, becoming so unhinged she used a broken glass to slash and stab them both. Brooke got the worst of it to her abdomen but on the side, while Caleb's neck wound was more superficial. But fuuuck. Janice Thorndike, super-model-turned-psycho-beast queen was locked in a padded room being restrained while our loved ones were in the hospital from her savage attack during a charity gala. The news media would have a field day playing off this story. For fucking decades.

Winter held on to my hand in a death grip. We hadn't spoken much about it yet, but we would as soon as we had a minute. We'd spent the remaining time in the car on our phones getting updates. Winter talked to Willow, and I got through to Vic to let everyone know we were on our way. The cat was now out of the bag about Winter and me. Everyone knew we'd spent the night together, so we were no longer a secret. It was one less thing to have to deal with in my view. *And fuck if I care. I love the woman by my side and will do anything for her. So, they can all finally fucking know how much I feel for her.*

I thought back on our own crazy encounter with Janice at the ball, wondering if I could have done something different to prevent her from staging a Hitchcock film noir scene at a formal fucking charity event. Probably not, but I still felt horrible for Caleb and Brooke being on the receiving end of such trauma. Brooke had been through too much already, and Caleb would be wrecked by guilt at this happening to her because of his crazy ex-girlfriend. I felt really fucking bad for them both. *Seven weeks pregnant too.* Damn. I hoped for the best and prepared for the worst. That was what we could do right now. And all of this madness had happened within the span of the few hours, while Winter and I were at my house in Sherborn fucking for the first time. With our phones off the grid. Unreachable.

The guilt just kept piling up like shit.

Lucas Blackstone added his share to the guilt-shit pile as soon as we came into the private waiting area attached to the surgical suite.

"Nice of you to stop by and check in," he sneered. "We were just hours away from filing a missing person's report with the cops, Winter." He was pissed, and probably all at me. "Willow and Roger left about fifteen minutes ago. They are exhausted from a long night of waiting for news on Brooke and trying to find you."

"I'm so sorry, Lucas, but we had our phones turned off until just a little while ago. We didn't know…any of this happened. Where is Caleb? How is Brooke? Can I see—"

"Why was your phone off? Nobody knew where you were! You could've been dying in a ditch somewhere from a road accident—God—who the fuck knows. So fucking irresponsible of you both—"

"I am sorry, okay?! It's not our fault Janice attacked and hurt Brooke last night. I was with James and we *left* the party. We turned off our phones, so we could have time away for one single fucking night." Winter could hold her own, but I also saw that she felt badly for causing extra worry for her family.

Lucas scoffed at her and nodded his head dramatically. "*Fucking* is the operative word all right." He pointed at her shoulder where the hickey showed through her hair. "Classy, sister dear, real fuckin' classy. Not so cool to be out getting your freak on with *him* while the rest of us are wondering if you're still breathing."

"You are being such an asshole right now. Didn't you ever take a night off from the rest of the world, Lucas?" Winter gave her brother as good as she got.

"Yes, he has," I answered for him. "Many nights I'd bet. He's not any different than the rest of us." I chose my words carefully for him, trying to keep my temper in check. "You are upsetting your sister for no good reason. Enough with the guilt trip you're putting on her."

"I cannot deal with you up in my face right now, Lucas. I'm going to find Caleb, and I'm seeing Brooke if they'll let me." She dismissed her brother with a middle-finger salute and left the room. *She is magnificent.* I had observed this trait in her before. Winter didn't waste her time on pointless shit. She'd come here to the hospital for a purpose, and she would see it done.

"So you—" Lucas turned his hostility on me. I knew what he was imagining. He was picturing his little sister tied to a rack in a room somewhere to be flogged, and gagged, and fucked by me. I wouldn't bother explaining to him that it was nothing like that with her, but strangely, I wanted to.

"I'm pretty fuckin' sure she doesn't need your permission for who she's with, and you need to chill. Winter's done nothing wrong. She's here for Caleb and Brooke right now, not you."

"So, please, the next time you go off for a night of fucking *my little sister*, could you leave us a number where you can be reached? You know, in case of a serious emergency or something fucking important like—"

"Get off my dick, you pretentious fucker—"

"Shut the fuck up, both of you." Thankfully, Caleb found us at the moment shit was starting to get real and put a stop to the nonsense. "You're in a hospital for fuck's sake." Lucas and I both turned, ready to take the ass chewing we definitely deserved. "You, Lucas, sit there, and James, there." He pointed us to our respective corners before pulling up a chair for himself in between us. He sat facing the back of the seat, folded his arms over the top and rested his chin down. The exhaustion in his face showed how long the night had been for him. He had a large bandage at his throat and hospital johnny for a shirt. "I want you to listen and not talk. Just listen to me. Can you do that?" He pegged us both with angry, weary eyes. I couldn't even imagine what he was feeling right now. If that were Winter attacked by Janice, I would want the bitch dead. Especially if she were carrying my baby. Fuck.

I nodded.

"None of this crap matters. *None of it.* It's all distracting bullshit to take you away from what's really important. There will be some immediate changes happening. Read that as, I am taking Brooke away the moment she is cleared to travel. So very far away from this shitstorm of drama, to give her a chance at some peace for once. She's been through so much…and I can't allow even one more bad thing to happen—"

Caleb's voice broke, but we all knew what he was going to say. He couldn't allow for Brooke to be hurt again by *anyone*. He would make certain it never happened even if he had to take her away somewhere secret to do it. I knew my friend well and understood where his head was at with this. Add in the fact she was pregnant, and he was going to be a father? Yeah, he needed a breather to get a handle on his emotions. I don't know how he wasn't passed out flat on the floor to be honest, but he scrubbed his face with his hands and continued, "We'll see you back here in a month, maybe longer. Lucas, that means you're the man who signs the checks at BGE in my absence. You might need to buy some suits and stay in the city during the week. You can use my office and sleep at my place if you want. I don't give a fuck."

As that information settled in for Lucas to digest, he turned to me. "James, you're going to be heading up everything of a legal nature, including keeping me apprised of the proceedings against the sadistic cunt responsible for this whole fucking nightmare. I know you'll have our best interests in mind." *He knows he doesn't even have to ask.*

"Whatever you need, Caleb, you have it," I said.

But he still had some more to say. "You are also my best friend, and even I had no clue about you and Winter. Brooke did though. She asked me about the two of you more than once. I just didn't see it and that bothers me, but I *am* really happy for you guys. Win told me last night was the first time the two of you were together, but I don't care about that part. I really don't. I might not want to think about you and my sister...well, yeah...since it's none of my business, but I know you love her and that's what's important to me. Seriously. Go and be with the one you love and never look back. Don't waste one more fucking moment of your life in a situation that takes you away from your happiness. I know I won't."

I had a thought as I got up from my seat to embrace my

friend in a sappy-assed bro-hug…eventually Caleb and I would be real brothers.

"WHY WAS LUCAS so hostile with you? Is there some kind of past issue between you two I should know about?"

Before I answered her, I remembered what Caleb had said to me at the hospital. I also thought about how Winter was cuddling on my couch right now, watching the hockey game with me. She was in my apartment, and she would be in my bed tonight. *By choice.* I had her legs stretched across my lap and her silky hair between my fingers as I played in it. Everything felt right for once. I didn't want to risk any of what we had attained in the last day and a half.

I won't risk it.

"He doesn't approve of me being with you because he knows where my dick has been in the past."

Silence. And then quietly, "Where has it been?"

"Nowhere important. I haven't been with anyone in the way I am with you for years. That's the truth." I hoped my answer was satisfactory, but figured it probably wasn't.

"I never knew you to date anyone after Leah, so what did you do for sex—who did you—where did you get it from?" As much as her questions pained me, I had to appreciate that she'd been paying attention to who I wasn't with, for five long years. I was a lucky bastard.

"Women I didn't know…and didn't care enough to know." I hated talking to her about them. It felt so very filthy a thing to bring others into our relationship, inserting them between the pureness of what we had.

"Escorts?" she asked with a tilt of her head.

"Along those lines, yes, but always in a safe, controlled environment with rules in place."

"So, like a kinky sex-club date or something, and Lucas saw you there?"

"Something like that. You would have to ask him, but I really hope you don't. I am not feeling your brother at the moment. He can fuck off for what he said to you earlier."

"He was being a jerk for real. I don't understand why so territorial though. It's not like Lucas to judge others so harshly. Why care about who you date when you're single?"

"Oh, he doesn't care about who I dated. He's worried about you being hurt or harmed in some way by a kinky fucker like me."

She changed her position so she could face me, and put her hand to my cheek. "Did you just refer to yourself as a kinky fucker, James?"

"I did." Her expression went from surprise to amusement. "Do you think I'm a kinky fucker when I'm with you, beautiful?"

"I don't know, because you are incomparable to other men for me. I don't want to equate what we do together to a thing that's been defined by a label. I think the way you are is just right for me, though, and *I know* you'd never harm me intentionally. Please don't ever change your kinky-fucker-self on my account, James Blakney." *I love this girl. She couldn't be more amazing.*

I kissed her, because there were no words that would have been good enough. So, I showed her instead, pressing her onto the couch and helping her out of her clothes until she was splendidly naked. I kissed her everywhere, worshipping the body I had grown to know intimately in such a short period of time…but would crave indefinitely until I took my very last breath.

After I made her come the second time, when she was in that boneless sensual subspace I loved for her to be in, I arranged her how I wanted. Pulled to the very edge of the couch with her arms up and over the back for holding on to, her ankles pressed against her ass with her long legs spread wide, her pussy wet and ready for being fucked by my cock.

We both watched me sink it deep into her tight, wet cunt. Over and over again, the metal doing its job, dragging against our hot flesh on sensual overload, until I was dying for release. But hoping it didn't come and end this moment in time with her. I couldn't stop it though. Eventually, biology took over my body. I lost myself to my own kind of subspace as I came powerfully hard inside her, a handful of her long hair wrapped in each of my hands. Her hair pulled back, her graceful neck exposed for her throat to be licked and marked with my teeth. Kissed and loved…and told with words all that she meant to me.

After a while, I carried her sleeping into my bedroom and put her in my bed. I watched her peaceful breathing and wondered yet again, how we'd found ourselves here. It seemed impossible to believe she was finally mine, but it was also terrifying to fear this might not last. I was confident I could be with her sexually and keep myself in check. I'd just done it. No restraints or discipline of any kind—and it was fucking hot while we were in it. I didn't need any more than that from her. Winter was my perfect partner just as she was. *Always*.

I realized my head was fucked from what Leah did. I knew it was wrong to bring my past into my new relationship with Winter. It wasn't fair to her. And so, I knew what I had to do. I wouldn't try to change her for my needs—I'd change myself to meet hers. But there was no regret. Only the most wonderful peace. After many dark years.

But my terror was fucking real, and it was always with me.

I couldn't go through that again. I couldn't lose my Winter for any reason. Which was why wanting my ring on her finger and my name at the end of hers had become my new obsession, and it had absolutely nothing to do with her trust fund. There would be no *on-paper-only* marriage between us.

One week later.

"YOU KNOW WHAT the best part of the game was for me?" Winter asked as we came in from the Bruins game at the Garden to have a quiet dinner at home.

"Was it Marchand's hat trick in the third period?"

"Um no…Licker had to go and bring out his tongue again. Seriously? Why would that be my best part of the game? Dumb, James."

I laughed at my beautiful girl who was turning out to be quite the hockey fan, impressing the hell out of me. Deadly serious about ice-time, there was no talking or otherwise distractions of any kind allowed while the puck was in play. But during intermissions she would chat up whoever was next to us in our seats. She'd hit it off with an older woman who was there with her husband and was deep into a conversation with her when the special holiday kiss-cam found us. Winter was so involved in her convo with her new friend she would not stop to kiss me even though I kept trying. It was hilarious, and the crowd loved it. When the kiss-cam came back to us a second time, Winter was ready for them. She jumped in my lap and made out with me in a big show for the cameras. I needed to find the clip and save it in case they ran it on *NHL Live* later tonight.

My phone pinged with a picture and a message, and when

I comprehended what I was seeing, I showed it to her. "Win, you need to see this." We looked at the screen together.

The picture was of Caleb and Brooke in the doorway of the stone church on the island. *At their wedding?* Caleb's lips were pressed to the back of her hand as Brooke smiled at him, completely in love. The message said simply: **We took the advice of a very wise man, and decided to hold on to our happiness, and each other, starting tonight. With Much Love, Caleb & Brooke Blackstone xoxo**

"No way. They got married without us there? They didn't tell anybody…" Winter took my phone from my hand and went over to sit on the couch with it. She stared at the picture for a long time.

"Are you okay, beautiful?" I asked as I came over to sit next to her.

She swiped at her eyes to brush away a few tears and nodded, but still kept staring at the picture. "Yeah, I am. I will be." And then she looked at me and smiled bravely. "It was a shock seeing that picture…at first…and feeling left out of such a big thing. My brother got married tonight, and we didn't even know? He didn't ask us to be at his wedding, James."

"I know, it's a surprise to me too. I always imagined that I'd be at Caleb's wedding just like he was at mi—"

I stopped my rambling and wished I could turn back time for just two short seconds. That day with Caleb is carved in my memories so clearly. He was the one who had to walk me out of the church, because I would have stayed all fucking day waiting for her to show up. Caleb was the one who convinced me to walk right out the fucking front door of the church with my balls still attached to my dick instead of slipping out the back where the guests wouldn't see. He'd said something important to me that I'd always remembered. He'd said the day would come when I'd marry the right girl. It wasn't the day, and Leah wasn't the right girl, and in time I would be glad she hadn't shown up to the church. He was right of course.

"It's okay to talk about that day with me, James. I'm so thankful you didn't marry Leah."

So am I. Because the right girl—is you.

"Me too…but I think I understand why he did it like this, Win. Don't you?"

She leaned into me and nodded a few times. "I think so. I'm just feeling a little selfish for missing out, but I can understand where he might be coming from. We knew he was taking Brooke away for rest and recovery, so I suppose marrying her wasn't too far off from his plans, especially since they have a baby on the way. It must have been a personal decision that they felt it needed to be just the two of them." I had no doubt it was the best thing for both of them. Brooke was the best thing to ever happen to Caleb, and I'd loved watching her bring his sorry-ass back to life.

Like Winter is doing for mine.

I rubbed her arm and kissed her on the forehead. "Maybe you can throw a party for them when they're back in a month. I'm sure they'd be honored with an after-wedding celebration."

She smiled again. "That's a good idea. I'll talk to the rest of the family about it. I really am thrilled for them. My brother is a married man now, and once I get over my FOMO I'll be good again."

"I can make you a married woman very easily, you know, to help you get over your FOMO a little faster. I know a guy."

"Do you now?" She rolled her eyes at me. "I know a guy too. He's wickedly hot in bed and very easy on my eyes, but I certainly don't have to marry him to enjoy being with him."

That's me told.

I'd keep working on her though.

Someday, I'd ask my Winter to marry me and she would say yes.

CHAPTER TWENTY

Winter

January

"Hello, Winter Blackstone, why are we seeing you today?" The doctor looked up from my chart to greet me. She also looked like she'd been up for far too long without sleep. I used the clinic around the corner from the South Boston Youth Center because it was convenient, not because it was free. I'd suggest to Caleb and Brooke the clinic be placed on a list for sponsorship via the philanthropic arm of BGE. I had plans to do big things in the near future—which was another reason I needed to take care of this issue regarding my birth control before I really messed up. Brooke's surprise pregnancy was still fresh in my mind, and even though it was a joyful surprise for our family, I needed my own situation squared away. James and I were in a great place in our relationship, but it was still very new.

We'd only been together for a little over a month, and we'd had a lot of sex in that month. Pretty much daily doses of amazing and fabulous sheet-clawing sex. I had no complaints, and I know James didn't, but dropping a pregnant bomb on him might send him running for the hills. Even though it would be completely different if I were pregnant, he'd been through it before and had been hurt badly. I wanted to have babies with him sure, but after we were married, and after I was settled into my career. James kept dropping hints about the marrying-me part, so I guessed a ring would be in my near future, but he hadn't given me one yet. One thing I was certain about was that I didn't want it forced onto my finger because of an accidental pregnancy. I was nowhere close to ready for motherhood.

The last weeks had been just so ridiculous from changes within my family and at BGE, we'd hardly stopped to take a breath since we'd gotten together. James was heavily involved with the BGE legal department since taking over the top spot at Caleb's request. I'd been busy completing my master's in the last month, volunteering at SBYC, and getting registered with the Association of Social Work Boards for the State of Massachusetts. James and I both had been forging through these additional stressors for weeks while trying to settle into our brand-new relationship. Lots of adjustments all around. Caleb had even hinted at something for me in the way of a job taking shape, but we hadn't discussed anything formally yet. He and Brooke had only returned from their month-long honeymoon less than a week ago.

"I just need my Depo shot," I said as I read her badge. Cassandra Wilton, M.D. didn't look much older than me. She was probably one of those genius kids who'd been to university at fifteen years old or something.

She read over my file again, but I already knew what she would find. "I'm overdue, I missed my last shot."

"I see that your last Depo was more than six months ago. Were you trying out a different type of birth control or something?"

Emotion bubbled up in me as quickly as the question fell off her lips. I shook my head no and tried to tamp down the sudden urge to cry. "No, I—I j-just missed my appointment and then I ig-ignored the follow-up reminders..." So much for getting a grip on my emotions. Instead, I found myself sobbing my heart out on the shoulder of a doctor I'd never met before, who couldn't be a day over twenty-five. *Awkward much?*

"I THINK YOU NEED to be kinder to yourself, Winter. You lost your father and broke off an abusive relationship all in the last eight months. That's a lot." She rubbed my back in a slow circle. "It'll be okay. Have faith and know you're doing the right thing by being seen today."

It was plenty. It still is. And I am a first-class idiot for putting myself in this position.

"So, can we talk about your sexual history? What method of birth control were you using in lieu of the Depo?"

"Nothing." I winced as I answered her. "But, I wasn't having sex until a month ago. That's when I started seeing James, my boyfriend."

"Are you getting your periods?"

"No, I've not had one in a year. And honestly, that's the reason I wasn't super concerned, as no period means the Depo is still working, right?" God, my reasoning sounded so fucking dumb as I said it.

"That is a good sign, yes," she said carefully, "but I want to do a test before giving you another shot. And remember, you had antibiotics with your hand injury, so I can't rule out the interaction of certain drugs on a hormonal contraception like Depo Provera. It's not common, but it can certainly happen."

"Okay…but how accurate is the test? I mean, could a

positive result even show up this early? We've only been active for a few weeks." A small flame of worry had started to flicker to life inside my chest.

"Very accurate. As early as fourteen days from conception…and it only takes *one* little swimmer to get the job done."

James

I COULD TELL something was wrong by the look on Marguerite's face. She'd been working for me for a long time, so I knew whatever it was couldn't be good news. Marguerite ran my law office with true efficiency, making sure I didn't waste my time on stupid shit, or people, who could fall into line and wait their fucking turn.

"James, there's a Dr. Cassandra Wilton on the line. She's calling from the South Boston Clinic on Munroe where…ahh…Winter is there with her. She says you need to come down right away and pick her up." *Why couldn't she call me herself?*

SHE. WAS. HYSTERICAL.

I didn't know what I was expecting when I walked into that clinic, but Winter bursting into tears that streamed down her face wasn't it. The instant she saw me, she broke down into sobs and turned away, refusing to meet my eyes.

I was a problem solver by nature. Always had been.

Especially when it came to people I knew, because I wanted to help them fix their problems. That's something important to me as an attorney, one of the better parts about my job. But this situation was far beyond a job. This was Winter—the woman I loved—behaving completely out of character. Winter didn't have emotional breakdowns or hysterical bouts of crying that I'd ever witnessed over the twenty-plus years I'd known her. She was terribly upset, yes, but what really struck me was how she would not look at me.

As if she was ashamed...

So, I assessed.

Winter was in a medical clinic around the corner from where she volunteered...having a motherfucking meltdown. But she didn't look hurt or sick, or injured in any way that I could tell. So, my inner Sherlock Holmes took it a step further and studied the evidence in the room. A small plastic cup of what looked like probably urine, swabs, long thin white test strips with blue ends, and most importantly, one shell-shocked girlfriend. My mystery-loving, deducing-ass figured it out as my heart thumped out of my chest and flopped around still beating on the floor of that exam room.

She's pregnant?

"Winter? Can we talk about why you're so upset? I'm here...and you need to know there is nothing you could tell me right now that will change how I feel about you or...us." I knelt on the floor in front of her and picked up her hands to hold them in mine. I caressed the back of her hand and stroked my finger over the scar along her thumb, remembering the night when she'd come to me bleeding and terrified. Everything had started between us because of it. That one event could be the difference between us as we were now, and never finding our way to be with each other.

So, I'd have to take that one as fate. *And I fucking love fate right now.*

I take this new surprise as fate, too. If we were having a baby together, then all my self-doubt pondering if I could keep her was in my fucking past. Winter would be my wife and the mother of my children. I'd just been given the keys to the kingdom of my happily ever after…with the love of my life.

This was one enormous thank you to God, from me. *I'll be sure to thank you in person next time I'm in church, big guy.* I might have to make a special trip to St. Clement and light a candle before then, though, because I didn't show up there very often.

"I love you, Win. Focus on that while you find your words to tell me what's got you so upset. I'll wait until you can." I didn't coddle or try to force her; I was patient…and simply continued to trace my finger up and down her scar.

She shifted her head and turned toward me, her long hair falling forward and clinging to her tear-streaked cheeks, eyes still tightly closed. I gently tucked her hair behind her ears to get it out of her face, but nothing else. Winter had to be the one to go first.

She let me finish fixing her hair before leaning a bit more toward me, as if closing the physical distance between us was giving her strength. I really hoped that was the case. Then, on an anguished whisper she said, "James…" Simply my name. Then, a terrible shuddering breath came out from her chest and her sad green eyes finally opened to mine.

I was waiting with a smile, ready to wait forever if I needed to.

"I'm pregnant." She whispered it, utterly devastated as she spoke those two words out loud.

"I kind of figured that one out all on my own, beautiful, and I can see just how much it's upset—"

"It's my fault. I did this—oh my God. James, I told you that first time…when we were together…I said I was protected, but I wasn't. My shot—I missed getting it after Dad died and I just didn't go and get another one. I…I…I…*lied*…and I don't even know *why* I lied. I'm sorry—I am so…s-s-sorry for doing this to us—"

She broke down into more crying and couldn't speak anymore after that, so I held her in my arms until she was able to walk out of that clinic with me and let me take her home.

Winter might be devastated now, but I hoped it was temporary devastation. We had a lot to discuss and major plans to make. We could start just as soon as the shock wore off and she was ready. Why was she so…devastated and why had she thought she'd lied? That wasn't Winter's MO at all, so she must be in need of some time to evaluate and process. It was certainly much more of an issue for her than it was for me. I couldn't do anything about changing that part for her, though. She knew what was in her own heart, and she would have to come to terms in her own way.

For the second time in my life I'd been given the same news. Leah's announcement had blindsided me with doubt and filled me with worry. This time, with Winter, neither was present. Instead, the news was my salvation. The answer to prayers I'd never have the balls to actually say, even to myself. Complete opposite reactions coming from me.

I hoped she could come around in her feelings about the baby we'd created; reasoning as simple as the fact she could never leave me if she was having *my* child. My reasoning was flawed, of course. But then, that was often the case when reasoning with your heart's desire. Winter was my heart's desire and she always would be.

It wasn't what I'd expected to happen, or an outcome I'd sought. But it *had* happened. We were having a baby, and we were getting married, and now, *in my mind*, those two things were certain. The deep Catholic roots had taught us the rules. Rules that destined us to carry pregnancies to term. Rules that dictated we marry the person we made a baby with if it was legally possible. This was the way it was done. We both knew it without having to voice the points at all. Our families would demand it from us regardless.

ONCE I HAD HER back to my place, I did something nearly identical to the night she came to me after cutting her hand. I took her into the bathroom, sat her on the countertop, and talked to her. But unlike that night, she wasn't falling in and out of consciousness. Rather, she was hyper-aware, experiencing a much different sort of trauma. And I could clearly see just how traumatic it was for her, which was what worried me the most. She hadn't spoken a word to me in the car on the way home, because she wasn't able, and I knew better than to push. Instead she'd been quiet, staring out the window at the winter gloom and the sprinkling of rain blowing from the clouds. My very traumatized Winter on a wintery day in January.

"I'm running you a bath, okay?" She nodded once, her face a storm of emotion and worry. "It'll be okay, Win. I know we will all be okay."

"But…how do I…how do *we* have a baby right now?" she asked finally, the suffering in her voice very clear.

"We just do." I took her face in both hands, so she would see me when I said the most important part. "We'll do it…together." It made me realize why I felt nothing but calm at that moment. *We'll do it together.* Nothing really mattered now I had Winter as my own, because from now on, everything was *with Winter. God.* She truly had no clue how much she'd brought to my life.

On that note, I stepped away to start the water before coming back to undress her. I knew what to do. "I'm taking your clothes off." Not a question. She didn't respond other than to be soft and pliable as I worked, helpful even, until I had her exquisitely bare beneath my hands. I caged her in with my arms, loving that I now had her captive, able to focus only on me. Which was all she needed right now. I knew best how to help my Winter.

I took a finger to her brow and traced it down her cheeks where the tears had fallen. I drew it down her neck, and then on farther down between her breasts, before circling one perfect globe in a spiral with my fingertip. She gasped sharply, arching into me when I took her nipple into my mouth to soothe the tightened flesh I'd made. So responsive. So finely made. So beautiful, inside and out. *Mine* to love.

"You are so beautiful to me. I don't think you're even aware of how much, "I whispered to her as my mouth covered the other breast and sucked on the nipple until it was tight and tipped dark pink from the attention I was giving it.

Another moan was her response. I kissed my way down until my mouth hovered over her flat belly, the smooth skin hiding something precious behind it. I couldn't help but think about what was happening inside her body. A baby was growing—our baby. "Every time you give yourself to me I love you even more. Always so generous, I am in awe of you." I replaced my mouth with my hand and splayed it out on her stomach. "We have something precious between us right here. Something that's part you and me together…that was made with love."

I felt the change in her body as she heard me, the battling of emotions silently screaming inside her as she processed the truth I'd spoken. I was torn between leaving it there and pushing her for just a bit more.

"Look at me, Winter."

She lifted her head and locked her eyes with mine, tears flowing anew. One word. It was all she was able to say, but it was a good word. It was enough to show me what she felt beneath all of the fear and the shock.

"Y-y-yess."

I kissed and touched her all over with as much love as I could until she was soft again underneath my hands and mouth, and I knew she was ready for me. I picked her up and carried her into the bath where I helped her into the water first. I stripped out of my clothes before her, silently commanding her to watch me as I got naked. I stroked my cock a few times and studied her expression, her eyes widening for just an instant before growing hooded. She swallowed deeply and adjusted her legs under the water. Her breasts above the water's surface were tinged pink from the heat...and desire. *She wants me.* More like she needed me. My Winter needed to be taken away by pleasure from the fear of the moment.

My specialty.

I stepped in and settled into position, grateful the tub was so large to accommodate both of us easily. "Come here, beautiful. You need to be fucked first and then we'll talk." I reached for her, bringing her over my lap to straddle me. I did not ask. Instead, I split her wide and thrust my cock into her slippery heat quickly and deep. She was so ready it was easy, even with the added friction of the water.

For once she didn't take it silently.

Winter needed to let off some of the tension while being fucked this time apparently. She told me she wanted it harder right before she came the first time. So, I fucked her harder and did some things that put marks on her flawless body...and mixed in a little bit of sweet pain with the pleasure. Her words and cries told me I got it right as she came the second time with me.

Whatever my girl needs.

AFTER THE BATH—*and one more hard fuck*—she was ready to talk about it. I didn't mind her process. In fact, I found it brutally honest. Giving the body what it needed so your mind could do what it had to do was about as honest as it got.

She was also a fucking gorgeous sight with her head thrown back, tits shaking, her long hair trailing down to brush my thighs as she squeezed her cunt around my cock. I knew I'd never tire of watching her come.

I settled us side by side in the bed and smoothed her hair back from her face. She was tired, but her mind was busy when the first thing she asked was, "How can you be so easy with this, James? Why is this not making you angry? I don't understand your reaction at all."

"You love me?"

"Yes, of course I do."

"And do you trust me?"

"Yes, always. But what I did is the same as Leah did to you."

Hell the fuck no. "This is *nothing* like what that bitch did. Let me be very fucking clear on this, my love. Leah cheated with a colleague who was a partner in my father's firm. She got pregnant with his kid and told me it was mine. She would have married me anyway, but my father intervened and made sure she didn't...and in the most humiliating way possible to me. But only so he could call in favors later—when he wanted something—and had the person by the balls trapped in his spider's web of lies." Which he now had, with Ted Robinson beholden to him as well as dying of cancer. Karma was a vicious bitch sometimes...and not my fucking problem today.

"I'm so sorry, James. For what happened before with her, and for now...with me. I lied about being protected. I wasn't completely sure, and I didn't do a thing about it for over a month."

"I'm not sorry."

"How? Why aren't you feeling betrayed by my lying to you about my birth control?"

"Okay then, let me ask you this. Why did you lie?"

She looked down, feeling the full force of her shame, I guess, but I wanted to hear her answer anyway. "I didn't care. That first night…I'd wanted you for so long…and once I knew you wanted me too, I refused to allow anything to stand in my way of having you. I…I…really don't know. I told you point blank it was okay for you to come in me. You asked me if you needed to pull out because we didn't have condoms at the house that first night we were together. I told myself the shot was still working when even I considered it might not be." She shook her head slowly back and forth. "It was so irresponsible of me and goes against everything I know and practice in my life and my work."

"I don't care, and I'm still not sorry it happened."

"Why not, James?"

"Simple." I took her face in my hand and held her firmly then put my other hand low on her belly. "Because this baby was made with the right girl. *My* right girl. And I love you, and now *our* baby, very much."

Her eyes filled with tears again. I knew then that I loved her tears when she cried, because they were mine. I owned them…much like Winter owned my heart. This woman had cried *for* me…feared for *my* heart, when she had possibly hurt me. But what she didn't realize was that her instant reaction proved her love for me beyond words.

She was *mine* to love forever.

And my heart was now safer than it had ever been.

CHAPTER TWENTY-ONE

Winter

One week later.

"I suppose I won't ever have to worry about a want of grandchildren, will I? At this rate adults in this family are going to be outnumbered by babies in a very short time." This was my mother's attempt at making light of a situation that was anything but light for me. I had to give her props for not being a bitch about it though. She'd always adored James, so she was genuinely thrilled with our news. Which surprised me only because she hadn't been as thrilled about Caleb and Brooke when they'd announced they were expecting. Granted she'd been out of town then, staying in Charleston with her aunts and cousins over the holidays when Brooke and Caleb found out she was pregnant. Married in secret a week later, then away for a month-long honeymoon, they were now happily living life as they waited for their baby to be born. Without input from her or anyone else.

I was not feeling so fortunate as my brother. Caleb had skills for dealing with our mother that none of the rest of us could match, and he always had. She didn't get away with manipulating *him* very often, the lucky bastard.

"Three weddings in six months will certainly be a challenge, even for me," she said cheerfully, "but I think I can pull it all off with a flourish."

"Not three in six months, Mom."

"Yes, you and James of course, Willow and Roger in July, and something to mark the event for Caleb and Brooke."

"I don't want to get married before the baby is born." I knew this would go over like a lead balloon for her, but I wasn't going to budge on my position. She couldn't force me. "James and I have already decided. We're waiting until after the baby to have our wedding."

"Oh no, Winter, you most certainly are not. I cannot accept that from one of *my* children. Even Caleb married Brooke as soon as they could possibly manage it."

Even Caleb? What the hell did that mean? Sometimes she said things which made no sense. Still a mystery to me most of the time even though we'd always had a decent mother-daughter relationship; my mom was ever a supportive parent. But I'd known she'd react this way even before we showed up tonight. Her position certainly wasn't a surprise, annnnd I was regretting the madness of coming to this dinner for the purpose of telling our parents they were going to be upgraded to *grandparents* in about seven and a half months. I looked to James sitting to my left and asked silently for his support in backing me up.

We'd talked about it and he had agreed to let me set the pace of things. I was still in a bit of shock about his attitude about the whole thing to be honest. He accepted the pregnancy bomb like it was the best news he'd ever been given. He said it wasn't anything different from what he wanted to do with me eventually; we'd just sped up his plans up a bit. *Ya think?* From the moment I'd told him, James had been very relaxed about everything. If he had doubts about being a father and a husband, he didn't share them. He was probably shielding me, because he *knows* I'm a total mess over it. I'm scared I'll be a terrible mother. I don't know how to be a mom. Maybe his eight years on me has helped him cope with impending parenthood. I don't know…*anything* anymore.

When James smiled at my mom and then at me without speaking, I tilted my head at him and glared.

"Your thoughts, Robert and Vanessa?" My mother bypassed me altogether and went to the judge for input. Asking Vanessa for her opinion was merely a courtesy, because we all knew she would agree with whatever her husband decreed. I was not thrilled with having to toe the line for the judge in any way, shape, or form. Fuck him. I'd told James that already. I had limits and Judge Beastly went far past mine a hella long time ago.

He smiled his fake reptilian smile at me and then turned to look at his wife. "Vanessa and I've discussed it at length and feel that our only son deserves a wedding that befits the Blakney name—and Blackstone, of course." Vanessa looked especially miserable tonight as she sat beside her husband at my mother's dining table. If I didn't know better I'd say she was in pain—and it didn't sit well with me at all. I needed to reach out before I lost my mind over whatever was going on with her. I decided I'd speak to her alone the first chance I got. Meanwhile, the judge droned on, "As both James and Winter are descended from founding fathers of New England, the honor carries with it certain responsibilities to uphold our worthy place in history and to be seen in society *well*. A marriage of our children cannot be something slapped together on the haphazard efforts of a few weeks. The guest list for this wedding will need to be curated with careful attention."

Curated with careful attention? Is this idiot for real?

The judge was dreaming if he thought I was putting on a celebrity-scale wedding event to appease his absurd political aspirations. That sort of event would *definitely* not be what my wedding was about. Part of me wanted to get up from the table and leave, but I held my tongue and watched the circus instead.

My mom raised a perfectly shaped eyebrow and gave the judge her version of high-society-stink-eye. "I am well aware of that, Robert, but my daughter is pregnant. We don't have the luxury of months to plan a society wedding. She's not walking down the aisle to marry James in one of those hideous maternity wedding gowns."

The judge gave it right back to her. "I agree...*our* children have jumped the gun by putting the baby before the wedding, Madelaine, but that matter is rather out of our hands now. I suppose we'll just have to swallow this misstep and have the wedding after my grandchild is born." He could play the sympathetic victim so well it was almost entertaining to watch. *Almost, asshole...almost.*

And so incredibly rude to be talked about as if I wasn't sitting in the same fucking room as them. I now had a much better understanding of Caleb and Brooke's decision to go with marrying in secret. Maybe James and I could do something similar...

Which made me wonder why my beloved was now mute.

I elbowed him and whispered tightly, "Say something."

Startled by my poke, he quickly found his voice. "Ahh, Madelaine, we considered a few options, and honestly I'd be happy with any scenario that ends with our names on a marriage certificate." He looked at me and winked, letting me know he was on my side. "I'd do it tomorrow in front of a justice of the peace if that's what Winter wanted. But a rushed marriage is *not* what she wants, nor will she consider upstaging her twin sister's wedding in July. So, we've decided to plan ours for somewhere around six months *after* our baby is born. He or she will be able to be there with all of us on our big day when we say our vows."

Perfectly said by my man. He reached for my hand and clasped it, giving a little squeeze. I loved him so much. My James and his understanding of how to give me what I needed—always. I'd probably never grasp any logical reason for his way of loving me.

"Oh." Mom opened her mouth to say more and then shut it again. James was a master at explaining things in such a way that made arguing the point…difficult if not impossible. I almost felt a twinge of sympathy for my mother being silenced on the subject of my wedding. *Almost.*

I TOOK MY OPPORTUNITY with Vanessa when she was in the bathroom and the others were occupied with coffee and dessert. I surprised her when she came out by being the first thing she saw when she opened the door. "Oh, my goodness, you startled me, dear."

"I know, I'm sorry for accosting you like this but I really wanted to talk to you *alone.*" I reached out my hand and covered one of hers. I didn't want to be pushy, but I felt I needed to move quickly and make a connection with her, and touching a person was a good way to do it. "Vanessa, you know I'm a social worker, right? I really love my job. I love helping people. I don't want to offend you in any way, or make you uncomfortable, but I am feeling most profoundly that you may be in need of some support, and if I could get that support to you it would mean the world to me, and to James of course, to be able to help you. James adores you, and we'll be family very soon. We already are really, because you're my child's grandmother. You don't have to say anything to me—here or right now. I only wanted to make the offer."

"What is the offer, my dear?" I saw understanding in her

eyes, so I felt confident enough to say the rest.

I slipped my business card into her hand and then closed it by folding her fingers over and hiding it inside her palm. "This is where I work. I can help you with *anything* that you may need it to be…or put you into contact with the right people who can. You are also invited come down and tour SBYC and decide for yourself if you might like to be a volunteer there. Sometimes people are most comfortable beginning their relationship with support services by volunteering." I smiled gently. "No pressure at all, and if what I've said is way off-base, please disregard it as my hormonal pregnant brain taking over my mouth, okay?"

She didn't say anything at first, but her eyes held mine and I sensed that maybe I had reached through to her. Vanessa was so proficient at hiding her feelings that I truly had no clue what she'd been subjected to over the years. But her husband was an egotistical tyrant, and if what I suspected was true, Vanessa had suffered at the very least emotional abuse for many years. I hoped it wasn't physical, but nothing surprised me these days. A moment later, she drew me into her arms for a hug and whispered in my ear, "Thank you, Winter, you'll never know what this means to me."

Judge Beastly interrupted us about ten seconds later. I panicked that he'd guessed what I'd been up to when he drew her away from me by the hand possessively. "It's time to go, Vanessa. For the moment, we've settled everything here." I worried he might confiscate my card and expose my covert efforts to help her—hopefully to escape *him*. But he'd taken her hand without the card, or maybe she'd slipped it up her sleeve and out of sight before he saw it. Either way worked for me.

Dear God, thank you!

"Just some girl-talk with my new mother-in-law is all. You may have her back, your honor." I faked my sweetest most sugary smile and put my hand on the bathroom door as if I was going in.

"Oh, please call me Dad, Winter. You must." He said it as an afterthought, like he was used to family members referring to him as *your honor* on a regular basis.

That will never happen, you fucking monster.

I TOLD JAMES what I'd done in the car on the drive home.

He was silent at first, his knuckles turning white from the force of his grip on the steering wheel. "She actually said that to you— 'Thank you, Winter, you'll never know what this means to me.' —and took your c-card?" The stammer gave away just how much I'd shocked him. By now I was well aware of the *many* times James and Victoria both had reached out to their mom offering their help to her in leaving the judge and starting a new life if she wanted. But never once in all the years they'd tried to open a discussion with her about her obvious unhappiness, had she admitted a thing to her two children. They knew something was wrong, but whatever it was remained a deeply buried secret.

"She did, James."

"I can't believe it." As he looked over at me, and even in the darkness I could see the surprise in his eyes. "I'm fucking glad, but I still can't believe she even entertained the thought of doing anything other than pretending all is well."

"Sometimes when it's a person removed from the situation offering the help it's easier. Like me inviting her to volunteer at SBYC might be the way in. Your dad has a hold over her…with something. That much is apparent, and I could see it clearly in their small encounter when he came to find her to leave. Your mom is making a choice to stay with him. Her choice. That only she can make, James. No matter how much we try to help she has to be the one to ask for it."

"I know that. Vic and I've known it for a long time. She's miserable with him but she won't say why or do anything to change her situation. Trust me, I've spent countless hours worrying about my mom. I accepted a long time ago that whatever it is between my parents…I may never know."

"All we can do is try and let her know we'll be here for her when she's ready."

"Thank you, Win." I heard raw emotion in my James's voice. I sensed he wanted to say more to me but couldn't. It wasn't the right time or place for it while driving us home.

I must have dozed off in the cozy warmth of the car, because I woke up to something much different. James smelled so good. The realization that I was resting against his hard chest as he carried me in his strong arms…was heaven. "Mmm…did I fall asleep again?"

"Yes, beautiful, you do that a lot now. Growing our baby makes you tired, but I don't mind because that means I get to carry you around more often like this."

"I love when you carry me." He did carry me often, so I trusted he liked doing it for a reason. I'd also discovered James was very particular about how he touched me—or more so in placing me *where* he wanted me. He arranged me into positions or put me in places where he then had a purpose for something more to come. I could tell this was one of those times. The whole feel of his body changed. His muscles flexing against me, and the way he was carrying with determination told me he had plans for me tonight.

I didn't ask him either.

I knew if I asked he probably wouldn't tell me anyway.

Because my James was a fan of plans…and surprises. And so was I. *But only with him.*

The first surprise was that we weren't home in Boston but rather at his house in Sherborn. We hadn't come here since the first night we were together. He told me he bought it before he was supposed to marry Leah. I'd considered he avoided coming here so he wouldn't be reminded of her, but I wasn't completely sure. James had his demons…as did we all.

"Are we staying the night here?" I asked when he brought me in through the front door, carrying me effortlessly, as if I weighed nothing—which was definitely not the case.

"Only tonight." He kissed me before setting me down carefully in front of the fireplace which was already lit and cheerfully warming the room, most likely from Enzo's efforts. There were blankets and pillows and drinks and appetizers set out too. It looked like my surprise was going to be a slumber party by the fireplace with James. *Yes, please.* "Is that okay?" he asked.

I nodded slowly, my smile taking over as I realized what he'd planned for us. "This really is a beautiful house, James."

His hands gripped my hips loosely as he stood before me. "Your beauty makes the house pale in comparison, but it's served its purpose I think. In a good way. And now I'm ready to let it go for something else altogether. Other people will find it useful I hope, especially with your help."

"You're selling?"

"Something like that, beautiful." He smiled at me, a rare one that lit up his whole face. "You're a hard one to buy gifts for, Winter Blackstone, do you know that? I've wracked my mind for weeks trying to figure out the right engagement gift, and then tonight I knew what it should be. It came to me so easily while you were sleeping in the car."

"Why do you need to give me an engagement gift? I

don't have a gift for you, and we already discussed this."

"Oh yes you do, beautiful. *You* are my gift because you love me and you're having our baby. Your gifts are…everything to me…so much more than any single object I could ever give to you."

"Oh James—"

He silenced me with another kiss and then he knelt in front of me and put his lips to my belly. He looked up at me with his sludgy green eyes that held the power to make me melt and said, "Winter Leigh Blackstone, I have loved you for a long time. I've watched you grow into the most amazing woman in the world…to me you are. One who is not only beautiful, but kind, and lovely, and so smart I am in awe half the time. The other half the time I have to pinch myself that you love me and want to belong to me. So, this house is my engagement gift to you. You already told me you didn't want a big diamond ring and wouldn't wear one anyway, so what can I give to the woman I love who holds my heart?" He looked around the room and then back up to me. "A house, one I don't need but could be used for those that do. It's yours to have as a starting point for a shelter or administrative offices or whatever you'd like it to be. There's room for expansion too, because the land itself is just under five acres. You can have horses here, there's a barn with outbuildings and everything. I'll take care of all the permits and legalities for you, and you can do what you do best. Help the people who need it and make your dreams a reality. You have your safe house, my Winter."

I ended up on the floor with him because my legs couldn't hold me up anymore. Especially with him kneeling and his mouth too far away for my lips to kiss.

Help the people who need it and make your dreams a reality. This man. I was speechless actually. Without even mentioning the specific things I needed, he provided. My starting point.

Because he loves me. He hadn't only given me my safe house, though. He'd given me his heart, and nothing—*nothing*—would ever eclipse that.

MANY HOURS LATER I woke in his arms. Enveloped in his warmth and the soft blankets of our love nest beside a fireplace glowing with embers, I'd never felt so loved. I don't even know how I lived my life without James loving me this way before he started. I've also never cried as much in my life as I have in the last few weeks. But it didn't matter, because he'd told me once that he loved my tears. He owned my "love-tears" as he called them.

Much like he owned my heart.

CHAPTER TWENTY-TWO

Winter

February

They say every family has a few skeletons in their closet.

Whoever "they" were, they weren't lying.

I may have just had an out-of-body experience at dinner tonight when my mother told us all that Caleb was the love-child of my father and a British housemaid who worked for them the year my parents married. When she died just three weeks after he was born of a brain aneurysm, my parents made a pact to raise him as their firstborn, even moving to Houston for a few years to conceal the secret.

Mind-fuck much?

That one was going to take me a while to process, but some of the oddities of her behavior over the years had now started to make some sense. Still, my father's indiscretion was a total shock. My mother was adamant that his final wishes were for Caleb to never know…but now that truth *was* known. And we would all have to move forward and figure out what it meant for each one of us. Caleb had then gone the additional step of announcing his purchase of the old Blackwater estate with the intention of converting it into the Sanctuary at

Blackwater, a safe house shelter for women and children in need. Brooke's initial idea had morphed into a real opportunity for our family to do some good works and make a difference. I was thrilled for about two seconds before being completely blown off my feet by him offering me to run the whole show, as the Director of the Board of Operations.

Overwhelmed, I cried some more, blaming my tears on pregnant hormones, even though nobody was buying my story. I felt like I could barely keep up with the changes. And now, with a shiny new job of not only Sherborn, but also the Sanctuary at Blackwater to organize into operational safe houses? I needed a day, or ten, to let everything sink in before I tried to do much exploration with my feelings. Caleb assured me I would have all of the help I needed, of course, but it was still a huge amount for me to take in.

James took one look at me and announced he was putting me to bed, picked me up, and carried me out of Caleb and Brooke's place in his arms. "I guess it's a good thing we live in the same building as them," I said admiring the hard set of his jaw, "because you don't have to carry me very far."

"I would carry you until my arms fell off."

"Oh, please don't do that, because I love your arms best when they are attached to your god-like physique."

He laughed as he set me down to unlock the door. "God-like? Really?"

"SOOO GOD-LIKE. Will I be seeing this body in my near future?" she asked in her sweet voice.

"Normally I would say yes, of course you can see it, touch it, lick it, suck it, fuck it, but right now you're going to bed...*to rest.*" She pouted, sticking out her bottom lip at me in protest. *I'd really like to suck on that bottom lip for about a year.* "Do I detect some displeasure from my woman over my orders?"

"Yes, that would be some very extreme displeasure you are detecting. Please remember that I *am* pregnant, and my libido is pretty much off the chain right now."

I groaned at the thought of just how fine her *off-the-chain* moments could be during sex. *Hot as FUCK.* "You can take it out on me later if you want, but I'm going to hold firm that you need some rest right now. That was *a lot* just now at dinner with Caleb and Brooke. I saw the look on your face— and it's still there by the way. You've just had some major shocking family news dropped in your lap, on top of taking on a huge project in the span of about twenty minutes. I'm using my prerogative as your man to see that *my woman* is cared for how she needs to be."

She was quiet as I led her into the bedroom and started to undress her. I loved the way she always turned so soft and pliant whenever I did this. Taking care of her was so important to me. Seeing that her needs were met and that she was comfortable was always my number-one. She had far too much on her plate right now. On that matter I was very fucking certain. I doubted that she would agree with me though. I might have to call a timeout on the work with the safe houses. She was pregnant, and our baby was going to be put first regardless of anything else that was thrown at her. Human biology would make sure. And so the fuck would I.

"I love you, James, so much. You are going to be the best father ever. I hope you know that." She yawned as I slipped her nightgown over her head, yet still doled out compliments even when she could hardly keep her eyes open.

I was going to give it my best, but even I was fucking

terrified that some of my father's parenting traits might have been passed down by default onto me. I wouldn't admit that to soul, and pretty much refused to even entertain the idea. I wouldn't be anything like my father.

"I love *you*…so much. I cannot wait to see you holding our baby in your arms." With her endlessly kind heart, she was going to be an incredible mom. I helped her into bed, tucked her in, and gave her a kiss. "Sleep all the sleeps now, beautiful."

She was out like a light before I left the room.

I went to make myself a stiff drink…and to worry about her in peace.

Winter

Two weeks later.

"HOW DO YOU like your new school?" I asked Shane and Brenna as they gobbled down bananas on crackers with peanut butter.

Shane answered first, his mouth crammed full of his snack. "It's good and I met a new friend. His name is Trace and he invited me to come to his house on Saturday, but Mom said we have to ask you if it's okay."

"I think we can arrange a playdate for two friends on a Saturday." I ruffled his new haircut and pointed to his plate. "Don't talk with your mouth full, buddy." Brenna was a complete contrast to her brother. She ate her snack daintily. She did not try to speak with food in her mouth. And she looked freaking adorable in her new navy school uniform jacket and her cute bobbed haircut as she grinned happily at me. "How about you, Brenna?"

"I made a friend too. Her name is Michelle and she has a black and white pony. She showed his picture to the class. She calls him Joc."

"Oohh, ponies are the best. Soon we'll have some of our own ponies here in our barn and you can start riding lessons. Would you like that?"

"Yesssss!" they both screamed in unison.

"Good grief that's loud. Finish your snacks, and then go and change out of your uniforms like we talked about, kids. Hang up your jackets *on hangers* this time, please," Alanna scolded gently, "then you can play for a while before we start on our homework and chores."

Watching the scene before me was pure joy. Alanna and her twins were now safely installed as residents of SafeHouse-Sherborn. One of my very first acts as soon as James signed it over to me was to call Alanna and offer her a place to live where the kids could go to a good school, and she could work for me, indefinitely if she wanted. When she accepted my offer, she became the very first employee of SafeHouse-Sherborn, working tirelessly to help in setting up the main office, ordering furniture, equipment, supplies, but mostly just organizing the zillion tasks it would take to get the place ready to open. It was amazing. Sometimes people made the worst decisions because they couldn't see any other options. Alanna wasn't a bad person at all, but someone who'd fallen on hard times and tried her very best to work with what she had. Despite her lack of opportunities, she was smart, and already enrolled at Mass Bay Community College, determined to finish her associate degree. She was a godsend really, and I could now sleep at night knowing the kids were safe and thriving in an environment where they could grow and just be six-year-olds in peace.

Again…pure joy for me to witness. Good things were starting to happen, and it was all thanks to my James. I realized this as I settled in at my desk and got back to work.

YOU NEVER KNOW when people will finally find the precise moment to ask for help, but I've learned to be grateful whenever it happens. It's the very first step, and it doesn't matter so much *when* as much as *starting*. For my future mother-in-law that moment happened when she called me tearfully from her car and said she wanted to divorce her husband.

"I…I can't do it anymore, Winter. I am leaving him…today with your help if it's possible."

It was a challenge to keep the excitement out of my voice but I tried my hardest to be professional. "Do your children know, Vanessa?"

"No." Sounds of agonized weeping met my ears as she tried to compose herself. "It's always been so h-hard for m-m-me…to talk about it with James and his s-sister."

"All right, that's okay. I'm going to give you an address. You go there whenever you are ready. Take clothes and necessities, but not your phone or your car because they can be tracked. You are to get a ride and pay with cash. Do you understand everything I've said, Vanessa?"

"Yes."

"It's a safe house where you can stay until we decide what you want to do next. "You are so incredibly brave for doing this, and I know with absolute certainty James and Victoria will support you in every way. They love you very much. But also know that whatever you decide to do will be kept confidential until you tell me otherwise. You'll be safe here and incognito for as long as you need to be. Once you arrive, your name goes in the system and your case is a matter of record. That's the law, and *nobody* is exempt, not even a federal judge sitting on the bench of the First Circuit Court of Appeals."

At her quiet mumbled, "Thank you," tears sprung in my eyes. So many thoughts begged for attention, but the most dominant was pride. I was proud that I'd had the intuition—*and guts*—to say something to a woman desperately needing a supporting and understanding hand. And I was incredibly proud of Vanessa, because what she was doing took more bravery than I had even in my little pinky. I knew from some of my semesters studying the psychology of abuse, that many women believed they deserved the emotional and/or physical abuse inflicted on them. And that could well be Vanessa Blakney. *But she was walking away.* Now I understood James's love for his mother. Now, she had my love and total respect as well.

I WAS EXHAUSTED when I got home and my back hurt. I wanted to soak in the tub and take a nap before dinner. Dinner, which would definitely be delivered to our door. The stress of the afternoon had done a number on me, as well as the added burden of keeping quiet to James that his mother was right this minute *in* Sherborn trying to take steps for a much-needed change in her life. I felt sure she would be ready to talk to him and Victoria tomorrow after a good night's sleep, but when a new case is opened it's usually best to let the person have a day or two of solitude to process everything. I'd left her in Alanna's care with a cup of chamomile tea and two little darlings on either side of her enjoying a read of *Cloudy with a Chance of Meatballs*. Best medicine ever for a broken heart.

While I was changing my clothes a text from James came through. **Beautiful, I have a mediation meeting at 6:00. I**

won't be home till 8:00ish. Love u and be naked when I get there. Ur kinky fucker xo

Yes, you are. I laughed out loud at his signature and felt some relief that I didn't have to deal with ordering dinner since he would be late. I could make some toast and soup and take my bath after all. Annnd be naked when he got home.

I was washing the dishes when the doorbell rang. I figured it was Brooke because she often popped by around this hour to go over Blackwater Sanctuary business, but she usually messaged me first. I wasn't up for meeting tonight though. I was just too tired and my backache hadn't gone away. I still wanted my soak in the tub.

I opened the door and realized my mistake in the same instant.

But it was too late because the door was open…and pushing his way into the apartment was the judge, looking maniacal and furious.

"Where is my wife?" he asked in a low but terrifying voice.

"Somewhere safe from you and your abuse. You have about ten seconds to leave before I'm calling the cops."

"Calling the cops on me?" His eyes bulged in outrage, and I really wished I hadn't opened the door. I didn't need this. Not tonight. But there was no way in hell he would find out anything about Vanessa.

"I don't think so, you meddling little bitch. I can now see that you're going to be a problem. I'll figure out what to do with you eventually, but right now you're going to fucking tell me where Vanessa is."

He scares me, but I will not be bullied by this animal. I didn't know what he'd done to Vanessa, but I now wondered how dangerous he actually was. Had I underestimated him? Because the signs were unmistakable that the judge was truly insane. Regardless, I stood my ground. For James, and for Vanessa, I would stand my ground.

"No, I'm not. In fact, I *can't* tell you. It's against the law for me to share confidential case information with anyone not authorized by the recipient. Surely I don't need to explain this to you, *Judge*."

"Where is James?" he demanded.

"He'll be home any minute. In fact he just texted that he's on his way," I lied, but hoping like hell it might be true.

"My son has done exactly what I told him to do with you by the way." His expression was smug…and hatefully empowered as he walked in and paced around the room as if he owned the place.

"And what might that be?" I shot back.

"Impregnate you and stage a big family wedding for the press."

"He did not, and you are fucking crazy. Get out now!" I pointed to the door.

"Oh, but he did. We have a deal."

"He's already told me about your ultimatum. I know all about it." The judge had hurt James before, so he wasn't to be trusted about anything *he* claimed to be true. Lying came very easy to him.

"Did he?" His face changed into one of intense triumph as he caught on. "Interesting. Perhaps this will help you *understand* who you are to him. To us." He tapped his phone and held it up.

JUDGE: "Trouble in paradise so soon?"

JAMES: "You need to back the fuck off if you want this to happen. I already told you her family doesn't know about us yet."

JUDGE: "Why the hell don't they know? What are you waiting for? Get this situation nailed down and settled or I settle it for you. Do your job and get her pregnant. It shouldn't be this hard, son." I could hear a pause and then a mean little laugh come from the judge. *"But maybe that's the problem for you. Your cock's not hard enough to get the job done. Do you need some help from another cock perhaps?"* Then a break in the audio. *"Marry a girl from a good family and get her pregnant. I am assuming you can figure that part of it—or get her pregnant first, and then marry her. In fact, a surprise pregnancy might work even better to endorse our support of traditional values with a thoroughly modern interpretation."*

A longer pause…

JAMES: "Are you even human, because sometimes I wonder. Audio noise. *And how do you suggest I do this?"*

JUDGE: "Are you even my son, because sometimes I wonder. Be a man and fuck your baby into that Blackstone bitch and be done with it. My God, the senate announcement is in less than two months."

JAMES: "You know, Dad, if you want to fool the voters into thinking you're a loving family man, you're gonna need to work on your game and have an ounce of patience. Winter is already mine— Audio noise. *I've done every fucking thing you asked of me. I knocked her up and we're getting married after the baby is born. What the fuck else do you want?"*

The audio ended abruptly after that last question from James, and I was left standing in front of the judge with my mouth agape.

I couldn't believe the conversation I'd just heard. All the air in North America had suddenly been sucked out of the room. I felt sick at the thought the judge might be telling the truth, but James wouldn't use me like that. *He loves me.* He wouldn't ever trap me into marrying him.

Like you trapped him?

But that conversation was definitely James speaking to his

father. He'd said clearly: *"I've done every fucking thing you asked of me. I knocked her up and we're getting married after the baby is born. What the fuck else do you want from me?"*

I suddenly felt violently sick. *Surely this isn't true. Surely there's a mistake.* I just wanted to get away from the judge and…everyone. My need to flee as immediate as taking my next breath.

I ran out the door and headed toward Caleb's penthouse through the stairwell. I was almost to the top when he caught me by my hair.

My feet came off the steps.

And down the stairs I went, falling backward as the brunt of the fall was absorbed by the lower half of my body.

There was no bracing myself for impact because my hands were in the wrong place—in front of me. I knew it was bad. I might have just killed my baby. As much as I prayed it wouldn't be true, I knew it was already too late the instant I hit the bottom step of the stairs.

My innocent little child who I would never get the chance to meet was leaking out of me in the stairwell while I cried the most dreadful tears I'd ever known.

I was alone while I cried out my mourning, anguished by the pain of my guilt for something I'd caused in a weak moment of selfishness with the man I'd wanted for so long, I couldn't remember when I didn't.

I'm sorry, Baby. Mommy is so, so sorry… And I'd never forgive myself.

Never.

CHAPTER TWENTY-THREE

James

Three days later.

She checked herself out of the hospital during the one hour I was away to shower and change my clothes. Before that, the doctors wouldn't tell me a whole lot because we weren't married. The only information I was given was that the miscarriage of our baby boy was *probably* a result of blunt-force trauma from the fall, but not certain because there were indications she might have been bleeding before she fell. Otherwise, she sustained no other serious injuries despite falling several feet down an unforgiving concrete stairwell. A miracle really.

She never lost consciousness and was able to make it to the elevators and up to Caleb's place after she'd caught her breath. She told the police everything once they arrived and reported her injury to the doctors at Mass Gen. My father was arrested for assault and for fleeing the scene of the crime. Security cameras caught it all. When asked if she wanted to press charges she answered, "Fuck, yes."

Other than that she didn't say much to me. Very little beyond "I'm so sorry" many more times than she needed to.

What did she even have to be sorry for? Obviously she felt guilt for the miscarriage even though we all told her it was not her fault. Her mom, her sister, Brooke, Caleb, Lucas, and even Wyatt came to sit with her; repeatedly assuring her *nothing* that happened was her fault. She wouldn't accept it from any of us, though. Stubborn as they come, nobody was going to change Winter's mind until she wanted it changed.

I didn't know where she went when she left the hospital or how to find her. My Winter was just…gone.

And my life was as good as over if she didn't come back to me.

One week later.

THERE WAS ONE THING that gave me an immense feeling of accomplishment, though.

Delivering to my father the terms of what would be my mother's divorce settlement. My only regret was that it wasn't from inside a jail cell. Unfortunately, when Winter left town, he couldn't be held without her statement. It didn't really matter, because I'd taken care of him, jail time or otherwise. I'd heard the spliced-together audio clip he'd played for her, rearranging my words from different conversations at various times to make it seem like I was using her at his direction. I think I hated him for that deception most of all.

"She will have the house in Weston and the beach house on Blackstone Island. Assets will be divided as such." I slid over the list of demands and a pen. "After you sign I'm presenting the restraining orders for my mother, Victoria, Winter and myself. If you violate any terms of this agreement you go straight to jail. No passing GO, or collecting anything other than a colored jumpsuit to add to your wardrobe. In my capacity of legal counsel to the above-mentioned people, you attacked a pregnant woman, and in doing so murdered the grandchild you wanted so badly. You are finished, Robert—with me, with everyone who's connected to you by blood or marriage." He was finished with being a judge too. Criminal record and all… *Thank. God.*

After he signed, I placed the documents in my briefcase and walked out the fucking door. There was more that I could have said to him, but I didn't need to. I'd never speak to him again if I could help it. Maybe I'd get my wish, maybe not. As far as I was concerned my father died the moment he put his hands on my Winter and hurt her so badly she had to run away.

Two weeks later.

I STARTED SENDING PICTURES to her phone. Pictures of good things that would show her there was happiness all around because of her good work. One was a picture of the two ponies now living in the barn at the Sherborn house. Shane and Brenna helped me choose them and named them George and Martha after characters from some books they liked. I sent a video of my mother leading Brenna around the ring on Martha for her first riding lesson. In the video, my mom looked genuinely happy, but she had grieved terribly over the last few weeks. Not for the loss of her bastard husband, but at being the reason Robert Blakney had set his anger and monstrous hands on Winter. That depth of pain would take Mom a while to recover from, and Victoria and I were doing our very best to assure her that we loved her and didn't blame her. And that Winter would have never blamed her either, but would be happy she was safe and out of my father's clutches.

My mom had been quite the equestrian in her younger years, and now that she was free from the devastating grip of my father's control she was coming back to life again. She wanted to start an equine therapy program at Sherborn for children and adults with special needs who could benefit from the unique healing treatment from the connection with horses.

I sent her a picture of Alanna with the kids holding a handmade sign that read: **WE LOVE MS. WINTER AND WE MISS HER VERY MUCH!** I never knew if she received the pictures or not because she might have changed her number. So, I sent everything to both of her emails just in case.

At night I slept on sheets I refused to wash because I couldn't bear to lose the scent of her. I wrote her many letters on paper with a pen. I didn't know how to get them to her but I still needed to write out the words for myself anyway.

And then, Caleb came to see me and told me where she was.

"She's in L.A. with Wyatt. She said she needed to be far away from everything that would remind her of sad things and of the people she's hurt. I'm assuming that's mostly you, James."

"No. The only way she's hurting me is by being gone." If I could see her—and she could see me—I *knew* I could make things right again. I knew what she needed. She needed me to love her and tell her to start living her life again. She needed that push to come from me. I knew it down to my very core.

"That's what I figured," he said evenly. "I was never here, brother. We did not have this conversation, okay?"

"Okay." *You'll never know what this means to me, Caleb.*

"Now, getcha ass going and bring my sister back home where she belongs."

"Get the fuck outta my way so I can leave for the

airport," I told him.

"I'd take you there myself but I was never here and we never had this conversation."

I bear-hugged him and planted a sloppy kiss on his cheek.

The next day.
Malibu, California

THREE WEEKS, FOUR days, and eleven fucking awful hours. That's how long I'd been without my Winter. That's how many hours I hadn't been able to touch her, kiss her, hold her... love her. But I felt my starved heart start to beat again when I spotted her walking on the beach. She was far off in the distance and walking in the opposite direction, but I knew it was her. She had on black shorts and a blue long-sleeved shirt. Those long legs carrying her down the beach, and that chestnut brown hair blowing in the Pacific breeze were unmistakable to my eyes. I knew what my woman looked like even from far away.

I gave a kid five bucks to deliver my letter into her hand once she sat down on the sand to watch the waves. I knew what I'd written by heart and watched her when she read it.

Winter

THE HAIR ON THE BACK of my neck started tingling the moment I stepped onto the beach. I sensed that something was about to change but had no particular reason for why I should feel that way. The familiar ache that had been with me for the long weeks was starting to lessen. But maybe that had to do with the emails I'd seen last night along with the pictures he'd sent. I'd almost called Alanna to get the details on the new ponies but lost my nerve at the last minute.

I'd stayed silent for so long, I was terribly afraid he wouldn't want to hear me if I tried to reach out to him now.

James...

I'd hurt him *and myself* so badly. I hadn't wanted to hurt him, but I had, and the devastation of that knowledge had pretty much cut me off at the knees.

I didn't know how to begin.

I needed help taking my first step...just like the people I mentored as a social worker.

"I'm supposed to give you this." A boy of about ten handed me an envelope marked simply "Winter" before taking off down the beach whooping with joy and waving a five-dollar bill.

I opened the envelope.

Dear Beautiful,

I need you. I won't stop telling you, or showing you how much I need you, either, until I'm dead. That's my promise to you, and I will keep it.

*I know you are feeling guilt about the loss of our son but you are not alone in that. I have guilt too, because guilt is an emotion we all feel when we **love**. I love you, and I loved our son for the short time we had him. I will not lose either of those feelings for as long as I draw breath. If you want to continue to feel responsible for our loss, I can't take it from you. It's yours to own. You have the free-will to feel as you do.*

251

But so do I. And my free-will tells me that I can't live without you in my life. I need you. I need you to come home and love me. I need to be loved by you. I need you to start living your life again. Yes, you will feel sad when you remember, but going forward means you can take that sadness and use it for something good. I know you will find a way to make that happen. Everything you touch is good. I don't know another person with as much goodness in their heart as you have inside your generous and beautiful heart.

It's time for you to come home now. There are people who love you who only want to feel your presence in their lives. And then there's me, who will not survive without you to love me. I know this. I can live without the rest if I have to, but not having your love…I cannot do.

We can get married today or next year…or never.

We can have more babies if you want to or we can have dogs or cats instead. (I would prefer dogs.)

We can adopt teenagers if you want—some real difficult little shits that'll joyride with my car and give me gray hair long before I should have it.

Point is, Beautiful, I'm not leaving this beach until you come over here to where I am waiting and tell me you love me, and to bring you back home where you belong.

Ever your kinky fucker,

James

I DON'T REMEMBER getting up, only that I was running and my legs were flying, taking me closer to my James. I didn't even choose a direction; I just went to…where he was.

And then he was in front of me standing in the sand, his god-like physique on full display for me to devour.

Every line of his sculpted body, his hard-set jaw, the eyes that spoke more volumes of words than I could ever comprehend—my beautiful man was here for me. He'd come for me…to bring me back home.

With his strong arms open—*waiting for me to come to him.*

His arms were open for me when I fell into them.

Heaven.

Once I was against him, I felt the most immense sense of peace envelop me. My whole universe clicked back into place and the incredibly painful tightness I'd borne within my heart for weeks began to dissolve. Just from being in his arms.

James healed me in an instant with only his touch.

"I love you, James Blakney, and I can't live without you either. I needed help taking my first step back to you, and back to my life in Boston. I needed help because I just wasn't able to make that first step on my own without you."

And nobody had known it except for James. He knew. He knew how to help me best and he always would.

He tilted my chin up with the side of his finger, so commanding and tender at the same time. The only man capable of holding my heart. "What's the other thing you need to say to me, beautiful?" he asked.

"Take me home and marry me, James Blakney."

"Are you proposing to me now?"

"Yes, because once you told me some rules. One of the rules was for me to be honest and to tell you what I needed. You said that if I told you, you would hear me. So I'm telling you now, James. I need you to take me home and marry me."

EPILOGUE

Winter

Six months later.
Fripp Island, South Carolina

"How is he doing, Caleb?"

"Funny you should ask, because he wanted to know the same about you." My big brother gave me a kiss on the cheek carefully so as not to damage my makeup. "But first, I need to tell you what a beautiful bride you are, and how honored I am to walk you down the aisle today. I know Dad is watching over all of us and he sees you, Win. He's thrilled with your choice of husband. Dad respected James very much, and I know Mom loves him too. You've done well, little sister."

"You'd better stop now or my makeup will be washed away and it took a really long time."

He took my hand in his and clasped it. "Got it. As to your question about your groom, well I can tell you he's still standing and able to answer yes or no questions…but that's about it. He's so ready to marry you." Caleb whistled and shook his head back and forth. "He told me he wouldn't be able to relax until he sees you walking down the aisle to him, and he isn't lying."

"He knows I'd run through fire to make my way down the aisle to him if I had to. He just likes to worry."

"I can't blame him for loving my little sister."

I thought I should change the subject to something a little lighter. "How is Lucas treating my man? Are the boys playing nice in the sandbox this evening?" I couldn't help asking, because James and Lucas still had spats from time to time even though they mostly kept the peace—or ignored each other.

Caleb chuckled, clearly finding the two of them and their contentious relationship amusing as hell. "I think they'll manage to keep the fisticuffs to a minimum since it's your wedding day."

"They'd better." I brushed at nonexistent speck of lint on Caleb's lapel and asked, "Has Mom even let Johnny out of her arms yet today?"

"Not really. She made sure he had an extra-long nap earlier, so he could be awake during your wedding because she's holding him in her lap front and center. He looks quite swank in his miniature tux. Silly for a two-month-old to be dressed up in formalwear, but hey, if it makes her happy." It was apparent to everyone in the family that Caleb and our mom were trying hard to have a relationship based on honesty. The birth of baby John William, affectionately called Johnny, was helping with that, because she was really into being a grandmother. She took one look at that baby on the day he was born and fell completely and totally in love with him. Nobody could deny what a very beautiful thing it was when a precious babe could bring people together in love. *It didn't matter that Johnny wasn't biologically related to Mom.* None of that mattered. Not anymore. Family was too precious.

James and I had chosen our wedding day rather strategically because this was the time when our son would have been born. We wanted to mark the occasion and the date with good and wonderful moments spent with friends and family, feeling this was the best way to honor his memory. One day, I'd discovered that James went to St. Clement regularly to light a candle for him. If I'd been able to love my James any more than I already did, then it would have happened that day. We named him Jeremy after a beloved grandfather on his mom's side. My dress had two interlocking Js embroidered into the silk. Many might not even notice or understand the significance, but I did and that's all that mattered. Two Js for my two J-men.

On the night that James and I attended *The Autumn Ball*, he'd put in a bid at the silent auction, but he never told me what it was for. Well, he won that silent auction, and then he sat on it for a long time before finally sharing with me. The prize was an exclusive destination-wedding package to Fripp Island, South Carolina for all our guests to enjoy. So, after our ceremony tonight, all those who'd planned to, were extending their stay on the island to include a beach holiday afterward. James and I were honeymooning. Not sure what the rest of them were doing because we had some very *private* plans of our own.

In lieu of gifts, we'd announced that donations were welcome to either of the safe houses, The Sanctuary at Blackwater or SafeHouse-Sherborn. I needed nothing more than to marry the man I'd loved for the past decade. The rest we would figure out together.

Willow poked her head in and told us it was time. She had all the girls lined up and ready whenever we were, she said. My sister was a newlywed herself, having tied the knot with Roger barely two months ago. Only the *identicals*, as Caleb liked to call Lucas and Wyatt, were left to fall to matrimony. I had a feeling Lucas might be next with a certain sister whose initials were V.B.

James and I didn't talk about them—like ever. Now, I

would have really *loved* to discuss exactly what was going on with my brother and his sister, being the nosey matchmaker that *I* am, but James—not so much.

"I'm ready," I said to my brother. "I want to marry my James now."

James

THE MOMENT I'D WAITED for was finally here. My greatest fear and greatest joy all rolled up into one big clusterfuck of emotion. My best man wasn't standing by my side today either—but it was for the very best possible reason.

Caleb had a job so much more important than simply calming my fucking nerves.

He was walking the bride down the aisle...and giving her away on her wedding day—*to me.*

Brooke came first, then my sis, and then Willow. Everyone in their places doing what they were supposed to do. Shane and Brenna were the last to come down the aisle before my bride made her grand entrance.

The ocean breeze was warm and gentle, the island sunset timing out like clockwork, the guests giving silent witness to our pledge to each other when I spotted her on Caleb's arm. Looking so bright and beautiful I was blinded just a little.

A little fucking much?

My knees might have buckled just a fraction, too, but I stayed on my feet.

She was radiant, and smiling just for me, and so beautiful in her dress that I had to close my eyes for two seconds, sealing that image of her away in my mind forever.

So I'd never forget how my bride looked at me that first moment when we saw each other on our wedding day.

Four days later.

WITH NOTHING TO DO but make love to my gorgeous wife and lounge around on the beach with her, I was pretty pleased with the destination-wedding I'd snagged from the silent auction last year. Fripp Island was flanked by several tiny, nearly deserted islands, connected by canals that ran through the marshy waterways. The beach side was the Atlantic Ocean. The whole area was one big wildlife refuge really. We saw a family of deer wander through the area this morning while eating our breakfast outside on the deck. Dolphins appeared everywhere you looked. Yesterday we kayaked to another tiny island, called Prichard's Island, where Win was so fascinated with the pile of driftwood she'd collected I was afraid we might capsize the kayak on the trip back. A dolphin followed us the whole way almost as if it were making sure we'd get back safely. It was so awesome.

While I appreciated the beauty of nature, it was Winter's beauty that I found so magnificent as she played in the sand with her collection of shells in nothing but a pink and black flowered bikini. *Fuck HOT.* Her tits were pushed up and out the sides from the top and her ass was hanging out from the bottoms, and she never looked better in my view—happy and healthy—just as she should be.

The last months had been spent finding our rhythm with how we wanted our life to go. It certainly wasn't quick or easy finding it either. I didn't want her to overextend herself trying to create two safe house networks from the ground up, so the pace on both projects was slowed. It was going to take some time. For now she was focusing on Sherborn and the equine therapy program it featured. Brooke and Caleb were the principals for The Sanctuary at Blackwater on Blackstone Island, where Winter was more of an admin and less hands-on than she was at Sherborn. I wasn't allowing her to get in over her head with work again…because we were trying to have a baby.

It wasn't something we'd talked about at first because neither of us felt really sure what the other one wanted to do. When you lose something you love in such a heartbreaking way, it's terrifying to put yourself, or the one you love, at risk for losing it a second time.

But my beautiful Winter is brave.

She is a fighter and doesn't back down from a challenge very often. So, when I asked her a month ago if she wanted to try again she didn't hesitate for even a tiny second. She just said, "Yes, James, that's what I want." And then she told me to get my ass naked as quickly as possible and to get started working on it with her.

Oh, I did. I still do. At every opportunity.

Probably the biggest surprise for me is her enthusiasm for the kink.

God.

She fucking LOVES being kinky with me. My major hesitation in the beginning for pursuing Winter turned out to be anything but a problem. My wife is a kinky fucker just as much as I am—maybe more sometimes.

She took me shelling earlier on a beach where we didn't see another soul the entire time. We found hundreds of perfect conch shells, some as long as my foot. She'd dragged as many shells as she could carry back to our place along with the driftwood, which she was now arranging carefully into a design on the beach.

"What are you making, beautiful?"

"See for yourself, handsome." She held out her hand to beckon me over.

I couldn't help but laugh at what she'd made with shells and driftwood. It was *perfect*. I reached for my phone to take a picture, because this masterpiece was going on a framed canvas, and then up on the fuckin' wall in my office.

Mr. & Mrs. Blakney

kinky fuckers in love

THE END

BLACKSTONE
FAMILY CONNECTIONS

The American Blackstones of Boston are related to the British Blackstones in the UK. For a fun look at just *how* they connect, please turn the page for a glimpse into Caleb and Brooke's honeymoon, when he decided to take her back to her native England for the holidays...in A BLACKSTONE CHRISTMAS. You might see a character or two that you recognize from *The Blackstone Affair*. (wink)

But please, make sure you've read *Filthy Rich* first. You don't want to miss Caleb and Brooke's love story. It's magical.

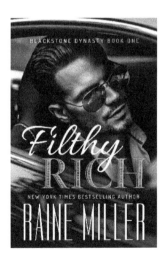

A BLACKSTONE CHRISTMAS

Caleb

"My cousin, Hannah, runs this huge old manor house as a B&B in Somerset, and she just won't take no for an answer about us staying the night. Are you going to be okay with that?"

I hoped my wife would tell me the truth about what she wanted to do. Brooke was the most undemanding person I had ever known in my life, so it was a crap shoot on whether I'd get this right or not.

"I will definitely be okay with it if you are, Caleb," she answered serenely, stretching languidly among the sheets, where she looked far too sexy to even consider letting her leave the bed, let alone our hotel room.

A day ago we were honeymooning in Hawaii, today London, but it didn't matter to me. I had my Brooke, and I'd go anywhere she wanted. This trip to London was for her, so it was going to play out exactly however *she* decided it would. Once she'd told me she hadn't been back to the land of her birth since she'd left to live with her grandmother at fifteen, and how much she missed London, especially at Christmas, I knew where we'd be spending our first holidays together. Being able to give her even the simplest gift of a visit back home to England felt like I was winning.

"I know we said London, but their place is a good three

hours by car, I can just call her back and say we can't swing it this trip if you'd rather just stay in the city—I don't want to force my family on you—"

She put two fingers over my lips and pressed down, effectively shutting me up without saying a word—something at which she was an expert. "You never force me to do anything, and I very much want to meet them. I need to know everything about my new husband—who spoils me rotten constantly—and that includes getting to know his English cousins, especially if one of them runs a B & B in a huge old manor house in Somerset." She moved her fingers away and replaced them with her sweet lips instead. "Now come back into bed and warm me up," she murmured softly. Her kiss kept my mouth silent, but who needs words when you have the most beautiful wife in the world naked in the sheets, hopped up on pregnancy hormones, with nothing but time to give her what she just asked for?

Have I mentioned what a lucky bastard I am? Or how, for like the first time in forever, I am digging the holidays this year? *Merry effing Christmas, and glad tidings of great joy, Blackstone. Don't fuck with good fortune when your wife needs you to fuck her instead.* I am probably going to hell for that filthy thought, but I'll worry about that at another time. I'm on my honeymoon with the love of my life, who at this very moment has her gorgeous naked body pressed right up against me in the bed.

Say what you will, but one thing about me is never in doubt. I am a man who definitely knows where his priorities lie.

Five hours later.

Brooke

THE UNUSUAL WINTER snow draped over the hills and dales like a white fur coat.

Absolutely breathtaking.

263

Even though winter was probably not the very best season for its full potential of beauty, I still soaked up the sight of the English countryside like drops of water melting into a dry sponge. The surprise Christmas snowfall was merely an added treat. I did not realize how much I'd missed the sights and sounds of home—and because so much time had passed since I'd experienced it—the blast of the reconnection was truly overwhelming for me. I struggled to control the rush of my emotions, and the pull of tears that threatened to spill over as I stared out the window at the lovely countryside of my homeland. The urge to tears was nothing new. I lived with it daily due to my PBA. It was easier to control these days now that I understood what had happened to me in that accident, thanks to Caleb and his endless research. If he hadn't figured it out, I would still believe I was just an emotionally damaged freak with no explanation whatsoever for my overreactive behaviors.

"Are you okay, baby?" Caleb whispered against my ear. He was so intuitive, and had been from the first. My husband amazed me with his patience and kindness whenever I had one of my "episodes." Quite simply, Caleb was the very best cure for my unwelcome melancholy feelings, hands down.

I nodded yes and gripped his hand with both of mine. I kept my eyes out the window and focused on the beauty of the scenery. "I hadn't realized how much I missed…just seeing it—being here. Thank you for bringing me." I let Caleb's strength and love support me through the moment until the intense emotions melted away, ever grateful he'd hired a driver to take us to Somerset, so I could have him beside me in the back seat where I could touch him. Caleb's touch worked miracles on me even though I was dealing with the effects of pregnancy hormones on top of my PBA. The next months were going to be *very* interesting.

"Good. I'm glad we came then. And I will always take you wherever you want to go," he said as he drew me back to lean against his strong chest, "as long as I can get the information out of you," he teased.

I nodded again, still focused on the countryside as he held me close. "Can you tell me a little about your family before we get there?" I asked, content and warm with Caleb wrapped around me like a blanket and the comforting view out the window.

"Sure. I think you're going to like them a lot. They already love you, and they haven't even met you yet."

I took a deep breath as I settled, listening to the steady voice of my husband as he described the people he clearly adored:

There was Hannah who ran the B&B at Hallborough House, the ancestral estate of the Greymonts, set along the scenic Somerset coast. He told me about her physician husband, Dr. Fred Greymont, and their three children—two older boys, Colin and Jordan, and a little girl, Zara, about five or six. Hannah also had a brother, Ethan, who had a country home nearby and would also be there with his American wife and baby daughter. Caleb and Ethan were about the same age and kept up with each other on Facebook, and even did some business between their two companies. He mentioned that Ethan and his wife, Brynne, hadn't been married all that long, describing their posh country wedding last year at Hallborough, and how all of Caleb's family had come over for the wedding. It was the final family trip for their father before he passed away. I'd also meet Jonathan Blackstone and his wife Marie. Jonathan and Caleb's dad had been close, and the backbone of the relationship between the American and British Blackstones.

It was a lot to take in, but I was grateful for the distraction. I was looking forward to meeting them all, they sounded so lovely, but truth be told, the country-manor-turned-B&B—Hallborough House—was what I found the most intriguing of all. There was something about the name of the house that rang a bell with me. I had my suspicions as to why, but couldn't be sure until I saw it with my own eyes.

Caleb

BROOKE HAD BEEN quiet in the car on the drive up from London, as if she were deep in thought, or maybe she was just processing the emotions from being back in England after such a long period of a time. We hadn't really done much at all since arriving in London, except for a quick stop to collect our warmer clothing, and a fantastic Christmas dinner last night in Covent Garden at a new place called Frog. In December, Hawaii and England are on such opposite ends of the thermometer, I'd called ahead and had a shopper pull together winter wardrobes for both of us, so we'd be set up for the wintry weather the minute the Gulfstream landed.

But it wasn't the snowy weather causing my Brooke to tremble. I'd sensed excitement from her as we came through the gates of Hallborough and up the drive to the front of the stately manor house. I had to help her out first, so I could deal with paying the driver and our luggage, but when I turned back to her a few moments later, I got the best surprise of the day. My wife was grinning from ear to ear as she took selfies standing in front of Hallborough House.

"So, I gather you like the house."

"It's beautiful." She gestured for me to come to her. "Take a selfie with me. I want pictures of us here."

I complied, but had to wonder why she was so excited by the house itself. But before I could ask, I felt little arms wrapped around my legs from behind along with the excited thumps from wagging dog tails.

"Uncle Caleb!"

"Who is that grabbing me, and why are there wolves attacking?" I teased.

She popped her head around with a giggle. "It's Zara,

and they're just dogs, not wolves. This is Rags and that one is Sir, Auntie Brynne's dog," she explained patiently with a pat to each dog's head as she named them. "They like playing outside in the snow."

"I don't blame them. I'd play in the snow too if I had their fur."

She just stared up at us in all her adorableness.

"Well, I am very sorry I didn't recognize you right away because you've grown so much since I was here the last time." I crouched down to her height so we could speak eye to eye. "How old are you again?" I asked.

"Five." She held up one hand with her fingers splayed out.

"Are you sure you're not twenty-five? You've grown a lot." I thought it was sweet she called me 'uncle' when I really wasn't. Obviously her parents had referred to me that way. Charmed the hell out of me, regardless.

She giggled again and nodded her head. "I *am* five right now, but I'll be six on my birthday," she explained patiently. She focused her attention on Brooke before asking, "Are you Uncle Caleb's native wife?"

Brooke bent down to join our little conversation, stifled a laugh and answered, "Yes, I am his native wife. I'm Brooke, and I'm pleased to meet you, Zara." She held out her hand.

"Pleased to meet you, and welcome to Hallborough House, we hope you enjoy your stay here with us," Zara answered back, shaking Brooke's hand with complete sincerity, as if she'd done it many, many times before. It made sense since she was used to guests coming into her home constantly, but seeing a little girl take on the role of concierge was priceless.

"Was it your mom or your grandpa who said Brooke was a 'native'?" I couldn't resist asking, and I knew she would tell me. Zara was honest to a fault underneath all that charm. If I ever had a daughter, I hoped she might be like her. This kid was one in a million.

"Uncle Ethan said it," she informed us.

Not a surprise. I knew Ethan would get a laugh out of the fact I married a Brit, especially since he'd recently married an American.

Zara took each of us by the hand and steered us toward the house. "Let's go in now, the boys will come for your bags and take them to your room." Hannah and Freddy were obviously raising their kids right, teaching them to help with the family business.

"Do you know what 'native' means, Zara?" Brooke asked as we walked, our footsteps crunching along the snowy ground.

"Yes," she said with a serious nod of her head, "It means you know the Queen, and can say your words properly."

I just about died laughing right there in the snow.

Brooke

IT SIMPLY WASN'T possible for us to have been made any more welcome by Caleb's family. Hannah greeted us at the door with open arms before doing the introductions all around. They were all there waiting impatiently for us to arrive, but it felt more welcoming than anything. They were just happy to see Caleb again, and to meet his new wife. The fact I was British, only made for some fun jokes to break the ice.

I could see that the UK Blackstones had been blessed by the same good genetics as the US ones. Hannah's brother, Ethan, had similar features to Caleb and his brothers, and just as easy on the eye.

Handsome men, every single one of them.

There was a darkness to Ethan though, almost unrecognizable at first, but definitely present. I could relate; the same dark shadows bounced around inside my head too. Seeing those shadows lift the instant his lovely wife, Brynne, or his baby girl came into view, gave me hope. Caleb did the same for me.

Little Laurel was such a gorgeous baby, and came right into my arms when I held them out. I needed to get in some baby practice because I'd have my own in less than six months, which was still a concept I was getting used to. I almost didn't want to let Laurel go when it was time for her to have a nap, but it was a good excuse to ask if I could have a tour of the house.

Hannah was more than happy to take me around, and Zara, her miniature assistant-in-training who slayed me with her charm when she informed me that the stunning portrait on the staircase was painted by Sir Tristan Mallerton in the early 1840's. When I asked her who the people in the painting were, she answered without missing a beat, "Sir Jeremy Greymont, Lady Georgina Greymont, and their children, Roderick and Anna-Marguerite."

"Are you sure you're really five? I don't believe it. You know too much to be just five," I teased.

She giggled up at me and nodded yes, swinging her hand clasped tightly to mine, as we toured the magnificent house I was sure my parents had visited on one of their many weekends to the country.

"How long has Hallborough House been operating as a B&B, Hannah?"

"Twelve years this coming spring."

And twelve years made it a definite possibility.

"My parents loved to take weekends in the country. They went everywhere, and stayed in places just like this when I was away at school. I think they might have even come here, because my mother used to send me postcards of the places they visited. I remember there was a beautiful house in Somerset, and I still have the postcard somewhere."

"We have postcards in the gift shop," Zara said.

"Well, then I must look at the gift shop's postcards and see if they are the same as mine."

"I can do better than that for you," Hannah said with a grin. "How long ago would your parents have come here?"

"It would have been about nine or ten years ago I'd guess. They were killed in a car crash seven years ago, so not recently," I explained as they led me to a bright room with a garden view that housed the gift shop. I could imagine the ladies of years past using it as a sitting room because of the great light pouring in from the Gothic arched windows.

Hannah went to a bookshelf and began ticking through the volumes while I studied the postcards on a rack beside the desk. Some were of other sights in the area such as Kilve Beach, and a very old seaside church that reminded me of Stone Church on Blackstone Island where Caleb and I were married just a few weeks ago. I found one of the house that I thought could be the same as the postcard I had, but I couldn't be certain.

"Let me see," Zara asked.

I showed it to her, and she looked less than impressed, but informed me that building on the house was started in 1785 and finished in 1789.

"You are just a fount of information, aren't you?"

"Yes." She was dead serious.

Ask a stupid question, Brooke. Zara was as hilarious as she was adorable.

As I looked around at the beautiful room I could finally

appreciate what drew my parents to leave the city and come to places like Hallborough for a getaway. I also found it ironic that they had died on one of their country weekends away, but I'd always taken comfort in the fact they were together and doing something they enjoyed immensely. "Can you check the registry for their names?" I asked Hannah hopefully.

"Of course, but even better are the photo albums. They may have a picture in one of the albums. Let's take a look, shall we?" She pulled out two leather volumes and brought them to the desk. "These are the years you mentioned, please have a look through." She gestured to the books on the counter.

I approached carefully, almost afraid to be disappointed, but too curious not to look. "You take pictures of your guests? I asked as I opened the first book.

"Only if they want to, of course, but most do. It's a tradition to take a Polaroid or two and make a page in the book with a message or whatever they want to share with other guests about their stay. The Polaroid stays with the book, but most everyone gets a picture of the finished page with their mobile, so they can take it with them too."

"Oh, that's lovely," I whispered, afraid to hope I might see a picture of the two people I still missed on a daily basis.

I turned pages slowly, reading the messages and seeing the happy smiles of lovers and friends and families who had all come to this place a decade ago on their travels from somewhere else.

I finished the first book and closed it before handing it back to Hannah who placed it back on the shelf.

"Feel free to look through any others if you'd like. The year is written on the spine." She gave me a hug and said, "We're so happy you and Caleb are here with us this year."

"Thank you," I managed to get out before my throat

seized up.

"I'm going to take this little monkey to the kitchen and leave you to it. Come find us if you need anything at all," she said gently, probably sensing that I was getting emotional. Zara gave me a sweet little wave as she left with her mum.

Once I was alone, I took the second book to a chair by the window and sat. For a few moments I just looked out at the beauty of the grounds covered in snow before I opened the photo album and started looking at pages.

Seven page-turns into the book and there they were. In life…in color…in a picture I had never seen before. Susanna and Michael. My mother laughing up at my dad as if he'd just said something incredibly clever. Happy. That's how they were in the picture. So happy. My eyes filled with tears, growing blurry to the point I couldn't even read the message on the page in the familiar hand of my mother's writing until I gave myself a minute.

Once I was able to read it, the message wasn't anything remarkable at all, just how much they'd enjoyed their weekend at Hallborough and that they would love to come back again someday. That never happened, obviously, but that wasn't the point. The important thing was that they *had* been here and enjoyed themselves together…spending time with each other and finding happiness in those precious moments they were given.

The warm weight of Caleb's arms came around me from behind. I was so absorbed in my trip down memory lane, I hadn't even heard him come into the room.

"Your parents came to Hallborough," he said softly as he studied their picture.

"They did." I reached a hand up and cupped his cheek, needing to touch him.

"That's why you were so excited about seeing the house.

You suspected they came here."

"You caught that from me?" The level of Caleb's intuitiveness amazed me. It must be why he was so good in business. He could read people.

He kissed the top of my head. "I like to think I can know what you're thinking but I don't. I just sense changes in your body language, and you were trembling when we drove up to the house, and then taking happy selfies in front of it two minutes later. When Hannah said you were in here looking through the photo albums for your parents, I figured it out."

"I'm glad you came to find me." I got up from the chair and went into his arms and let him hold me. Caleb's touch was my lifeline now. He balanced my highs and lows with his ever-present strength and love.

"Me too. I love seeing you so happy, it's the best gift you can give me. Well, that, and our baby," he said sweetly against my forehead.

"I love you, Caleb Blackstone, and I needed this trip so much more than I could have ever imagined, but you imagined it. You know me better than I know myself sometimes. Thank you for bringing me here, but more than that, for loving me the way that I am."

"I love you, Brooke Casterley Blackstone, and that *is* my most important job. It's what I do best."

"I know."

THE END

ABOUT THE AUTHOR

Raine has been reading romance novels since she picked up that first Barbara Cartland paperback at the tender age of thirteen. She thinks it was *The Flame is Love* from 1975. And it's a safe bet she'll never stop reading romance novels because now she writes them too. Granted, Raine's stories are edgy enough to turn Ms. Cartland in her grave, but to her way of thinking, a tall, dark and handsome hero never goes out of fashion. Never! Writing sexy romance stories pretty much fills her days now. Raine has a prince of a husband and two brilliant sons...and two very bouncy but beloved Italian greyhounds to pull her back into the real world if the writing takes her too far away. Her sons know she likes to write stories but have never asked to read any. (Thank God.) The greyhounds are likely to be in her lap while she writes the stories—both dogs at the same time. She loves to hear from readers and chat about the characters in her books. You can connect with Raine on Facebook at **Raine Miller Romance Readers** or visit her blog at **www.RaineMiller.com** to see what she's working on now.

BOOKS BY RAINE MILLER

HISTORICAL ROMANCE

The PASSION of DARIUS

The UNDOING of a LIBERTINE

The MUSE

CONTEMPORARY ROMANCE

CHERRY GIRL

PRICELESS

HUSBAND MATERIAL

BLACKSTONE DYNASTY

FILTHY RICH

FILTHY LIES

THE BLACKSTONE AFFAIR
NAKED, Part 1

ALL IN, Part 2

EYES WIDE OPEN, Part 3

RARE and PRECIOUS THINGS, Part 4

WRITING as *Vivienne Wilmont*
LORD BLACKWOOD'S VIRGIN

WRITING as *Brit DeMille*
CRUSHED, *Vegas Crush #1*

SIN SHOT, *Vegas Crush #2*

RED ROCKET, *Vegas Crush #3*

CPSIA information can be obtained
at www.ICGtesting.com
Printed in the USA
LVHW09s1033081018
592766LV00006B/97/P